Jed had always found himself powerless to resist the lure of a pair of beautiful eyes.

"I can assure you the pleasure was all mine," he replied. "Do you know your eyes deepen to purple when you're alarmed, Miss Caroline?"

"And what color would you say they are now, Mr. Fraser?"

"I'd say an exquisite azure, like the sky in summer."

Caroline Collins arched a curved brow. "Then if your theory holds true, Mr. Fraser, I guess that would indicate I'm no longer alarmed." She turned around and walked away.

Jed's appreciative gaze followed the sway of her hips as she struggled to stay afoot on the rocking train. The lady intrigued him. As complicated as they come, and sure as hell one beautiful female. Those eyes of hers would take a long time for a man to forget.

"You'd be wise to be alarmed, Miss Caroline," he murmured softly.

Turn the page for praise of Ana Leigh's romances

His Boots Under Her Bed

"Leave it to Leigh. . . . She's taken one stubborn woman, one sexy man, and a hidden gold mine and set them down in the Wild West—a surefire formula for a hit." (4 stars)

—*Romantic Times*

"*His Boots Under Her Bed* is an emotional and fun book! . . . A plethora of additional secondary characters provides lots of laughter and genuine emotion to the story."

—Romance Reviews Today

The Lawman Said "I Do"

"Winning . . . a very 21st-century light romance in a 19th-century setting."

—*Publishers Weekly*

"Quirky characters and witty dialogue fill the pages of this entertaining novel. . . . This will appeal to many audiences, from fans of the Old West, to readers who enjoy a good romance, to those who like books rich in humor."

—*Booklist*, starred review

"This novel is filled with funny moments and moments of poignancy. . . . Leigh is a wonderful writer who tells a great story."

—*Romantic Times*

"An enchanting Americana tale that . . . fans will cherish."

—The Best Reviews

The Frasers: Clay

"[Ana Leigh's] strong characters and their biting repartee and tender emotions touch readers' hearts, while the hardships of western travel are brilliantly portrayed in this tender, exciting western."

—*Romantic Times* (4.5 stars)

"Delightful repartee and scenes of comic relief abound. . . . The pacing moves along nicely and allows the readers to laugh and cry as the plot progresses to an especially heartwarming ending that leaves one anticipating the sequel. . . . Pick up a copy . . . and join in an historical adventure of grand proportions."

—Romance Reviews Today

"This intriguing western romance stars two fine protagonists [who] struggle not to fall in love while the reader chuckles at their failure. . . . A fine tale."

—The Best Reviews

Also by Ana Leigh

ONE NIGHT
WITH A
SWEET-
TALKING MAN

ANA LEIGH

Pocket Star Books
New York   London   Toronto   Sydney

Pocket Star Books
A Division of Simon & Schuster, Inc.
1230 Avenue of the Americas
New York, NY 10020

Copyright © 2008 by Anna Baier

First Pocket Star Books paperback edition March 2008

POCKET STAR BOOKS and colophon are registered trademarks of Simon & Schuster, Inc.

For information about special discounts for bulk purchases, please contact Simon & Schuster Special Sales at 1-800-456-6798 or business@simonandschuster.com.

Cover illustration by Jaime DeJesus

Manufactured in the United States of America

10 9 8 7 6 5 4 3 2 1

ISBN-13: 978-1-4165-5136-2
ISBN-10:   1-4165-5136-0

I dedicate this book to my son, Mike. One of the real heroes in this world, and not just a make-believe one.

CHAPTER
1

Jed Fraser swung his long legs over the side of the bed and propped his throbbing head in his hands. Cheap whiskey always gave him a headache. After a long moment, he stood up to open the window in the room. The scent of rotting fish in a barrel below punched him in the nose; he slammed the window shut.

The blond woman in the bed sleepily opened her eyes. "Where you goin', honey?" she asked when he began to dress.

"I have to walk off this headache. Go back to sleep, Millie."

She rolled onto her side. "You comin' back, Jeb?"

"It's Jed, not Jeb. And no, I won't be back."

He laid some bills on the dresser, picked up his seabag, then paused at the doorway and looked back at her.

"Thank you. You were great, Millie."

Surely no woman chose prostitution as a profession willingly. What had forced a sweet gal like Millie into it? And what would wanderers like him do if she hadn't?

The soft snores coming from the bed indicated she had already returned to sleep.

Outside he walked briskly to the dock, where he took a deep breath of sea air as his gaze swept the endless expanse of water. The sea had always lured him, and no matter what the port, the activity around the dock never failed to stimulate him.

And surely there was none more galvanizing than the thriving port of San Francisco, where East met West.

Heavy crates and barrels hoisted on pulleys swung through the air and were lowered onto a ship preparing to return to the Orient. The grunts and shouts of the American longshoremen loading the cargo clamored with the singsong chatter of the Chinese coolies who scurried up the gangplank carrying crates of cackling chickens or fresh vegetables and fruit.

Jed's eyes gleamed with pride as he gazed at the clipper ship nearby in dry dock. A maintenance crew was busy scraping the barnacles off the hull in preparation for a fresh coat of paint. Three-hundred-and-sixty-feet long from bow to stern, with a shiny black hull and bright-red mast and sails, the vessel was the best looking—and fastest—ship in the harbor.

The *Redheaded Belle* was Jed's true mistress. From the instant he had stepped on her deck twenty-four months earlier, he'd felt cushioned in the arms of a lover.

As first mate, his services wouldn't be needed for the thirty days the ship was in dry dock, so he intended to visit his brothers and sister and their families in the nearby Napa Valley. Each time he made port in San Francisco, one or the other had either a new addition to his family or would have one soon.

Clay's marriage had come as no surprise, since Jed's older brother had always talked about settling down as soon as the war ended. But he would never have guessed that those two lotharios, Colt and Garth, would follow so soon in Clay's footsteps.

Well, marriage certainly wasn't for Jed—he had found the only mistress he could ever cherish.

"Good-bye, Belle," he murmured with a lingering glance at the ship. "See you in a month."

Since he had two hours before the departure of his train, Jed went to the public bath, where he shaved and then climbed into a tub of hot water. He leaned his head back, closed his eyes, and smoked a cigarillo until the water cooled. After donning clean clothing, he entered the dining room of the nearby hotel.

As the waiter led him to a table, a voice called out, "Mr. Fraser!"

Recognizing the authoritative voice of Nathan Collins, Jed turned with pleasure.

Though the years had aged the man, Nathan Collins was still as imposing as he had been to Jed when he was a young seaman a decade ago.

Collins had been the captain of the *Virginia Lady*, one of several ships that had risked running the Yankee blockade of southern ports to carry much-needed supplies to the Confederacy during the late war.

Jed respected Nathan Collins more than any man except his own father. The captain had been a mentor to him and had taught him seafaring skills that had proven to Jed that it took more than merely the love of the sea to survive on it.

The two men shook hands. "Have you eaten, Mr. Fraser?" Nathan asked.

"No, sir."

"Then you must join us."

"I don't wish to intrude on your breakfast, sir."

"Nonsense, it's a pleasure to see you. Do you remember my daughter, Caroline?"

"Of course," Jed said with a polite nod to the lovely woman seated at the table. "It's a pleasure to see you again, Miss Caroline."

He'd forgotten the captain even had a daughter. Caroline Collins had been just a young girl when her father had sent his wife and daughter from Virginia to live with his brother in California just before the war broke out.

She dipped her head to acknowledge his greeting, but her expression was unwelcoming. Apparently she was displeased with her father's invitation to him.

Oblivious, the captain went on to say, "And this handsome young chap is my grandson, Garrett Collins. Garrett, I'd like to introduce you to Jedemiah Fraser. Mr. Fraser served on the *Virginia Lady* during the War Between the States."

The young boy stood up. "It's a pleasure to meet you, Mr. Fraser."

The lad couldn't have been much more than seven or eight but stood tall and held his head with a confidence that Jed found appealing in one so young. After his proper greeting, the boy broke into a wide grin as he plopped into his chair.

As soon as Jed sat down, a waiter hurried over to them with platters of scrambled eggs and strips of bacon.

His brown eyes gleaming with excitement, Garrett asked, "Did you really sail on Granddad's ship during that war, Mr. Fraser?"

"Yes, I did, Garrett."

"And what a time we had slipping past those Yankee ships," Nathan said. "Tell me, Jedemiah, what have you been doing these past four years?" Nathan asked as he spread strawberry jam on his toast.

"I went back to Fraser Keep for a short time, then I applied for my officer's papers and shipped out on a freighter. On a trip to China I transferred to a clipper ship, and for the past two years I've been first mate on the *Redheaded Belle*. We carry cargo and mail between here and the Orient."

"Who's the captain?"

"Benjamin Beningham, sir."

"Beningham! A good man," Nathan said.

"Wow, you've been to China!" Garrett exclaimed. "That sure sounds exciting. I wish I could go there."

"I'm sure you could convince your grandfather to take you someday."

Garrett propped his head in his hand and began to tap his fork against the side of his plate. "I know my mother wouldn't go. She doesn't like to sail."

The lad's sigh sounded pitifully despondent, so Jed said, "Well then, we'll have to try and convince her to the contrary, won't we, Garrett?"

"Don't bother, Mr. Fraser," Caroline said. "It won't do you any good."

"Are you that sure his mother would be so hard to convince, Miss Caroline?"

"I'm certain of it. I *am* his mother, Mr. Fraser."

His mother! Jed was thoroughly confused. He'd noticed she wasn't wearing a ring and had assumed she was unmarried.

She turned to her son. "Garrett, why are you squirming?"

"I have to pee," he said.

"Need I remind you we have a guest? Excuse yourself properly."

"Excuse me, Mr. Fraser, but I have to pee," the boy said.

Jed grinned and winked at him.

Caroline's mouth curved in an effort to suppress a grin, but her eyes failed to disguise her amusement.

"Garrett, I meant that is *not* the proper way to ask to be excused."

"Good Lord, Caroline!" Nathan declared. "If the boy has to pee, he has to pee."

Caroline sighed. "Father, you're not helping. Will you please accompany Garrett?"

The captain shoved back his chair. "Let's go, rascal—we're both in trouble now."

But Garrett was already halfway out of the room, with his grandfather in pursuit.

Chuckling, Jed turned his attention to Caroline.

"Kids. You never know what will come out of their mouths."

He found her grin enchanting. "So I've discovered. Garrett says the first thing that pops into his head. He's very like his grandfather."

"And is that so bad, Miss Caroline?"

"Not at all; it's one of the endearing qualities I love about him the most. However, some people are offended by his candidness, so my apologies if that was the case."

"None needed; the boy is the most refreshing person I've met in a long time. But I owe you an apology, Miss Caroline. I didn't realize you were Garrett's mother. Since your father introduced the boy as Garrett Collins, I presumed he was your nephew."

"Weren't you aware my father only has one child, Mr. Fraser?"

Jed tried to conceal his astonishment. If he interpreted her meaning correctly, she was implying she had never married. This whole conversation was not to his liking; he was beginning to feel like a dolt.

To his relief Garrett and the captain returned to the table, and within minutes the boy again began to restlessly tap his fork against his plate.

"It's difficult to imagine your dislike for sailing, Miss Caroline, considering your father is the finest seaman I've ever served under."

"No doubt he is, Mr. Fraser, but after what my mother and I endured, sailing around the Cape of Good Hope on the way to California, I vowed to never set foot on a ship again. It was the longest and most miserable ordeal I've ever experienced."

"That can be an arduous voyage. But that had to be at least nine years ago; now there are steam ships and clipper ships that practically soar over the waves. You'd find them considerably faster and more comfortable."

"I'm happy for you, Mr. Fraser, but I still never intend to step foot on a ship again."

She turned to her son and snapped, "Garrett, if you're finished eating, kindly sit up straight and put aside your fork. The implement is *not* a musical instrument."

Jed frowned at the unnecessarily sharp reprimand. Something else seemed to be annoying her; had he said something to anger her?

He picked up his coffee cup and gazed at her thoughtfully as he sipped from it. Was she embarrassed at bearing a child out of wedlock? After so many years that seemed unlikely, but perhaps that's why she appeared uncomfortable and silent throughout the meal. Ordinarily he'd be willing to cut her some slack, but now her skin had deepened in a blush and she looked ready to explode.

"Captain Collins, what are *you* doing in San Francisco? Don't tell me you're in port, too?" he asked to ease the conversation.

"You might say I'm in dry dock, Jedemiah. I sold the *Virginia Lady* years ago, and I'm a forester now. We have a sawmill and produce lumber for building ships."

"It's hard to imagine you as a landlubber, Captain Collins, but you didn't abandon the sea completely."

"I've abandoned it enough for you to stop address-ing me as 'Captain,' Jed."

"That will be difficult to do, sir. But since we no longer share a deck together, I'd be honored to do so, Captain. Ah, sir."

Nathan broke into laughter. "So how long will you be in port, Jed?"

"The ship's in dry dock for a month. I intend to visit my brothers and their families. They live nearby."

Caroline's head snapped up. "Your family lives in California?"

"Yes, not too far from here."

"Your whole family?" She sounded more alarmed than curious.

"No. Will and his family remained in Virginia. The rest of my brothers came here. Actually, Colt married and lives in New Mexico, but now with the railroad completed, he and his family will be able to come to California more often."

"Did you lose Fraser Keep to carpetbaggers when the war ended?" Nathan asked.

"No, sir. Thanks to Will and Emmaline's efforts, they managed to hold on to it during the war, and now the plantation's begun to thrive again."

"What of your sister Melissa?" Caroline asked. "Does she live here, too?"

"Oh, yes. And deliriously happy, I'm pleased to say. Immediately after the war ended, Lissy eloped to California with a Yankee soldier named Stephen Berg. She and Steve have three children now."

"I'm happy for her," Caroline said. "She was always

so friendly and sweet; I'm glad she got the happiness she deserved."

He looked at her, surprised by her unexpected warmth. "That's very kind of you, Miss Caroline. I'll be sure to tell her the next time I see her."

Caroline picked up her gloves and handbag. "Father, if you'll excuse us, Garrett and I will leave. I still have a few items to purchase, and I'm sure you and Mr. Fraser have a great deal more to talk over. We'll meet you at the station in thirty minutes. Don't lose track of the time."

"I won't, my dear. Garrett can remain with us, if you prefer."

"No, I rather he come with me," she said quickly.

Jed got up and pulled out her chair. "It was a pleasure seeing you again, Miss Caroline."

"The same to you, Mr. Fraser," she said coolly.

He offered Garrett his hand. "I enjoyed your company, young man."

"Thank you, sir," Garrett said and grinned when Jed winked at him.

Jed's gaze followed Caroline as she departed. *Despite how hard you're trying to appear conventional, Miss Caroline Collins, I suspect the jaunty set of that bright-red hat perched on those blond curls means there's another side to you.*

A strange woman, he reflected. Lovely face, trim figure, intelligent . . . Why did she seem so ill at ease?

"We have time for one more cup of coffee and a cigar, then I must be on my way," Nathan said.

"Are you taking the northbound train, sir?"

"Yes."

"That's a coincidence; I'm taking it, too."

"Delightful! We'll be able to visit together for al-most another forty miles. I'm sure Caroline will be just as pleased when I tell her."

Jed arched a brow. "Yes, sir, I'm sure she will be."

The train whistle was blowing its final departure warn-ing by the time Jed and Nathan arrived at the station. Jed could see that Caroline's displeasure increased when she saw that he accompanied her father.

"It's about time you got here, Father."

"I'm not a doddering old man, so mind your tongue, daughter."

"I apologize for delaying him, Miss Caroline," Jed interjected.

Garrett's wide grin at his beloved grandfather eased some of the tension. "Mama was worried that you'd miss the train, Granddad. You coming with us, Mr. Fraser?"

"Yes, then I'm continuing a bit further than you."

"Get on the train, Garrett," Caroline said.

Nathan patted the boy on the head and took his hand. "Come on, son."

They climbed on and just as Caroline followed up the steps, the train lurched forward and started to roll. She lost her balance and fell backward, but Jed caught her from the step below, preventing her from falling off as the train gained momentum. Their gazes locked for several seconds.

"Thank you, Mr. Fraser," she said breathlessly.

He'd always been powerless to resist a pair of beautiful eyes. "The pleasure was all mine. Do you know that your eyes deepen to purple when you're alarmed, Miss Caroline?"

She smiled slightly. "And what color would you say they are now, Mr. Fraser?"

"I'd say an exquisite azure, like the sky in summer."

Caroline Collins arched a curved brow. "Then if your theory holds true, Mr. Fraser, I guess that would indicate I'm no longer alarmed." She turned around and walked away.

His appreciative gaze followed the sway of her hips as she moved down the rocking train car. Caroline Collins intrigued him. She was as complicated as they come, and a hell of a beautiful female.

Garrett had sat by the window of one of the double seats facing each other. Nathan had taken the opposite seat, and Caroline sat next to her son.

"If you prefer not to ride backward I'll be glad to sit there, Miss Caroline," Jed said.

"Thank you, but that won't be necessary, Mr. Fraser."

"I think it's fun to ride backward," Garrett declared. "Don't you, Mr. Fraser?"

"Well, Garrett, I guess that if I had my druthers, I prefer seeing where I'm going, rather than where I've been."

"Hmmm." Garrett reflected for a long moment. "Mama, is that why you always tell me I never know if I'm coming or going?"

They all broke into laughter, and Caroline slipped her arm around his shoulders. "I wasn't just referring to train rides, sweetheart."

She leaned back and opened the book on her lap as Garrett returned to gazing out the window.

"What are you reading, Miss Caroline?" Jed asked.

"*A Tale of Two Cities* by Charles Dickens," she said.

"Are you enjoying it?"

"Very much so, Mr. Fraser. Have you read it?"

"Yes, several years ago. Do you enjoy reading, Miss Caroline?"

"I always have. Unfortunately, I have less opportunity to do so than I'd like." She shifted her gaze back to the page.

"Is your family expecting you, Jed?" Nathan asked.

"No. I thought I would surprise them."

"In a state this size, it's quite a coincidence we've settled so near to one another. Our home's in the Napa Valley, too."

"My brother Clay had hopes of becoming a vintner and was told the Napa Valley is a good region for growing grapes," Jed said.

"And has he succeeded?"

"Yes, very much so."

"I'm glad to hear it."

Soon the motion and the rhythmic clickety-clack of the rails had an effect on all of them. Caroline continued to read, Nathan slipped into deep thought, and Garrett slumped drowsily in his seat.

Jed was now free to ponder the riddle of Caroline. Everything about her was intriguing. It seemed incredible that a woman with her beauty wasn't married by now, especially with the shortage of women in the West. Even more, why hadn't she married the man who fathered her child?

As if sensing his gaze, she raised her eyes and for a moment they stared openly at each other. The expression in her gorgeous blue eyes remained enigmatic before she lowered them back to the page.

She made no attempt to disguise her dislike of him, but the reason for it was a mystery to him. Back in Virginia he had barely noticed the girl; he couldn't even remember ever speaking to her. He vaguely recalled that she was shy and rather bookish. He couldn't recollect seeing her at any cotillions or other social events.

"You said your family is not expecting you, Jed?" Nathan's question jolted him out of his reverie. "Yes, sir."

"I understand that you're eager to see your family, but I wonder if you would consider joining us for dinner and spending the night at our home?"

"That's very thoughtful of you, sir, but I'd hate to inconvenience you."

"Not at all. In fact, there is a matter of deep concern that I wish to discuss with you, but I can't do it on this train."

"I understand. If it's that important to you, I would be delighted, sir."

He glanced at Caroline. Her book had fallen into her lap and she looked horrified.

CHAPTER
2

When they arrived at the Collins's home, a yellow shape streaked across the yard to greet them.

"Buffer!" Garrett shouted joyously and jumped out of the buggy while it was still in motion.

The momentum of the barking, tail-wagging dog knocked him to the ground, and for several seconds the dog and the giggling boy rolled in the dirt.

Then Garrett jumped to his feet. "Beat you to the barn, Buffer!" He raced away. The dog stared up at Jed, gave a low growl, then chased after the boy.

"Was there hostility in that growl?" Jed asked.

"Just a warning shot across the bow, Mr. Fraser. You have just met the captain of this vessel," Nathan said.

"Now, Father, he hasn't deposed you yet," Caroline said lightly. "Garrett and Buffer are just very devoted."

"How long have you had him, Miss Caroline?" Jed asked.

"Eight years. He was born the same night as

Garrett, and they've been inseparable companions since."

"Really!"

Her eyes flashed with a sudden animation. "Yes, don't you think that's rather strange?"

"Perhaps the births were coincidental, but it's not unusual for a boy and his dog to be close."

"Ha!" Nathan cried out. "Thank you, my boy. Caroline believes that Buffer's birth was some kind of divine plan that God conceived."

"Are you implying Providence, Miss Caroline?"

Apparently he had failed some test, because her expression changed to annoyance. "I am indeed, Mr. Fraser. And if you laugh at me like my father, I swear I will shove both of you out of this buggy."

"Forgive me, ma'am, but I can't see anything provident about your dog happening to have puppies the same night you gave birth to your child."

"Even if it was a stray dog that crawled into our barn that night and gave birth?"

Jed shrugged. "If I may play devil's advocate, there is nothing unusual about a dog seeking out a quiet corner to have her litter."

"Aha!" she exclaimed smugly. "But it wasn't a litter; it was only *one* pup. She delivered it and then died. Now, wouldn't you say that was unusual, Mr. Fraser?"

He shrugged. "Obviously she'd been ill and couldn't survive the delivery. I'm no expert in veterinary medicine, but I was raised on a plantation where animals were breeding and birthing continually. And the only time I recall a dog delivering only one pup was because the rest of the litter was stillborn."

Nathan reached the house and reined the buggy to a halt.

Jed offered Caroline a hand, and as she stepped down from the buggy, she gave him a devastating smile that almost knocked the legs out from under him.

"Then you agree, Mr. Fraser, that apparently this birth was due to Providence."

"But I didn't intend to imply that . . ." He could have saved his breath, for she was already through the front door.

Jed followed and was about to enter when he heard Garrett's dog barking in the barn. He loved dogs and had never encountered one that didn't like him. Warning shot across the bow, indeed! He'd soon have that dog eating out of his hand.

The moment Caroline reached the privacy of her bedroom, she flung herself on the bed in despair. Why had her father invited that man here? The more he was around Garrett, the greater the danger of his guessing the truth. He was too clever not to begin putting the pieces together, and with his brothers living nearby, the result could be disastrous.

Jed Fraser's presence had resurrected her painful memories of Virginia, and once again her life was in turmoil.

She drew a shuddering breath. How she had hated her life there! Most of the other girls ostracized her, never inviting her to their teas or parties because they considered her bookish and unsociable. Not that she wanted to attend any of their stupid affairs, their endless chatter about hairstyles, ribbons and ruffles, and the men who came to call on them utterly bored her.

Books never bored her. They gave her knowledge, or carried her to a different time or place abounding with interesting and exciting people.

The Frasers were about the only ones who had been friendly and polite, though she doubted that most of them even knew her name when they nodded or tipped their hats in passing.

But all of the Fraser brothers were handsome devils, with every girl in the county chasing them.

And now, due to Jed Fraser's arrival, the only family who had shown her any kindness was the family she feared the most.

The tears Caroline was trying to restrain stung her eyes. She gave the pillow several whacks and buried her head in it.

But, dammit, it still hurt. She'd always felt awkward and unattractive, and though she'd shed the bitterness, the scars remained. And with some scars, nine years wasn't long enough for them to fade.

Later at dinner, Nathan told her, "My dear, I have some pleasant news. Mr. Fraser has agreed to extend his visit an additional day."

"But he can't," Caroline blurted out. "I mean, I intended to paint that room tomorrow."

She knew the lame excuse had failed to fool either of the two men and was embarrassed at her rudeness. But she was desperate to protect her son.

"If it's an inconvenience, I can stay in town, Miss Caroline," Jed said.

"Nonsense," Nathan declared in a huff, "I'll not hear of it. I apologize for—"

"I can speak for myself, Father. There's no need for you to do it for me." Caroline rose to her feet. "My apologies, Mr. Fraser; please forgive my rudeness. We look forward to your company. Now, if you gentlemen will excuse me, I have a headache." She hurried from the room.

Nathan flung his napkin on the table and shoved back his chair. "I'll not abide such conduct under my roof. If you'll excuse me momentarily, Jed, I'd like to speak to my daughter."

In all the years Jed had served under Nathan Collins, he had never seen him so angry.

"Sir, please stay where you are and let me handle this."

Nathan hesitated. "Very well. If you prefer."

"Thank you, sir."

Jed got up and headed out the door Caroline had disappeared through. It opened into a garden, and he caught a glimpse of her white gown in the moonlight.

"Miss Caroline, please wait." He hurried to catch up with her.

She halted but didn't turn to face him. "What do you want, Mr. Fraser?"

"I'm sorry you're feeling indisposed, Miss Caroline. Is there something I can do?"

"No, thank you. I just want to be alone."

She started to walk away, but he grabbed her shoulder and turned her to face him.

"Madam, what in hell have I ever done to you to

warrant this? From the first moment you saw me, you've made no effort to disguise your objection to me, so I can only assume this resentment goes back to some incident in Virginia."

"Assume what you wish, sir."

"In the name of sanity, madam, will you please tell me what's wrong? If something I said or did offended you, I apologize, and please believe it wasn't intentional."

"I guess seeing you again resurrected memories about Virginia that are best forgotten. I'm sorry."

She started to walk away again, and he joined her. "Are you happier here than in Virginia, Miss Caroline?"

"There's no comparison, Mr. Fraser."

"Life was so unpleasant there for you?"

She scoffed. "If I say yes, I'm sure you'll remind me that life is what you make it, as my father does."

"Why don't you give me a try and find out for yourself?"

For a moment, she studied him intently. Was he sincere, or merely scheming to gain her trust? Under any other circumstances, she would have found him charming and interesting. She had created this tension between them with her own fears and suspicions—and guilt.

Yet he had been gentleman enough to endure her discourtesy.

She gave him a contrite smile. "You've heard enough of my rudeness and self-pity for one day, Mr. Fraser."

"Not at all, Miss Caroline. I've sensed from the

beginning that you are troubled, and there's nothing I'd rather see than a smile returned to your lovely face."

These Fraser men *were* charming and irresistible. And despite the threat he presented, she felt an innate kindness about him.

As they sat down on a bench, she said curiously, "I don't understand you and your brothers, Mr. Fraser. You fought and risked your lives for Virginia, yet as soon as the war ended, most of you sought homes elsewhere."

"I've always loved the sea, Miss Caroline. I never planned on remaining at Fraser Keep and becoming a planter. Then Lissy's elopement with a Yankee soldier brought Clay and Garth to California when they followed her to bring her back. Colt always wanted to become a lawman, and while traveling, he became a deputy in New Mexico, then fell in love with the sheriff's daughter and married her. Ironically, all of my brothers married Yankee women, and considered the happiness of their wives more important than returning to Virginia."

"They all married Yankees! Then Clay didn't marry that silly Ellie Deveraux, after all."

"No." Jed chuckled. "Actually, Ellie married Elias Buford a couple of months before the war ended, and they moved to Vermont."

Her eyes widened in surprise. "Wasn't he that milksop shopkeeper with the thick glasses?"

"That's him."

"Elias Bufford!" Caroline giggled, then she clamped a hand over her mouth. "Oh, I'm sorry. I'm sure Clay was devastated when he returned from the war."

"Yes," Jed said solemnly. "It took a whole two weeks to recover."

What was she doing? Caroline thought with a start. She was falling totally under this man's spell. She had to distance herself; she should get back to her room at once.

"I heard you tell my father that your brothers have built their own Fraser Keep right here in California. Since your brother Will is the only one who remained in Virginia, do you feel it's fair to leave him alone to keep the home fires burning?"

Jed couldn't restrain chuckling. "Alone, when he has Emmaline, their children, Emmy's parents, and other family members born and raised in Virginia? Fraser Keep has always been a passion with Will; he and Emmy could never be happy elsewhere. And even though we signed it over to him and his heirs, the door is always open to any of us if we choose to return one day."

"So you think he never will come West?"

"Not to remain. I hope he will visit, though, because I'd like him to see how vast and spectacular this country is. And with a transcontinental railroad now, there's no reason we all can't visit one another.

"As a matter of fact, we're planning to do just that, even Lissy and Steve. They'll load up their families on the train and go back East together so that their offspring can see their birthplace, and their spouses are all anxious to see Fraser Keep. What a train ride that's going to be!"

"Do you intend to go with them?"

"I wouldn't miss it—even if I have to forfeit my commission on the *Redheaded Belle.* What about you, Miss Caroline? Ever think of going back to Virginia for a visit?"

She scoffed. "Not in the least! The only pleasant memory I have of Virginia is that Garrett was conceived there."

"Aha, so you *do* have one pleasant memory, after all."

She looked at him boldly. "Mr. Fraser, that isn't due to the pleasure of my son's conception, but rather the location where it occurred."

"You misjudge yourself, Miss Caroline. I'm sure Garrett's father would view it as pleasurable. You are a very beautiful and desirable woman."

"Mr. Fraser, I am not one of those brainless twits you and your brothers always chased after, so save your flattery for one who will appreciate it."

"All I'd like is your friendship, Miss Caroline."

"You're welcome to it, if you'll stop calling me '*Miss* Caroline.'"

"My pleasure. And please call me Jed."

"I imagine you're anxious to spend the time with your family, Jed."

"I am, but your father has a private matter to discuss with me, and he'd also like to show me his mill. In addition, the opportunity to spend more time with your son was too tempting to turn down."

"You're wasting your breath with that useless attempt at flattery again."

"It distresses me that you can't take it as truth, but I'm sincere, Caroline. I find Garrett delightful. I only hope the chip on your shoulder doesn't fall onto his."

She stopped short, her anger clear. "And why would that be your concern, even if it did?"

Why had he made such a stupid remark? The woman obviously had no sense of humor. About to apologize, he turned at the sound of a low growl. Buffer stood stiffly, his eyes glowing like yellow beacons in the dark.

"What is that dog growling at again?"

Caroline arched a brow again. "You, Mr. Fraser." She pivoted and left him.

Dare he chase after her, or would the dog attack him? He hesitated, uncertain whether to turn his back on the animal. When the growling ceased, Jed reached out cautiously to pet him. "Good boy, Buffer."

Another growl emitted immediately from the dog's throat, and Jed jerked back his hand. Deciding to take the bull by the horns, he turned and headed to the house, but he couldn't help taking a backward glance. The huge dog stalked behind him.

Jed ran the last few steps, charged through the open door, and ran smack into Caroline. For a long moment her startled eyes looked into his. The closeness of her lips was a temptation, but self-preservation prevailed, and he released her and stepped back.

"Rather clumsy of me, I'm afraid. My apologies, Miss Caroline."

Devilment danced in her eyes. "Did something alarm you, Mr. Fraser?" she asked, tongue in cheek.

"What happened?" Nathan asked, joining him.

"Nothing serious, Father. It appears Mr. Fraser must be afraid of the dark. Come on, Buffer." She turned away and started to climb the stairs.

Buffer gave Jed a final growl, then padded away and climbed the stairway.

"I'm sure you're ready for a brandy. Come and join me in my study," Nathan said.

Caroline's walk had done a great deal to relieve her tension as she entered Garrett's room. Buffer stretched out at the feet of the sleeping boy, and as she gazed at the face of her beloved son, her face softened with a tender smile.

"I love you, sweetheart," she whispered. "You're my life, my reason for existing. I won't let anyone come between us."

She placed a gentle kiss on Garrett's forehead, then straightened and looked at Buffer, who was watching her with large, soulful eyes.

"He's your life, too, isn't he, boy? We've got to take care of him and not let Jed Fraser ruin our lives."

The dog responded with a sweep of his tail.

Caroline gave him a pat on the head and left the room. She paused at the top of the stairway. The low sound of the voices of the two men carried up to her, but only loud enough to tell they were talking about the railroad. Since the situation affected her as much as her father, she was tempted to join them but decided to continue on to her room.

Jed's sudden appearance this morning had been a shock, but now she had her confidence back. She dare not allow herself to become too confident, though; the man was dangerously charming and persuasive. The next time she faced Jed Fraser, she would need a battle plan to cope with him.

Surely there must be something she could do, she pondered as she changed into her nightgown. Being unpleasant to him sure hadn't worked; it had only piqued his curiosity about her. And he might swing that curiosity at any time toward Garrett.

Didn't they always say one could catch more flies with honey than with vinegar? She could tell on the train and in the garden that she had caught his eye, so if she encouraged him, it might keep his attention on her. Surely he would be leaving in another day.

Caroline sat down at the dressing table and began to vigorously brush out her hair. Leaning forward, she studied her image in the mirror. Was she beautiful and desirable, as he had said? No man had ever said that before.

Her alter ego stared back at her. *Of course not. Flattery and charm is why those Fraser men are so successful at seducing women.*

"What if I turned the tables on him and gave him a taste of his own medicine?"

You're no Madame Pompadour. Flirting is an art you've never attempted, and you'd be up against a master.

"And Jed Fraser is no Louis the Fifteenth," Caroline retorted. "It shouldn't be too difficult to keep him at arm's length for another day, even if I had to suffer a few attempts at stolen kisses."

And what if he wants more? You know the reputation of those Fraser men. He will be very persuasive.

Caroline winked at her image. "Forewarned is forearmed, dearie."

Having convinced herself to make the attempt, she climbed into bed.

"If I'm to believe my father, Mr. Fraser, you're not one to shy away from a challenge. Well, sir, you may be brilliant and relentless in a sea battle, but let's see how you fare against a she-wolf defending her cub."

CHATPER
3

❧

"Let me see if I understand the facts, sir," Jed said. "You say this local attorney, Vincent Calhoun, has made an offer for a large section of your property on behalf of the railroad, and their intent is to run a private trunk line between Napa and Sonoma."

"That is correct," Nathan said, handing him a glass of brandy.

"And you have had no direct contact by correspondence or mouth with any other representative of the railroad."

"None whatsoever."

"Hmm, that is strange. I would think the railroad would have their personal corporate attorneys representing them in this type of transaction."

"I thought so, too, and challenged Calhoun on that matter, since a trunk line would affect other property owners, as well. Calhoun said the railroad doesn't have the manpower to handle all the land-owners involved, so they had to recruit local attorneys to represent them."

"There is some logic to that. But why buy the property? Wouldn't the railroad be satisfied with you giving them an easement to run the line through your land?"

"I offered to allow them to do that after we harvest the trees in that area," Nathan said.

"Then what is the problem?"

"For one thing, my sawmill is on that same property. But more important, the trees in that area aren't ready to be harvested for two more years. Calhoun claims the railroad can't wait that long. They want to move on it now, so the trees and mill would have to be removed."

Nathan slammed down his glass. "The price Calhoun offered doesn't come near the financial loss I would suffer if I lose those trees. It would take years for me to replace them, and by that time I'd be out of the lumber business. I'd lose contracts I have with the shipping lines, because they would have to seek their lumber elsewhere, so it would be useless to build another sawmill because I couldn't survive the financial loss. I'd have no choice but to pack up and leave.

"This is our home, Jed. My brother struggled to hold on to it the same way your family did with Fraser Keep during the war. My grandson was born here; my wife and brother are buried here. I'm not going to sell out."

"It sounds to me like you've pretty much made up your mind, sir. How does Caroline feel about it?"

"She's of the same opinion as I."

Jed thought for a long moment, then shrugged. "So simply don't sell. Of course I don't have to tell you that. There's something else you haven't told me, isn't there?"

Nathan smiled and refilled his glass. "You always were able to read my mind. It once annoyed the hell out of me, until I discovered how helpful it became during a crisis." He slumped down in a chair. "You must respect this confidence, because I haven't even told Caroline. I don't want to alarm her."

"You have my word, sir."

"Calhoun threatened that some harm might fall to Caroline or Garrett if I don't accept the offer."

"Surely that must be a bluff."

"I thought so at the time, because the man is a weasel and would barter his mother for the right price. But then last week, the day after Calhoun's threat, Buffer drove off a stranger who suddenly appeared when Garrett was alone fishing at the river."

Recalling his own confrontation with the dog, Jed knew his own impulse had been to run. He walked over and put a hand on Nathan's shoulder. "Sir, that doesn't mean the man intended to harm the boy. Under the circumstances, the dog might have been more of a threat to the stranger than the man was to Garrett."

Nathan shook his head. "What would a stranger be doing on the property?"

"Perhaps he was one of the lumberjacks."

"Garrett knows every one of them by sight and name, and since the next harvest isn't until fall, I only keep a couple of sawyers on hand during the summer."

"A mill worker, then?"

"The same is true. Garrett knows every one of them, and they all know him."

"Then the man may have been a lost traveler, or a railroad surveyor looking the place over."

"I wish I had your optimism, Jed." Nathan stood up. "It's time I get to bed, or I'll find myself blubbering in my brandy. Good night, Jed. We'll visit the mill in the morning."

"Good night, Captain Collins."

Long after Nathan departed, Jed stood with his glass in hand and stared out the window, where moonlight bathed the garden with tranquility.

Were the captain's fears justified? Had Garrett actually been in danger? Well, there was no way he'd walk away from it now without checking into it.

He took a final sip of the brandy, then went upstairs to bed.

The following morning Jed awoke early as usual, dressed, and went downstairs. Stepping out into bright sunshine and the promise of a pleasant day, he took a deep breath. The sweet aroma of roses and gardenias made him think of Caroline.

"All right, Mr. Fraser, fifteen times around the deck," he declared, in keeping with his morning ritual of walking a country mile when he was at sea.

When he returned, Caroline was just descending the stairway. "Good morning, Jed."

She was wearing a yellow-and-white dress and her bright, shiny hair was tied back with a white ribbon. The faint fragrance of lavender followed as she passed him.

"Good morning, Caroline. You look as pretty and pert as one of the daisies in the garden."

"I declare, sir, if you don't stop flattering me, you're going to turn my head. Did you sleep well?"

"Very well, thank you. And you?"

"I can't remember when I had a better night's sleep. It must be the peace of mind at having a big, handsome man in the house."

"I had the impression you disliked men in general, Caroline."

Her eyes widened with astonishment. "Perish the thought, sir. Wherever would you get such an idea?"

He followed her into the kitchen. "Then it must be just men from Virginia that repulse you."

"I declare, Jed Fraser, you're painting a bleak picture of me. Do I really appear that dismal to you?" she asked as she rolled out the dough she had mixed and using a glass, began to cut it into biscuits.

"On the contrary, you're a very vibrant woman."

"There you go again with your sweet talk. I declare, Jed Fraser, you're embarrassing me."

"Caroline, how long are you going to keep on playing a . . . ah . . ." He struggled for a word that would not be too offensive.

"Brainless twit?" she volunteered.

For a few moments he was speechless, then they both broke into laughter.

She turned away and popped the pan into the oven, and when she turned back, Jed had moved to her side. The heat of his body was as warm as the oven as he clasped her shoulders and pulled her nearer.

"Why, Caroline? Why this sudden change of heart?"

The throatiness in his voice and the intensity of his dark-eyed stare added fuel to the heat sweeping through her.

"I'm ashamed of how rude I've been to you, and I thought if I . . . if I— Oh, it was stupid of me, I know."

"It was delightful, and I enjoyed every minute of it. But there's a much more pleasant way of saying you're sorry." Gazing at her lips, he lowered his head toward hers.

Her heart beating faster, Caroline closed her eyes and parted her lips. But before he could kiss her, the kitchen door swung open and Garrett burst into the room, followed by Buffer.

"Good morning, Mama. Good morning, Mr. Fraser."

Jed dropped his hands and stepped away. "Morning, Garrett."

"Good morning, sweetheart." Caroline opened her arms and Garrett ran into them for a kiss and hug. "I hope you had a good sleep with pleasant dreams." She gave him a pat on his bottom. "Go get dressed, and tell your grandfather breakfast will be ready in fifteen minutes."

Then she turned to the dog, whose stare had never strayed from Jed. "Buffer, stop that growling."

"Thank you," Jed murmured.

"Come on, Buffer." Boy and dog exited as quickly as they had entered.

"Will you please explain why that dog continually

growls at me?" Jed grumbled. "I've never had a problem with any dog except this one."

Caroline tried not to laugh. "Well, they do say that dogs have remarkable instincts about people, and The Buffer is usually right."

"The Buffer!" he scoffed. "So the captain was right; the damn dog rules this household."

"He does indeed. Now, get out of my kitchen so I can get on with breakfast."

"Fine, but I should tell you, I'm known for my flapjacks."

She eyed him with a dubious glance. "Really?"

"Ask your father; he's eaten enough of them when we were at sea."

She tossed him an apron. "Then welcome to the galley, sailor. You'll find the ingredients in the cabinet next to the door."

A short time later she stole a glance at his broad shoulders as he stood at the stove, whistling and flipping pancakes. She'd already known he was dangerous to her life and Garrett's, but now there was an additional danger to fear—he excited her. Could she really hope to succeed against him in a battle of the sexes?

Garrett stuck his head in the door, interrupting her thoughts. "Mama, Granddad's at the table waiting for his breakfast, and he told me to tell you the fifteen minutes have passed."

"Tell your grandfather that patience is a virtue."

She picked up the pot of coffee and plate of biscuits and carried them into the dining room.

Jed glanced over his shoulder, and as soon as the door swung shut behind her, he broke off a piece of a pancake and tossed it to Buffer, who was watching his every move. The dog's jaws clamped on it before it hit the floor.

"Good boy," Jed murmured, just as Caroline returned and picked up a platter of bacon.

"Pancakes ready?" she asked.

"All set," he said. "Aren't we, boy?"

The dog gave him a muddled look but at least didn't growl at him. Smiling with satisfaction, Jed grabbed the platter of pancakes and followed Caroline.

Yes, sir. Just a matter of time, and that dog will be eating out of my hand.

After breakfast was over, Caroline tidied up the kitchen, then packed them a lunch. Nathan harnessed Belle to the buggy and then saddled their remaining horse Liberty for Jed to ride since there was only a single backseat in the buggy.

Nature smiled on them as they rode the five miles to the mill through the sun-kissed valley, the rough trail shaded by towering oaks and pine trees. White petals of Indian pipe lined the route, their fragrance blending with the spicy scent of pine.

Unlike the flat, arid land of the grape-growing Napa Valley, this area had a river running through it, a hot spring, an artist's tapestry of vine-covered hillsides, and brightly colored wild flowers amid the groves of oak, maple, and Douglas fir trees.

The trail ended in a woodland clearing. Several yards away stood a large rectangular building, a small cabin, and a third building next to the cabin.

Garrett scrambled out of the buggy with his usual

enthusiasm when Nathan reined up in front of the cabin.

"Garrett, you stay nearby," Caroline called as he raced off with Buffer at his heels. Then she disappeared into the cabin. Jed walked over to a nearby hillside that was devoid of any trees or shrubbery; several chutes had been gouged into the earth.

"The chutes were made by trees being slid down the slope into the river below," Nathan said, joining him. "We rotate the sections that we cut and skid the trees from the cutting area to the river, then float them to the mill."

"As long as you have to haul them this far, why not take them directly to the mill?" Jed asked.

"We harvest them faster than we can mill them. We cut and jam them in fall and winter, and mill them in spring and summer. The water protects them from insects and fungi, as well as a fire."

"But what keeps them from continuing to float downstream? Surely you don't dam the river."

Nathan chuckled. "No, we string a raft that jams the logs but keeps the water flowing. We might lose one now and then, but we depend on the river current to operate. Come along, I'll show you."

They approached the large building set on the river's edge.

"This is the actual mill. See that water wheel at the back of the building? It's rotated by the river's current."

Two men with cant hooks were standing on a log-jam, manipulating the trees onto a conveyor powered by the water wheel.

"Inside, you'll see more reasons why the river's current is so important to our operation."

The smell of sawdust tickled Jed's nostrils before they even entered the building. Once inside, he saw that the tree on the conveyor was being stripped of bark and then flushed down a chute into the teeth of a saw, where it was measured and sliced lengthwise. The ends were then trimmed and smoothed by waiting hands, and when completed, the lengths of lumber were taken outside and stacked to dry out.

"An interesting operation, sir," Jed shouted above the screech of the whirring saws.

"Most of my lumber is sold to shipyards. We delivered the last of that two weeks ago," Nathan said, moving outside. "We send it downriver on a raft to Napa. That's easier and faster than freighting it down in wagons. We only have a skeleton crew of buckers and boom men now, for some smaller pieces that go to furniture builders in Napa and San Francisco."

"So you depend mainly on shipbuilders. But most ship hulls are no longer made of wood, since iron is more protective—especially in battle. How much demand can there be for lumber?"

"Enough to keep us thriving. The shipping industry is booming. There're more ships now than there's ever been, and with a greater demand not only for more passenger cabins, but larger and more luxurious ones. That calls for a lot of wood.

"Steam may be replacing sails on ships, but it leads to explosions and a greater potential for fires. And even when they perfect those steam engines, there'll still be a demand for wooden masts and hulls." Nathan winked at him.

Jed laughed and slapped him on the shoulder. "And there'll always be a need for an old sea dog like you at the helm."

At the sound of an explosion, he spun around. "What the hell!"

Nathan chuckled. "Nothing to be alarmed about. It's just Bomber blowing up tree stumps that are too big to dig out."

"I'd have thought a blast would be too damaging to an area," Jed said as they walked over to a nearby hill.

"Not the way we do it. Bomber's a master at the art. You'll see for yourself."

They climbed the rise to where a man was sprinkling gunpowder at the base of a wide stump. "Bomber, this is Mr. Fraser. He was a crew member on my ship during the war."

The man looked up and nodded hello.

"Captain Collins said you're a master at the art," said Jed. "Why gunpowder? Wouldn't dynamite be easier?"

Bomber shook his head. "Too powerful, Mr. Fraser. It takes too much along with it when it blows. Gunpowder and a long fuse is easier to control on a smaller job like this and will only uproot the stump. That way nothing more than you want is destroyed, and nobody gets hurt."

"The uprooted stump is then hauled away by oxen," Nathan added, "and we use what we can as firewood here in the office and bunkhouse."

"If you two are gonna hang around, you best take

cover behind them rocks up the hill here," Bomber said as he ran a fuse up to the rocks.

Jed and Nathan took cover as Bomber lit the fuse, then watched as the flame crept along it toward the stump.

The hair on Jed's neck prickled when he heard Garrett shout, "Where are you, Buffer?"

Fearing the worst, he stood and saw Garrett racing up the hill toward the stump. "Garrett, get back!"

Mindless of his own safety, Jed raced toward the boy, then knocked him off his feet, covering Garrett with his own body just as the gunpowder exploded.

Rocks, earth, and hunks of tree roots flew through the air, raining down on him. When the smoke cleared he sat up, bleeding from the temple. "Are you okay, Garrett?"

The boy was wide-eyed and shaking. "I think so, but your head's bleeding, Mr. Fraser."

As Bomber and Nathan rushed up to them, Jed stood and lifted Garrett into his arms. "Let's get you someplace where we can check you out."

At that moment, a barking Buffer came racing up the hill, with Caroline in close pursuit.

"What happened? Is Garrett hurt?" she cried out.

"He says he's fine," Jed said.

"Jed, you're bleeding!" she exclaimed. "Give him to me."

Jed stepped back. "I'll carry him."

"We're wasting time. Let's get both of you down to the office," Nathan said impatiently.

A desk, chair, table, file cabinet, and cast-iron stove occupied practically all of the floor space of the room. By the time Nathan, Bomber, and Buffer followed them inside, there was barely enough space to move around.

Caroline swept some papers off the table. "Put him here."

As soon as he set Garrett on the table Jed sat down in the nearby chair, feeling a little dizzy.

Caroline gently ran her hands and fingers across Garrett's back and shoulders, and then along his arms and legs. When she finished, she sighed in relief. "Looks like nothing's broken." Then she frowned. "Garrett Collins, you know better than to get that close when Bomber is blasting stumps!"

"I didn't know he was blasting there. I didn't see a red flag."

Bomber shook his head apologetically. "He's right, Miz Caroline. Got to talking to the boss and Mr. Fraser and forgot to put up one."

"Oh dear—Mr. Fraser!" She pivoted and looked at Jed sitting with his head in his hands. "I'm so sorry. I forgot about you. How are you feeling?"

"Dizzy for a few seconds, but I'm fine now."

"Just the same, let me look at that wound."

Nathan lifted Garrett off the table and took Garrett's hand. "We'll wait for you in the buggy."

"Don't let him out of your sight, Father," Caroline called after them as the two men, boy, and dog left.

"I'm fine," Jed said. "It's just a scratch. It's even stopped bleeding."

She patted the table. "Just the same, sit over here and I'll clean you up a bit. Would you like a cup of coffee?"

He sat on the table and dangled his legs over the edge. "If you haven't anything stronger."

She came back with a cup of steaming coffee, and when he took a swallow of it, his eyes popped open in surprise. "Wow, you make a potent cup of coffee, lady."

She grinned. "I thought you'd like it. My father keeps a bottle of whiskey in the bottom drawer."

Jed breathed in the tantalizing fragrance of lavender when she stepped between his legs to sponge away the blood on his forehead. His loins tightened in response to her nearness, and he fought the desire to pull her against him.

"Am I hurting you?" she asked.

"You have no idea."

"Well, do you want it lying down or sitting up?"

Good God, she had read his mind!

Then he saw she had picked up a bottle of iodine and was waiting for his reply.

"Sitting up's fine," he grumbled.

"I hate to do this, but—"

"I know, it's going to hurt you more than it does me."

"No, it's going to hurt *you*, Mr. Fraser."

He gritted his teeth when the astringent liquid hit the open wound.

"Fortunately it's not a deep cut, but you really could use a couple of stitches to close it up," she advised. "I don't want it to start bleeding again."

He grinned at her and stood up. "Why, Miss Caroline—I didn't know you cared."

As she blushed, he winked at her and left.

CHAPTER
4

$\textbf{O}$n the way back, they stopped at a spring to water the horses. Caroline spread out a blanket and unpacked the basket.

"This was the best I could do on short notice," she said as she laid out thick slices of bread, cheese, and fruit.

After they ate and drank their fill of the cool spring water, Nathan stretched out in the shade and fell asleep. It wasn't long before Garrett and Buffer curled up beside him and did the same. Jed sat silently watching Caroline repack the basket.

She could feel his stare and felt a heated tingling in the pit of her stomach. "You're staring at me, Mr. Fraser," she said without raising her head.

"I'm enjoying the view."

His low voice was seductive, and she felt a hot flush of response to it. She knew if she looked up, she would see the desire in his eyes. As flattering as it was to be wanted by a man as attractive as Jed, she dare not look at him.

Sitting down, she leaned back against a tree

trunk. "This is my favorite spot. I come here when-ever I feel the need to be alone. It's always peaceful and quiet here."

"You shouldn't wander these hills alone."

"Nonsense. I know this area like the back of my hand."

"So you've got everything you want right here?"

"I'm contented here, if that's what you mean. But I hope that one day I will marry."

"I can't imagine a woman as desirable as you doesn't already have a special man in her life."

"Right now I actually have two." She glanced at the sleeping pair.

"You need more than that, Caroline."

The soft lilt of her laughter was like the riffle of a harp. "No, thank you. I have my hands full with just the two of them."

"I mean you need a man to take care of *your* needs. To remind you of how beautiful you are, how pleas-ing it is to listen to your voice or hear the sound of your laughter."

His voice was hypnotic, drawing her deeper and deeper into the spell he wove so artfully. She yearned to close her eyes and succumb to the picture he painted. Hadn't she often thought of what it would be like to be held and loved by a man she loved?

Yet her needs paled beside the consequences of surrendering to such whimsy. The man in her fanta-sies must not be, could never be, Jed Fraser. No mat-ter what the temptation, she must not weaken from that resolve.

"And what of your needs, Jed? Do you have a

special woman in your life?" A smile tugged at the corners of her lips. "I know the girls in Virginia were tripping over their party pumps to get your attention."

He couldn't help grinning. "Now, how would you know that, Caroline? I don't recall you ever attending a party in Virginia."

"Ladies do talk," she said archly.

"I'm surprised—you don't strike me as the kind to kiss and tell," he teased.

"I'm not; I merely listen."

"All joking aside, did you really hate Virginia that much? There's so much bitterness when you mention the word, and I hate to think you can't put it behind you and get on with your life."

She lifted her chin. "Then perhaps you'd be wiser not to mention the word." She stood up and went over to the spring. For a long moment she gazed into the water, her arms folded across her chest. Then she turned back with a smile.

"You've avoided answering my question, Jed. Is there a special woman in your life?"

"Very much so."

"That doesn't surprise me. Are you married?"

"You could say that."

"Now who's being evasive? Either you are or you aren't. But I won't pry any longer. It's none of my business." She started to walk away.

"I'm married to the sea, Caroline." She halted and turned back to him. "I've loved her from my youth. No woman could ever hold my heart and soul the way she does."

"That's very poetic, but not very realistic. You speak of my needs and then allude that yours are incorporeal. Yet your conduct shows that your needs are no less earthy than mine. Do you really believe you could never love a mortal woman?"

"I would like to believe that there is a special woman for me out there. I just haven't met her yet. Maybe my next port, or the one beyond that. But since I'd be gone at sea most of the time, I would make a poor husband—and father. Did you regret your father's lengthy absences?"

"I thought about him often and missed him when he was gone. But on the other hand, it made every moment he was home more precious to me. I would never wish for any other father."

"But how would you feel if it was a husband, the man you love?"

"I couldn't bear not being with him and would never understand why he wouldn't feel the same about me; the man I marry must hold the love of his family foremost in his heart.

"I want him beside me when I wake in the morning and close my eyes at night, not have him off on some distant sea or foreign country. I want to see his clothes hanging beside mine in the closet, smell his pipe smoke in the evening as we sit in front of our fireplace talking over the day, see him holding our children on his lap as he reads to them."

For a long moment she sat in reflection, then looked at him and smiled. "I guess we should wake the others and be on our way."

"As you wish."

He stood and reached out to pull her to her feet, his gaze never leaving hers as his warm hand closed around her own. A jolt of excitement went through Caroline, and she could see he'd felt it, too. His mouth was so close she thought he was going to kiss her, and she braced herself against her waning resistance.

Then he released her hand and stepped back. "I'll hitch up the buggy."

By rote, Jed harnessed Belle and then saddled his mount, his thoughts on his conversation with Caroline. She had cleverly fielded his questions, while finding out the answers to her own. Beauty and brains: a lethal combination.

This battle of the sexes between them was developing into an interesting duel, but unfortunately it was coming to a swift end. Tomorrow, after he talked to the local attorney the captain had mentioned, he would be leaving for Clay's. Maybe he'd stop back to say good-bye to the Collins family on his return to San Francisco.

Caroline Collins was unquestionably the most mysterious woman he had ever known. She had an ever-changing shift of moods, and he would have liked to remain longer to try and figure her out, especially the reason for her resentment toward him. But there wasn't any point to it; she had made her position very clear. She was looking for a land-based man who would give her the love she sought, and that certainly wasn't him. He hoped she found what she was looking for, though.

As for himself . . .

Jed suddenly had a prickly tingling on the nape of his neck and sensed he was being watched. He turned his head and saw that Buffer had awakened and was standing up, watching him.

"What?" Jed snapped. "You got something to say?" It was bad enough to be outwitted by a woman without having to cope with a damn dog.

After several more seconds of the stare-down, the dog issued a low growl, then trotted back to the others.

"Yeah, good riddance to you, too."

"Are you talking to me or yourself?" Caroline asked, suddenly appearing beside him. She put the blanket and picnic basket into the back of the buggy.

"What the hell's wrong with that mutt? Anybody can tell you that dogs usually like me," Jed grumbled as he swung into the saddle.

"Perhaps it's that Southern accent of yours, Mr. Fraser."

Frustrated, he threw his hands up in the air. "You even resent our accents? Aren't you carrying your resentment toward Virginia to an extreme?"

"On the contrary, sir. I find your accent very pleasant and soothing—when you're not shouting." She sat down in the rear seat of the buggy. Nathan and Garrett quickly climbed on, and Nathan took the reins.

"Granddad, since we'll be home soon, can I drive the rest of the way?" Garrett asked later.

"You know your mother says you're too young to handle a buggy. Belle's old, but she's still got some run in her."

"Mama's asleep," the boy said. "Besides, how's a person to learn if I can't get to practice?"

"All right, you can drive for a couple of miles," Nathan said and handed him the reins. "But I'll have the devil to pay if your mother wakes up and sees you."

"Driving's not hard," Garrett said proudly as they rode along. "I like it."

"I feel the same way about sailing, boy. I imagine you do, too; don't you, Jed?" Nathan called over.

Jed nodded. "Nothing can compare to it. You're doing a good job of keeping that buggy on this bumpy road, Garrett."

He'd no sooner spoken when a bevy of quail, flushed from the surrounding brush, fluttered across the road. Spooked by their flapping wings, Belle reared on her hind legs and Nathan was tossed off the seat. The horse bolted, and Jed goaded Liberty into a gallop to catch the runaway.

Caroline awoke sharply when she was thrown out of her seat. She tried to reach Garrett, but the careening buggy rocked for the length of several gasps of breath, then the rear end collapsed. The horrifying screech of splintering wood combined with Garrett's screams as the buggy's tongue splintered and broke off and the vehicle tipped over on its side.

Garrett, who had the reins wrapped around his fists, was dragged along the ground by Belle.

Jed jumped from his mount onto Belle's back and reined the runaway horse to a halt. Though the whole incident couldn't have taken more than sixty seconds, it left a trail of devastation behind it.

Buffer was licking Garrett's face by the time Jed dismounted. The dazed boy sat up and Jed quickly unwound the reins from Garrett's bleeding hands.

"Don't move, son, until I can check if anything's broken."

"I'm okay," Garrett said, "but my hands sure sting."

"We can take care of them right away. Are your hands the only thing that hurts?" Jed asked as he continued to check the boy for any further injuries.

"Yeah, but don't tell my mother: I peed in my pants," he whispered.

"If that's the only thing wrong, pal, I don't think your mother will care." He studied the youngster's eyes. "I'd say you look pretty good for what you've just been through."

"Oh, she's gonna care, all right. Me and Granddad are gonna be in trouble, 'cause I ain't supposed to be driving the buggy."

Jed glanced up and was relieved to see Caroline and Nathan running toward them. "Well, we'll soon find out." He helped Garrett to his feet as Caroline rushed up to them.

"Oh, thank God you're okay! Thank God! Thank God!" Tears of joy streaked her cheeks as she hugged and kissed Garrett. She tenderly wrapped a handkerchief around one of his hands, then ripped the ruffle off one of the sleeves of her gown to wrap around his other hand.

"That feels better, Mama," Garrett said as she wiped away her tears with the skirt of her gown.

"Are you hurt, sir?" Jed asked Nathan.

"No. These old bones will be aching for a couple

of days, but it wasn't as bad as getting tossed from a horse."

"What about Caroline?"

"She was just scared about Garrett. She got over her pain when she saw the boy on his feet. It was all my fault—I never should've given him those reins. I'm beholden to you, Jed. You saved my grandson's life."

"Don't give me the credit, sir. If it was his time to go, he would have been killed. How bad is the buggy?"

"I didn't even look at it yet. Reckon a rear wheel must have rolled off to make it tip over like that."

"And how far is it to the house?"

"Just over the next rise."

"Good. We've got two horses, so we can ride double. If we can wrench Garrett out of Caroline's arms, you and he can ride my mount since it has a saddle. Caroline and I can ride bareback on Belle."

"Since she's grateful to you right now, she most likely won't give you an argument. But there's sure going to be hell to pay when she's over her scare."

After Nathan and Garrett rode away with Buffer beside them, Caroline asked, "Would you mind if I walk a while? I'd be more comfortable."

Jed slipped off Belle. "I'll walk so you can ride on ahead. The sooner you get into a hot bath the better your aches will feel."

"I think if I stretch my legs, I can walk off some of the stiffness."

Jed lifted her down. "All right, but if you tire, let me know. We can always rest for a while."

"We only have about a mile to go."

"Do you ride very often, Caroline?"

"No, I'm not comfortable astride a horse. I find it very awkward."

After walking a short distance more, Caroline stopped to rest. "Just give me a minute."

"Do you want to sit down?"

She shook her head with a smile. "If I sit down, I probably won't be able to get up. Besides, this gives me the opportunity to thank you, Jed. If you hadn't been here, Garrett would have been dragged. . . ." She choked back her words. "I don't know what I would have done if he'd been killed."

Jed slipped an arm around her shoulders and drew her to his side. "It's over, Caroline. It didn't happen, so don't dwell on the thought."

"How do you expect me not to?" she said. "Twice today my son could have been killed, and you prevented that from happening. I'm frightened—something feels very wrong."

"I can understand your anxiety, but I doubt Garrett would have been killed in that explosion this morning. More likely he would have suffered a minor injury, like I did."

"Father told me you threw your body across him as a shield, so I can't believe he wouldn't have been seriously hurt."

"I can imagine how you must be feeling, Caroline. But growing up with brothers as I did, there were more times than I can remember when one or another had close calls."

She glanced aside at him. "If I recall correctly, you

Fraser boys often seemed to be in trouble. How did your poor mother endure it?"

He laughed. "With patience and faith. I have to admit, I initially thought you were overly protective of Garrett, but now I see why. He's like a cat with nine lives."

They resumed walking. "If so, he used up a couple of them today. Nothing like today's events has ever happened before," said Caroline.

"Does he have any playmates his own age?"

"No, our house is pretty isolated. My uncle owned the property originally, and this was where we came when we left Virginia. Uncle Frank died five years ago and Father was his only heir. When the war ended, my father put himself in 'dry dock' as he says, and joined my mother and me."

"So Garrett hasn't had an opportunity to be around children his own age. What about schooling?"

"I tutor him."

"You've done a great job. He's a smart little boy."

"And he's not completely without companionship; he and The Buffer are inseparable. Maybe that's why he hasn't had any narrow escapes—Buffer has always looked after him." She grinned at him. "He's even more protective of Garrett than I am."

"So The Buffer lives up to his name, is that what you're saying?"

"Exactly. He's not only my son's best friend and dearest companion, but also a buffer between Garrett and any danger. He's always been a buffer for me, too: I always had peace of mind knowing that he was always looking out for Garrett."

"I seriously suspect that this is leading into that *Providence* conversation again," Jed said.

Caroline's eyes lit with triumph. "Ah-hah! I think I've made a believer of you."

"Not quite, madam. Where was The Buffer when Garrett walked into the path of that explosion? If I remember right, Garrett was calling out for him."

"I'm afraid I'm to blame. I put Buffer into the office while Garrett was in the privy and called to Garrett to come to the office when he was through. I had heard that Bomber was going to blow stumps and wanted the two of them someplace where I knew they'd be safe. I guess Garrett didn't hear me. I should never have taken Buffer away from the privy door."

"This is all ridiculous. Your father takes the blame for the buggy accident, and—"

"Maybe he should! Father knew I think Garrett's too young to drive it," she declared.

"Just the same, he's no more responsible for the buggy accident than you are for the other one. For someone who believes in Providence, you sure are contradicting yourself."

Caroline looked confused, and they continued on in silence until they reached the house.

After Garrett bathed and had his hands properly bandaged, and Caroline's and Nathan's aches and pains had been soothed in hot baths, all the Collinses opted for an early bedtime.

Jed lingered downstairs for a smoke and walk in the garden before retiring. Now that the Collinses were all tucked away safely in their beds, he had a chance to reflect on the day's events. This family had come to mean a lot to him in this short time.

He sensed that Caroline still distrusted him, though. Why? Despite her recent attempt at friendliness, there was still an undercurrent of wariness toward him.

You can't win them all, Fraser. Too bad, because he found himself looking forward to being with her. Or was it just the challenge to win her over?

Well, he was leaving tomorrow so what in hell did it matter? But not before he spoke to this local attorney, Vincent Calhoun, as he had promised Nathan he would. Something about this railroad buyout smelled like three-day-old fish.

Jed ground out his cigarillo and went up to bed.

CHAPTER
5

Bright morning sunshine streamed through the ruffled curtains of her room, teasing Caroline awake. She opened her eyes and lay remembering the previous day's activities.

It had been a frightful day and she couldn't help fearing what the outcome might have been—and that was the rub. From the moment Jed Fraser had entered the picture, she had wanted him gone. Yet if he hadn't been there . . . She fought back tears of relief.

Despite the threat Jed presented, she had to admit she found him interesting; she enjoyed the quiet conversations they had together. Given her dangerous attraction to him, it was a good thing he was leaving today.

At the sound of voices outside, she got out of bed and crossed to the open window. Her father and Jed were preparing to depart in the buckboard. Was he leaving so early? And without even saying good-bye? Garrett would be devastated.

As if feeling her stare, Jed glanced up and saw

her. He smiled and tipped his hat. "Good morning, Caroline."

"Good morning." It was embarrassing being caught in the act of spying.

"I apologize for waking you."

"I was awake," she said. "Are you leaving so early? At least let me make breakfast before you depart."

"We're just riding out to see if we can salvage any of the buggy," Nathan said.

"Oh, then you'll be back." Her heartbeat quickened.

"Of course!" Jed exclaimed. "Do you think I'd leave without saying good-bye to you or my little pal?"

"I'm glad to hear that. I'll have breakfast ready by the time you get back."

Caroline turned away and started to dress. As she brushed her hair, her thoughts continued to dwell on Jed Fraser.

He was an incredibly handsome man. *All* those Fraser brothers were handsome and personable. That was the trouble—and the downfall of any woman who met them.

She congratulated herself for not having buckled under that smooth charm. Within a few hours, he'd be out of her life forever. Caroline lifted her chin. "Told you I could do it," she said to her image in the mirror, but her alter ego just stared back at her despondently.

Caroline tied her hair back with a ribbon, then went to wake Garrett.

Jed wore a worried frown after examining the shattered buggy.

"What's bothering you?" Nathan asked.

"It all happened so quickly, but let's go over the chain of events. It began with the rear of the buggy collapsing, right?"

Nathan nodded. "I was pitched off it when we bounced off a rock, the buggy slammed down, and the rear collapsed."

"That's how I remember it, too," Jed said. "Then the front of the buggy was dragged a few feet, tottered, and then tipped on its side, causing the tongue to break off and the harness to snap. So if all the resulting damage occurred *after* the rear collapsed, what do you think caused the rear end to collapse to begin with?"

"I assumed one of the rear wheels rolled off," Nathan replied.

Jed shook his head. "That was my assumption at first, too. But take a look—both of them are bent or smashed from the crash. That means neither one rolled off, which means the rear axle splintered and caused the collapse."

"I would say," Nathan said.

"I took a closer look at the rear axle, and the broken ends are smooth—not splintered. That axle was sawn through almost entirely, and when the rear hit that rock, the axle snapped and broke *before* the buggy bounced back. Then it tipped over and the tongue broke off."

After a brief examination, Nathan looked up at Jed, his eyes wide with shock. "My God, man, you're right! Who would do such a thing? I can't believe even Vincent Calhoun would be a party to such a dastardly deed. And who would even have access to do so?"

"Didn't you stable your horses and the buggy in Napa when you went to San Francisco?"

"That's right. Fortunately, we use the buckboard more than the buggy, so the axle didn't snap until it hit that rock."

"I think I'll take a look at the underside of that buckboard," Jed said. "Whoever did it to the buggy may have done the same to the buckboard."

He slid under the buckboard, and when he was satisfied the axles hadn't been tampered with, he crawled out from under it.

"Everything looks fine," he said, dusting himself off. "I think we should leave the buggy as is and bring the sheriff out here to see it."

"He took a prisoner to Sacramento. He won't be back for another week."

"Then we might have an additional problem to deal with. But if I were you, I'd still report this to the law. You all could have been seriously hurt—if not killed."

Nathan looked so downcast that Jed went over and squeezed his shoulder. "There's nothing more we can do here now, sir, so we might as well get back to the house."

He salvaged the blanket and picnic basket from the buggy's ruins and put them in the buckboard. "You realize, sir, for the sake of Caroline's and Garrett's safety, you're going to have to make her aware of the danger."

Nathan sighed deeply. "Yes, I see that now. I was

hoping I could avoid alarming her, but I'll have to tell her what's happened."

"Have you considered leaving the area until this issue with the railroad's been resolved?"

"No. This is my property, and I won't allow a weasel like Calhoun to drive me off it. And knowing Caroline, I think she won't consider leaving, either."

"Not even to secure Garrett's safety? After all, Calhoun threatened both of them."

"That might convince her, but even if she agreed, I don't know where I could send them."

"I could take them to my brother's home, sir. They'd be safe there. But before we do anything, I'm talking to Mr. Calhoun. I'd like to sit in on this pot and find out what kind of hand is being dealt. And if it ends up a bust one, you're all coming with me."

Caroline clearly wasn't thrilled when Nathan insisted she and Garrett accompany them to Napa.

"There's no reason why we can't say good-bye right here," she declared. "I'm still aching from yesterday, and the thought of being jostled about in a buckboard is not appealing."

"Caroline, there's a very good reason for going with us," Nathan said.

"What reason?"

"Do you mind if I talk to her privately, sir?" Jed asked.

Nathan took Garrett by the hand. "You come with me, and we'll feed the stock and saddle Liberty for Jed to ride."

"I don't keep any secrets from you guys," Garrett grumbled as his grandfather led him away.

"Jed, what's going on here?" Caroline asked.

"Let's take a walk." He put his hand on her back and guided her out into the garden. "Your father and I discovered something very disturbing about that buggy accident. It wasn't an accident."

She stopped short and looked at him, confused. "What do you mean?"

"We discovered the rear axle of the buggy had been sawn nearly through. It took just a bad jolt to make it break apart."

"My God, who would do such a thing?"

"Your father suspects Vincent Calhoun."

She looked incredulous. "Why would he think that? I know Father has always distrusted Mr. Calhoun, but I can't believe the man would endanger our lives. Is this related to the railroad wanting to run that line through our property?"

"Yes. Nathan said Calhoun threatened that something might happen to you or Garrett if he didn't agree to it."

She paled in shock, and he led her over to a bench. "I intend to speak to this Calhoun before I leave today, and the Captain's afraid to leave you and Garrett alone here. That's why he insists you come along."

"Why didn't Father warn us? When I think of how we let Garrett run free with only Buffer as protection . . ."

"That hound is as good a protection as an army would be. And don't blame your father. He had no way of knowing if Calhoun was merely bluffing, so he didn't want to alarm you unnecessarily. And with the sheriff out of town, he didn't know who he could trust. I trust your father's judgment, Caroline. I've seen him in battle before."

"He still should have warned me. I would have kept a closer eye on Garrett. Look at yesterday's accident at the mill—"

"We can't blame Calhoun for that, Caroline. Garrett just wandered into the wrong place at the wrong time."

Seeing her pallor and fear, he gathered her hand between his own. "Honey, he's still got a lot of growing up to do. You can't protect him from genuine accidents."

"I know, but I can't help trying."

"Then come with me. I believe the railroad should be informed of Calhoun's threats. If he's done it to you, he's most likely done it to others, too. I suggested to your father that the three of you come with me to my brother's. You'll be safe there until this situation is resolved."

Surprisingly, she looked even more distressed. "What did my father say?" she asked.

"He refuses to be driven from his land, but he's concerned about your and Garrett's safety."

"I'm remaining with my father."

"That will be keeping you and Garrett at risk, Caroline."

"I'll make certain we remain close to the house."

Jed shook his head. "For how long? You have no way of knowing the amount of time it will take to resolve the situation."

"It can't take much longer; it's been an issue for almost a year now." She drew a deep breath. "Look, Jed, I appreciate your concern. If necessary, we'll hire a couple of men to protect us. We can use the help anyway—the barn and fences need some repairs. We'll be just fine."

"Your father's showing more common sense than you are, Caroline. At least he acknowledges the danger."

"I'm not making light of the danger, but we can hardly go hide without knowing how long it will take to resolve it."

"And you'd risk your life or Garrett's waiting to find out? You've got more common sense than that."

"Exactly. I was shocked and frightened when you first told me, but the more I think about it, the more outrageous it sounds. We're assuming Calhoun's behind it all, but the buggy accident might have had nothing to do with the railroad issue."

"Get your head out of the sand, Caroline; it *wasn't* an accident," Jed exclaimed, exasperated.

"I'm not implying it was. But it could also have been caused by a disgruntled employee Father fired, or a spiteful suitor that I turned down."

"Do you have anyone particular in mind?"

"Yes. Gabe Ryan was furious when Father fired him for drunkenness that almost cost the life of one of the loggers. He told Father that he hadn't seen the last of him. And when I turned down a marriage proposal from a former neighbor, Ben Slatter, he said an 'ungrateful whore' like me was making a big mistake and that I'd be sorry when I didn't have my 'daddy' around to take care of me and my 'bastard' son."

"I'd like to meet this Slatter," Jed said grimly.

"It no longer matters. The bank foreclosed on his land, so he's no longer a neighbor. He's just a big-mouth drunk."

Jed nodded thoughtfully. "Do you believe either one of those men would seek revenge by harming a child?"

"I don't know. But anyone familiar with us knows that we don't allow Garrett to drive the buggy or buckboard. So if Garrett wasn't their target, damaging the vehicles would make sense."

"Would you gamble his safety on that?" Jed asked quietly.

She turned away in despair. "I want to believe it." Tears glistened in her eyes when she turned back to him.

Her agony was so real, so raw. Jed gathered her into his arms and leaned his forehead against hers. "I know you do."

When he pressed a kiss to her temple, she drew back. For a long moment they stared into each other's eyes, then he gently wiped away a tear sliding down her cheek, lowered his head, and claimed her lips.

Sizzling sensation surged through her, and she felt the loss when he broke the kiss. Too breathless to speak, they stared at one another.

Surprise and shock was on her face from the excitement his kiss had generated.

Bewilderment was on his, as to why he should be so shaken by a kiss.

"I won't say I'm sorry, Caroline," he finally said. "I've wanted to kiss you for a long time."

"I understand. It's been an emotional time for both of us. And since we may never meet again, it was only natural that we'd kiss good-bye. I'll never forget you, Jed. Every time I look at my son, I'll remember how indebted I am to you."

"Then do me a favor and come with me to my brother's."

She shook her head. "I'm sorry, but I can't."

Nathan called from the doorway, "Ready to leave anytime you are."

Jed released his grasp on her, and she slipped from his arms.

When Jed rejoined them for the trip to town, Garrett was sitting between Nathan and Caroline on the buckboard seat. Buffer was stretched out in the bed of it, and Jed tossed his seabag next to the dog. Buffer raised his head, sniffed it, then stretched out again.

Jed mounted Liberty, and as they rode away, he turned to look back at the Collins's house, feeling an odd sadness to be leaving.

CHAPTER 6

The ride to town was quiet. The men talked softly to each other, Caroline read a book, and even Garrett silenced his usual chatter and crawled into the back and lay down next to Buffer.

By the time they reached the town, Jed had two hours remaining before his train was due to arrive. He agreed to meet the others for lunch in thirty minutes and departed in search of Vincent Calhoun's office.

A shiny brass-trimmed sign indicated he'd located the attorney, and the gray-headed man seated behind a massive oak desk glanced up when he entered.

"Good day, sir, I'm looking for Vincent Calhoun," Jed said.

"You've found him." The man rested his lit cigar in an ashtray and rose to his feet. Portly and short, Calhoun appeared to be in his sixties. He reached across the desk and offered his hand. "What can I do for you, stranger?"

"Mr. Calhoun, my name is Jed Fraser,"

They shook hands, and the attorney indicated for Jed to sit down.

"Fraser. Sounds familiar. Where are you from, Mr. Fraser?"

"Virginia."

"Hmmm, there's a passel of Virginian Frasers up at the end of the valley. Wine growers, I'm told. You related to them, Mr. Fraser?"

"I'm proud to say that I am, Mr. Calhoun."

"Seems a lot of you Virginians have come West. We've got a couple more right here. If we get many more of you, we'll soon have to change the name of the state to West Virginia. Oops, there's one of those already." He chuckled at his own joke.

When Jed failed to be amused, Calhoun cleared his throat. "So what brings you to Napa, Mr. Fraser? You figure on settling here?"

"I'm here as a guest of my former captain, Nathan Collins."

"Zat so." His leery gaze swept Jed. "I'm well acquainted with the family."

"So I've been told."

"Are you Nathan's attorney, Mr. Fraser?"

"No, I'm just looking out for their welfare. I have a few questions regarding this railroad transaction."

"I'm sorry, but if you're not their legal representative, Mr. Fraser, I'm not at liberty to discuss their private affairs with you." He shifted his gaze to the door. "Sorry I can't be of any further help. I'm sure you can see your way out."

"I intend to do so, Mr. Calhoun, as soon as you show

me that you're authorized to represent the railroad."

"I would be glad to, Mr. Fraser, but since there's no mortgage or lien against the property, you apparently have no financial investment, either.

"As I said I'm just a family friend."

Calhoun studied him intently, then asked, "On second thought, maybe you do, Mr. Fraser?" After another long inspection, Calhoun nodded. "Yes, I think I see. Possibly a physical one, Mr. Fraser.

"What do you want, Mr. Fraser?"

"Yesterday the Collinses had a serious accident, and Garrett was almost killed. I'm here to suggest it better not happen again."

"I have no idea what you're talking about." Calhoun leaned forward, his eyes as cold as steel. "Are you threatening me, Mr. Fraser?"

Jed rose to his feet. "If any more *accidents* occur to any member of that family, I assure you that you'll suffer the consequences. In the meantime, I'm advising the railroad of the tactics you're using to acquire that property on their behalf. I'm sure they don't want their reputation blemished by an unscrupulous shyster."

Calhoun burst into laughter. "Blemish their reputation! When was the last time you read a newspaper, Mr. Fraser?"

"I stand by what I said, Calhoun."

"Strong words for a man who has no dog in the hunt, Fraser." Calhoun stood up. "Without any proof to back up your allegations, I'll sue you and the Collins family for every square inch of that property."

"We have proof to show that the axle of the buggy has been sawn through."

Calhoun snorted. "What proof is there that *I* had anything to do with it?"

"Captain Collins has a distinguished reputation. I'm sure his word will stand up in any court, as will my own testimony. He informed me of your threat to his daughter and grandson."

Calhoun laughed again. "Distinguished reputation? A couple of gunrunners during the war? Any judge west of the Mississippi—and most certainly the judges in the California courts—would be happy to see you both hanged for your treason during that war.

"And as for you, sonny, your word ain't worth spit in the wind. You tell Nathan Collins that I've withdrawn the railroad's offer. I'm gonna buy his property myself. I'll give him ten cents an acre, and he'd be wise to take it and clear out of here while he has the chance, or he'll be leaving in a pine box. Now get the hell out of my office, or I'll have the sheriff haul your Rebel ass out of here."

"Court or no court, I don't back down from Yankee carpetbaggers. So save your breath for someone who'll swallow your bull."

Jed paused at the doorway. "And if anything happens again to one member of that family, I will settle with you personally."

The moment Jed entered the restaurant, Caroline sensed the news wasn't good. Funny how in such a short time she had grown to recognize some of his body language. Could he do the same with hers?

His handsomeness and carriage were obvious, but what she found even more attractive was his aura of confidence. At first she had mistaken it for arrogance, but she'd realized it wasn't cockiness at all, but his positive attitude about life.

If only he wasn't a Fraser. She sighed and forced the thought from her mind as he ruffled Garrett's hair and sat down next to her son. Jed genuinely liked Garrett; that was clear. And there was no question that Garrett worshipped the ground the man walked on. Another complication in her already muddled life.

"What luck did you have with Calhoun?" Nathan asked.

"Not good, sir. Matter of fact, I may have exacerbated the situation."

"In what way?"

"In the beginning Calhoun denied any connection with the buggy incident, but by the time we finished, he was threatening you'd leave here in a pine box and told me to tell you he's withdrawing the railroad's offer and will pay you ten cents an acre—like it or not."

"That blunderbuss! Who does he think he is?"

"A very dangerous man, Captain Collins. I think you should take his threats seriously."

"Are you suggesting I sell out, man? That's practically stealing the land. I have no intention of selling, no matter what the snake would offer."

"I think he's very aware of that, sir. That's when he interjected the pine box into the conversation."

"What are you going to do?" Caroline asked.

Nathan slammed his fist on the table. "Not bow to his threats; that's for certain."

"Mama, what did Mr. Calhoun mean when he said Granddad would leave in a pine box?" Garrett asked.

"It's just an expression, sweetheart. Have you decided what you want for lunch?" She glanced helplessly at Jed. "I think we should order. You have a train to catch."

"You just don't want me to know what you're talking about," Garrett said.

Nathan chuckled. "You're a smart lad, my boy. You do your old granddad proud."

"You ain't so old, Granddad. Bet you could beat the tar out of that Mr. Calhoun if you wanted to."

"Garrett, that's no way to talk," Caroline said.

"Well he *could*, Mama."

"Your mother's referring to the word *ain't*, Garrett. It's improper." Jed winked at her.

"And you know your mother don't like no improper grammar," Nathan teased with a twinkle in his eye. "Ain't that right, honey?"

Caroline sighed in exasperation. "How can you two grown men make light of this situation? We have a serious problem."

Garrett's eyes rounded in astonishment. "Just 'cause I said *ain't*?"

Try as she might, Caroline couldn't keep a straight face when the men started laughing. Garrett looked perplexed as he glanced around the table, then he added his boyish laughter to theirs.

Their laughter was a momentary release to their tension, but once it ceased, Caroline's thoughts returned to the seriousness of the situation they faced.

What chance did the three of them have against the power of Vincent Calhoun? Could a man's greed for wealth threaten their well-being? Was a piece of property worth jeopardizing the lives of the two people she cherished more than anything on earth?

When she looked across the table at Jed, his gaze was on her. She didn't have to be told that he had no intention of deserting them. But he was only one man.

She picked up the menu. "Shall we order?"

As they lingered over coffee, Nathan reminded Jed it would soon be time for his train to arrive.

"I know I can't be of much help, sir, but if you have no objection, I'd like to hang around for a while longer."

"Jed, this isn't your fight," Nathan said.

"I made it my fight when I spoke to Calhoun." He glanced at Caroline. "Do you have any objections if I remain?"

Of course she objected; she wanted him out of their lives. But at the same time, she welcomed his protection. They had no one else to turn to.

"Only the same as my father's, Jed. There's no reason you should put yourself at risk for our sake."

"I can think of three good ones," Jed said.

"What are they?" Garrett asked innocently.

Jed smiled. "They're all seated at this table, Garrett."

"Can he stay, Mama?"

"That decision is between your grandfather and Mr. Fraser, honey."

The boy looked hopefully at his grandfather. "Can he, Granddad?"

Nathan grinned. "He's too big a fellow for me to wrestle, son."

"Yippee!" Garrett swung his glance to Jed. "I'm sure glad you're staying, 'cause I like you a lot."

"I feel the same about you, pal. But I don't think your dog will welcome the news."

"Oh, don't worry about Buffer. He just don't like having strangers around.

"He *doesn't* like strangers," Caroline corrected.

"See, Mama agrees. Once he gets to know you, he'll like you, too. I'm going outside to tell him the good news." Garrett dashed outside.

Caroline stood, too. "While your presence will be a relief, Jed, be careful you're not jumping into waters that are over your head."

"I'm pretty good at testing the waters."

"The water might be deeper than you think, so be careful you don't drown, sailor," she warned.

Jed grinned. "I'm a pretty good swimmer, lady."

Caroline enjoyed this little sparring between them, but the physical attraction she felt to Jed made it dangerous.

As she reached the doorway, the bright sunlight momentarily blinded her. Suddenly a hard shoulder slammed into her, and only Jed's body behind hers prevented her from falling.

"Oh, it's you," Ben Slatter grumbled. The smell of alcohol was strong on his breath.

"Yes, it's *me*. And as usual, Ben Slatter, you're reeking of alcohol," Caroline said in disgust.

When he started to shove past her, Jed said, "I believe you owe the lady an apology, sir."

The man stood eye to eye with him, with a withering glare. "Who in hell are you?"

"Name's Jed Fraser."

"Is that supposed to mean something to me?"

"Mr. Fraser is a close friend from Virginia, Ben. He served on my father's ship during the war."

Slatter snorted. "Yeah, I can see he was a *real* close friend. So he's the little bastard's daddy."

Despite Slatter's size, Jed grabbed a handful of the man's shirt, lifted him off his feet, and slammed him against the wall. "The apology, Slatter."

Slatter's alcoholic bravado was no match for the fury in Jed's eyes. "Okay, okay, I'm sorry."

"Tell that to the lady." Jed fortified the command with another slam against the wall.

"Excuse me, Caroline," Slatter grunted.

Jed released him, and the dazed man slumped against the wall.

"The lady accepts your apology, Mr. Slatter."

"I see you're still sword rattling, Mr. Fraser."

Jed swung around to see Vincent Calhoun smiling smugly at him.

"Miss Caroline." He tipped his hat to her and moved on.

"The more people I encounter in this town, the more I wonder why you want to remain," Jed grumbled as he adjusted his clothing. "Didn't you say that you turned down Slatter's proposal?"

"Yes, and it appears that I've made an enemy for life."

"I wonder if his resentment is enough to drive him to harming you or Garrett."

"You said Vincent Calhoun admitted to threatening us."

"He didn't come right out and admit it, but Calhoun strikes me as the kind who wouldn't dirty his own hands. He'd use an accomplice to do the dirty work."

Nathan and Garrett were waiting on the buckboard when they reached it. Jed helped Caroline climb on, then mounted Liberty. As they rode past the railroad station, the conductor shouted, "All aboard."

"Jed, it's not too late for you to change your mind. You can still get on that train," Nathan said.

Jed winked at Caroline. "I prefer the company I'm with right now."

Garrett giggled. "Even Buffer?"

The dog raised its head and was staring at him intently, as if waiting to hear his reply.

"Well, I guess there's no utopia, pal."

"Mama, what does utopia mean?" Garrett asked.

"It's an imaginary perfect place to live, honey."

Unable to resist, Jed interjected, "Like Virginia."

A faint smile curved her lips. "As I said, sweetheart: it's imaginary."

Garrett hugged his faithful companion, who was stretched out with his head on his lap. "You know what, Buffer? Sometimes adults sure are hard to understand. I'm glad you and me don't have that problem."

With the shrill toot of a whistle and the hiss of clouds of steam, the train slowly puffed out of the station.

Jed glanced back for a final look. *What have you got yourself into this time, Fraser?*

CHAPTER
7

Later that evening, having tucked Garrett into bed, Caroline sat down at the piano. Playing usually calmed her, but tonight she couldn't concentrate on the music. The fragrant scent of roses carried into the room and soon drew her to the open door.

The garden was bathed in moonlight, and she stepped outside, leaned back against one of the porch columns, and took a deep breath of the sweet fragrance as she gazed up at the stars, so close she felt she could reach up and pluck one out of the sky.

She found solace in the garden's sweet-scented serenity. A light breeze dallied with the hair on her temple, and she pulled out the pins that restrained it and shook out her hair. The heavy mass dropped to her shoulders, and she brushed her fingers through its thickness, then raised her face to catch the breeze.

A figure stepped out of the shadows. "Moonlight becomes you, Caroline," Jed said.

The butterflies that his nearness always awakened began fluttering in her stomach.

"Do you have any idea how beautiful you are?"

The soothing sound seemed to stroke her soul.

She leaned back against the column again. "I was enjoying the night's tranquility."

Jed walked over and set his hands against the column, confining her between his arms. His closeness and the desire in his eyes were an irresistible draw. And she had been naïve enough to believe she could fight it. Lord, how she was losing the battle!

"I know how worried you are, Caroline, but I won't let anything more happen to you or your family."

She looked directly into his mesmerizing brown eyes. "And what about you? If Calhoun is willing to harm one of us, he certainly won't have any qualms about doing the same to you."

He cupped her cheek in the palm of his hand and she closed her eyes, savoring the comfort of his touch. "Don't worry. I've been looking after myself for a long time. Nothing's going to happen to any of us."

"Promise, Mr. Fraser?" she asked lightly, trying to ignore the arousal his touch was generating.

"Promise, Miss Caroline," he whispered tenderly.

For a long moment he gazed deeply into her eyes. Holding her breath, she waited, torn between fear and hope. Then he dropped his hand and kissed her on her forehead, and moved away.

The man was lethal; she had been too tempted to surrender to the comfort he offered. Her whole body was trembling, and she folded her arms across her chest to appear indifferent.

"This whole situation just doesn't make sense to me," she said, hoping her voice wouldn't crack. "Why would Mr. Calhoun want our land? He's not married and has no heirs. He's not interested in the mill and has never shown any desire to own property. If he did, there've been dozens of opportunities to acquire some in the past. My uncle even offered to sell him part of the south section at one time, and Calhoun wasn't interested."

"Obviously he's had second thoughts since the railroad came into the picture," Jed said.

"But why? It seems that what he would gain from the railroad easement rights is hardly worth threatening people's lives for. And certainly not worth the cost of buying the land."

"Just winning or having power over others is often worth it to some people, Caroline. Does Calhoun hold any local office?"

"He has his fingers in just about everything. Mayor of the town, chairman of the bank's board of directors, as well as that of the school board. He handles all of the whole county's legal transactions, and—"

"Hold up a minute. Are you saying he's the one who issues and files any property deeds for the county?" Jed asked.

"Yes. Why do you ask?"

"Think how easy it would be for him to falsify any such records."

Caroline paused for a moment. "I suppose so, but I've never heard any rumor that he has. As I said, he's never been interested in being a landowner. Besides, it's rumored that he's considering moving to Sacramento to go into politics, possibly running for governor in the next election. So why buy property if he intends to leave?"

Jed thought for a long moment, then snapped his fingers. "That's it!" He picked her up and swung her around. "Honey, that's the missing link that ties it all together. Unless I've misjudged him completely, he sees this as an opportunity to make a big profit. He's in a position to falsify any property claims—he's most likely forged your father's name on the easement agreement already. He tries to intimidate him into selling out cheaply, and when the time is right, Calhoun will produce that deed, falsely dated, that indicates your father didn't have legal ownership of the property when he signed the agreement. Then he'll produce *his* false claim of ownership and increase the easement cost when it's too late and too expensive for the railroad to pull out. They'll have no choice but to give him what he wants."

"How could he possibly get away with it?"

"From what you've told me, he sounds sly enough to get away with anything. When his mission is accomplished, he'll resell the land for twenty times more than what he bought it for. Add it all together, and the result is a very tidy profit for Mr. Vincent Calhoun. As clever as it is crooked."

"That may be, but he's incredibly wealthy already. Father heard he struck it big during the Gold Rush of '49."

"Which only makes him a big fish in a little pond.

It will take a lot of money for an unknown like Calhoun to be elected governor. He knows he'll have to
buy the election, to pay off every crooked ward boss
in the state to deliver him the votes."

"But who would believe us? It's his word against
ours—and he's the one with the money," Caroline
said.

"Exactly. That's why I'm hoping you'll reconsider
my suggestion of going to my brother's home, where
you and Garrett will be safe."

"That would only be a temporary cure, Jed. Without knowing how long this situation will last, it
wouldn't solve the problem because we can't stay
there indefinitely. We need a solution now, so that we
don't have to live in fear."

Jed nodded. "We need to beat Calhoun to the
punch. Knowing you and Garrett are safe would give
your father and me the time to go to Sacramento and
speak personally to Leland Stanford, the president of
the Central Pacific Railroad. It shouldn't take more
than a couple of days."

"Stanford has a reputation for being crooked and
unscrupulous."

"I know, but your father told me he met Stanford
when the man was running for governor and they
became quite friendly. And according to my brothers, Stanford's admired more than he's condemned.
Think of it, Caroline: if it weren't for visionaries like
him, this country wouldn't have a transcontinental
railroad. That accomplishment is so great, people are
willing to forgive the methods he used. Maybe once
Stanford knows what Calhoun intends, he won't

want to blemish that achievement by having any-thing to do with a shyster like him."

"Stanford probably hired Calhoun because he *is* dishonest. Birds of a feather, you know."

"I still want to at least make the attempt. Since Calhoun's threats to you and Garrett have failed, I suspect he'll move quickly to eliminate Nathan to make his plan plausible. Your father's life is at risk every moment we delay."

"Then Garrett and I will go to Sacramento with you. We'll be just as safe there as we would be at your brother's."

"You don't know my brothers. They're an army unto themselves."

"Sorry to interrupt you, but I'd like to speak to you in my den, Jed," Nathan said from the doorway.

"It's been a busy day," Caroline said. "Good night." She kissed Nathan on the cheek and went upstairs.

"Close the door, Jed," Nathan said, when Jed fol-lowed him into the room. "I've just made out a new will which I'll have certified in Sacramento tomor-row."

"Sir, once we expose Calhoun's intentions, he wouldn't dare try to harm you."

"Regardless, I put a change in my will that relates to you. I've made you the executor of the will. As Garrett's father, I know you can be trusted."

"Garrett's father! What are you talking about?"

"Jed, this situation with Calhoun is getting too serious to continue to deny it. If Calhoun carries out his threats, I could end up dead or a pauper. I want to make certain that my daughter and grandson—your son—will be provided for according to the terms of my will."

"Sir, I swear on my honor that I am not Garrett's father! I never had any kind of contact with Caroline before you left Virginia."

"Jed, you're like a son to me. Why are you denying the obvious?"

Jed couldn't believe what he was hearing. "What do you consider the obvious, sir?"

"Why, the boy's a Fraser from head to toe. I can't believe I didn't recognize that sooner, but seeing you two together is living proof of it. Same color of hair and eyes. Same nose and jaw. I'm disappointed that you didn't have the honor to do right by my daughter and your son."

"Sir, it's not unusual for people to have similar features. Why, my brothers and I all have the same . . . Oh, my God, my brothers!"

Nathan appeared similarly shocked. "Could one of your brothers possibly have fathered Garrett?"

Jed jumped to his feet. "There's one sure way of finding out the truth."

"Where are you going?"

"To get Caroline."

"But she refuses to name the father."

"She will to me," Jed declared, already out the door.

He scaled the stairs two at a time, went directly to her room, opened the door without pausing to knock, and strode in.

Caroline was sitting up in bed, reading. Startled, she pulled up the sheet to cover her nightdress.

"What is it? What happened?" she asked in alarm.

Jed looked at her implacably "Tell me, Caroline. Which one of my brothers is Garrett's father?"

Caroline had feared Jed would discover the truth every day since his arrival, and the dreaded moment had now arrived.

"How dare you burst into my room without knocking! Please leave at once."

"Don't pull that indignant routine with me, lady. Thanks to you, a man I've respected for over fifteen years has just accused me of dishonorably fathering your son."

"I never said you were Garrett's father!" she protested.

Jed slapped his forehead with the palm of his hand. "Now I see why Calhoun and Slatter made those comments." He pulled the sheet off her, grabbed her arm, and pulled her out of bed.

"What do you think you're doing? Get your hands off me!"

Grabbing the robe at the foot of the bed, he shoved it at her. "Put this on. I want your father to hear the truth from *your* mouth, not mine."

Caroline planted her bare feet firmly on the floor and crossed her arms. "I'm not going anywhere with you. Now get out of here."

As he forced her arms into the sleeves of the robe, she tried to slap away his hands. "I'm not budging from this spot!"

"We'll see about that." He swept her up in his arms.

Caroline struggled to free herself as he carried her downstairs, then plopped her down in the chair in front of Nathan's desk. "Now, start talking. We want some answers."

She jumped to her feet. "Father, are you going to let this bully continue to manhandle me?"

"Caroline, he only wants the truth, and so do I."

"Which one of my brothers, Caroline? They're all happily married now with families of their own, so you can have the pleasure of complicating one of their lives as you have your son's."

"How dare you question my motherhood!"

"You've denied Garrett a father, haven't you?"

"For a good reason."

"No reason is good enough. My brothers are all decent, hardworking, and totally devoted to their wives and children."

Caroline scoffed. "Are we referring to the same boys? Back in Virginia, everyone in the county knew how wild you Fraser boys were."

"Wake up, lady. My brothers aren't boys any-more—they're men. They've fought a goddamn war, saw their buddies shot or blown apart, and buried people they loved. And if any one of them knew he fathered a son, you can be damn sure he wouldn't deny him. So look in the mirror, and you'll see who needs some growing up."

"Enough, both of you," Nathan declared. "Nothing is gained by this squabbling and name-calling."

"All I want to know is which of my brothers is Garrett's father."

"You must tell him, Caroline. Jed is right; you can't conceal such a truth from the father of a child. A man has the right to know."

She leaned over his desk and looked him in the eye. "And what of my rights, Father? I'm the one who bore him, nursed him, healed his bruises, and dried his tears. I laugh when he does; I cry when he cries; and my heart bleeds when he bleeds. I don't need 'the man who fathered him' to do it for me."

Unimpressed, Jed snorted. "Countless mothers have done the same before you. That doesn't change the fact that my brother is entitled to know he has a son."

"Honey, tell him who it is," Nathan said kindly.

"So he can come and take him away? Garrett's my life, Father. I won't give him up." She turned to Jed. "You said yourself that it will only complicate your brother's life. So why does he have to know?"

"Your feelings and my brother's aren't the only ones at stake here. A boy needs the chance to know his father, and his other siblings. If you love Garrett as much as you claim you do, then you owe it to him to tell him."

Jed hated the whole damn mess. There was no way either Caroline and one of his brothers wouldn't be hurt by it, but there was no way he could turn his back on it now. And he trusted the integrity of his brothers enough to know that any one of them would want to do right by the boy.

Caroline drew a shuddering breath, then her shoulders slumped. "Andy is Garrett's father."

Jed pivoted sharply, his anger renewed. "What in *hell* are you trying to pull with a damn lie like that? Don't you have any conscience at all?"

Bewildered, she asked, "What do you mean? I'm telling you the truth."

"Andy's dead. You damn well know it, and now you're trying to have a dead man take the blame."

Caroline paled. "He's . . . he's dead? I had no idea." She sank down in the chair. "How? And when?"

"In sixty-three. He was killed in Pickett's Charge at Gettysburg."

Tears glistened in her eyes when she looked up at him. "I'm so sorry." Her chin trembled, and she fought to hold back her tears. "He was so sweet. So kind and good. And all this time, I thought . . . I swear, I had no idea—"

"I don't believe you. Andy was just a kid—he couldn't have been more than sixteen when you left Virginia."

"And I was only fifteen," she railed in her own defense. "Was I any less of a child than Andy?"

"Did you know you were pregnant when you left?"

"No. I didn't realize it until we were at sea."

Jed turned to Nathan. "Did you know that, sir?"

"Of course not. I would have insisted they marry, had I known."

"That still doesn't excuse why you didn't write him, Caroline, to let him know. You certainly had enough time to do it before he was killed."

"I did write him," she declared. "He never answered."

Jed had never felt such anger. He curled his hands into fists, yearning to pound the wall in frustration.

"My brother went to his grave not knowing he had a son. My folks went to theirs without knowing they had a grandson to keep the memory of their son alive. Did it occur to you he may never have received the letter?"

"Since I never heard back from him, I assumed he didn't want anything to do with us."

"You really thought a kid with aspirations of becoming a minister would abandon you and his child? I don't believe you."

"I was sixteen when Garrett was born—just a child myself. I was ashamed and felt guilty for bearing a child out of wedlock. Is that so difficult to understand?"

"Didn't it occur to you to write to my parents and at least inform them of their grandchild?"

"Why? So they would force Andy into a marriage I believed he didn't want? Your arguments are coming from an adult. Try looking through the eyes of a sixteen-year-old."

"But you're no longer that sixteen-year-old, Caroline. What about now? Does it *occur* to you now?" he shouted. "No, you still want to deny Andy's son any knowledge of his father. At least you could have told me the truth when we met again."

"I was petrified—why do you think I tried to drive you away? Not knowing Andy was dead, I knew you would tell him. I feared he'd insist on raising Garrett and take him back to Virginia."

"Your fears are just starting, lady."

"Don't try to threaten me, Jed. Since Andy and I weren't married and his father is dead, you have no legal claim on Garrett."

"Garrett's a Fraser, so this is a question of family

honor. And as long as there's breath in me, he's going to be raised a Fraser."

He turned to Nathan and stood at full attention. "Captain Collins, I am asking your permission to marry your daughter."

Caroline erupted. "Marry! That's ludicrous! Now who's thinking like a child?"

Nathan sighed. "Jed, nothing would please me more for the sake of my grandson's welfare. Of course you have my permission, but it's Caroline's decision whether or not she will marry you."

"And my decision is *no*."

Jed ignored her. "Then may I ask another favor, sir? Will you consider signing ownership of this property and mill over to Garrett, with me as the executor?"

Jed waited on edge as Nathan gave a long look, and he saw the moment when Nathan figured out the bluff he was trying to pull on Caroline.

Nathan stood up to shake his hand. "I can't think of anyone I'd trust to do a better job," he said.

"Thank you, sir. I only have Garrett's welfare in mind."

Aghast, Caroline stared at her father. "You would do that to me, Father?"

"Only to assure Garrett's interests, Caroline. And by so doing, I know your interests will be protected, as well."

"Do you think I'd remain here as long as Jed is in charge? This is the only home Garrett's ever known! He loves it here. It would break his heart if I took him away from here. I can't believe you'd risk that on the word of this man."

She glared at Jed. "The minute you walked back into our lives, I knew you would be trouble."

"I'm sorry our relationship has to end so bitterly, Caroline, but business is business, and we Frasers look after one another's interests. I suggest you reconsider my marriage proposition."

"When Hell freezes over, Mr. Fraser." She walked out with as much dignity as possible when one is barefooted.

CHAPTER
8

The following morning, anger lay like an ember under Jed's skin, waiting for the minutest spark to set it ablaze.

He had anticipated a royal battle from Caroline, perhaps even an announcement that she wouldn't accompany them to Sacramento.

Surprisingly she appeared quite calm when she joined them for breakfast and offered a morning greeting to all, although she didn't speak directly to him.

He was certain she had some plan in mind, but it wouldn't do her one damn bit of good. He had admired her spirit and grit, but whether she liked it or not, he intended to decide the outcome of this situation regarding Garrett.

Throughout the night he had pondered the situation. Even if she was telling the truth and written the letter, which he doubted, there was no excuse not to inform the rest of the family about Garrett's existence in the years that followed. Her courage and struggle to raise Garrett were commendable for one so young, but he just couldn't justify the decision she made that followed.

Jed put aside his napkin. *So why keep trying?*

The time had come for her to face retribution for the deed. *Like it or not, Caroline Collins, we are getting married. And then my brother's son will rightfully bear the name of Fraser.*

The sound of her voice invaded his thoughts. "Honey, don't go outside after breakfast."

He glanced up and saw she was speaking to Garrett. For a few ludicrous seconds, he had thought it was to him.

"We're going to Sacramento later today, so I don't want you to stray away. Stay in the house or the garden."

"Do we have to go?" Garrett questioned.

"Your grandfather and Mr. Fraser have some business to attend to, and we're going with them."

"Can Buffer come with us?"

"No, he'll have to stay behind and sleep in the barn at night. It shouldn't be more than a couple of days."

"But who's gonna feed him?"

"You know he's capable of finding his own food and water. He's done it before."

"But, Mama, Buffer doesn't like staying behind. I want him to come along."

"Sweetheart, it's out of the question. Now go and do as I said."

Garrett trudged upstairs.

"So you intend to accompany us to Sacramento without any further argument?" Jed asked her.

"I told you that last night in the garden."

"I thought that perhaps the discussion that followed might have changed your mind."

"I have given that discussion a great deal of thought." After a glance at her father, Caroline said, "I've come to the conclusion that the wisest course I can pursue for my son's welfare is to agree to marry you."

"Honey, that's wonderful news!" Nathan said. "I knew your common sense would prevail."

"Let's hope Mr. Fraser's will, too, when he hears, what else I have to say. Last night you declared your terms, Jed; now I'll declare mine. Had you shown patience and understanding, I might have grown to care about you, even love you in time. But you've destroyed that possibility by forcing me into a marriage."

"I regret that, Caroline. But I know Garrett will love my family, and they'll love him as well."

"That is good to know, but under no circumstances will I or Garrett reside anywhere except in my father's house. When you are in port, feel free to stay here or wherever else you choose. It doesn't matter to me. Do you agree?"

"Yes, I don't find that to be a problem."

"And under no circumstances do you take Garrett anywhere without advising me of your intentions. At that time either my father or I will accompany you. Do you agree?"

"Did you discuss that intention with that bizarre hound you call a watchdog?"

Ignoring his sarcasm, she repeated, "Do you agree?"

"I think it's ludicrous, but I agree."

"Next, this marriage will be in name only. We will not share a bed or bedroom. Do you agree?"

"Definitely not. I will neither tolerate locked doors between us nor having to knock on a door in order to enter my wife's bedroom."

"I'll consider that, but it will not include the marriage bed."

"Are you aware that the marriage bed is one of the rewarding privileges between a husband and wife, Caroline?"

Caroline blushed, and gave her father an embarrassing glance. "I agreed to marry you, Jed, not to be a wife to you."

"I have no intention of forcing myself on you, if that's your concern. But the door connecting our rooms is to be kept unlocked."

Nathan jumped to his feet. "I've heard enough of this absurdity. Good God, woman, a man has needs!"

"I am quite aware of that, and he should have considered them before coercing me into an unwanted marriage."

Nathan gave Jed a sympathetic look, then strode from the room.

"So you agree," she pursued. "The marriage bed—"

"Will only be at your time and choosing, madam. You have my word."

"Very well, then I accept your proposal. Have you decided on a date?"

"The sooner the better. But since Hell has officially frozen over, now that you've agreed to wed me, will we need additional time to let it thaw?" he asked.

She pursed her lips to keep from smiling. He could be too damn amusing at times. "The date, Mr. Fraser?"

"I would like to have my family there. Since there are only three of us, we can go to them as soon as we finish our business in Sacramento. But for the sake of our future marital tranquility, Caroline, I'll point out that your attitude about this is beginning to wear on my patience."

"You should have thought of that before issuing your ultimatum." She calmly left the room.

Well, what did you expect, Fraser, a kiss and a hug good morning? Jed thought as he watched her walk away with that slight sway of her hips that always caught his eye. It tweaked his appetite enough to be curious what was beneath that gown.

Those demands of hers were more of a challenge than an annoyance, and he looked forward to showing her how wrong she was about not wanting to share a bed with him.

You may think you're dealing this poker game, sweetheart, but I'm about to raise the ante.

Caroline absently took a gown from the armoire, her mind on the scene with Jed at the breakfast table.

He had always remained poised and in control of his emotions before, but his anger last night had been unbearable, frightening. The tenderness they had shared so shortly before had changed to loathing in a blink of an eye.

She had reacted to it with the same emotion, instead of waiting it out and trying to come to a better decision after he cooled down. Once people lashed out with ultimatums, pride usually kept them from not backing down. "Act in haste, repent in leisure," as her mother used to say.

Perhaps he *was* right. Perhaps she should have made a greater effort to inform Andy of the birth of his son. But if the decision she made when he didn't answer her letter was wrong, there was no changing it now. What was done was done.

Why should it raise so much anger and bitterness in Jed?

She started to close the lacquered door of the wardrobe, then lovingly stroked the walnut veneer of the panel, embossed with pink roses and trailing green ivy. It had been one of her mother's most cherished possessions. Her father had brought it home from England on one of his voyages, and after her mother died, he had moved it into her room.

"Oh, Mother, I miss you so much," she murmured softly. "And I need your gentleness and wisdom more than I ever have. How I wish you were here now to tell me what to do."

Caroline walked to the window and stared out blindly. It seemed an eternity since her mother had died, and yet it had only been two years.

Since then, other than brief chats on Sunday mornings with the pastor's wife, there'd been few other females in her life. There were no neighbors nearby, none of the loggers had wives, and Garrett had no schoolmarm since she taught him herself at home.

She missed having another woman in the house, a

female voice other than her own, someone to talk or laugh with while hanging out the wash, shelling peas, or baking a cake—the things she and her mother had enjoyed doing together.

And oh, for a girlfriend her own age to giggle with, or share their deep secrets and wants!

Caroline moved to the mirror and stared at her image. In retrospect, she never *had* had any close female friend other than her mother.

So what makes you think you need one now? Stop the whining and think about the bigger problems at hand.

"Oh, shut up and go away," Caroline grumbled. "You're no help at all—you never have been. You don't even have a voice." She spun on her heel and walked away in disgust.

She finished packing, then went down the hall to Garrett's room, but he wasn't there. She peeked into the open door of Jed's room, which was empty.

When she checked the garden, he wasn't there, either, and she began to feel uneasy.

Her father had dozed off in a chair in his den, and Caroline woke him. "Father, have you seen Garrett? I can't find him anywhere, and I warned him to stay inside."

"Don't worry, honey, Jed's with him. The last time I saw them, they were in the barn."

"Have you packed a bag for overnight?"

"Yes, I'm ready to go whenever the rest of you are."

"If we're to catch the train to Sacramento, we'd better think about leaving soon," she told him, and headed for the barn.

The barn door was open, but there was no sign of either of them. Then her heart leaped to her throat when she saw that Liberty's stall was empty.

She rushed to the door of the barn and shouted, "Father, Father!" at the top of her voice.

Nathan came hurrying down the path. "What is it, Caroline? What's wrong?"

"Garrett's not here. And Liberty's gone, too. He took him—I know he took him."

"You mean Calhoun? You think Calhoun took Garrett?"

"No, Jed. Jed's kidnapped him."

Nathan relaxed and shook his head. "That's ridiculous, Caroline. Since they're both gone, no doubt they're together. And obviously Buffer is with them, too."

"They're together, all right, and I'm going after them. He's probably taken him to his brother's in Calistoga."

"If so, I'll go with you. But not until we're certain that is the case. I think they're just off somewhere and will be back soon."

"I can't believe you can take this so lightly. The man has kidnapped your grandson!"

"Honey, Jed is an honorable man; don't start accusing him of foul play."

"You're too blind to see that he's hoodwinked you," she said, frantic with fear. "No doubt he planned this from the start. He probably recognized the resemblance when he first saw Garrett, and staged that scene last night in order to throw off suspicion! Oh, he's treacherous."

"Caroline, I know that man. We fought a war together. He's neither dangerous nor treacherous."

"You've always been obsessive about him, Father. Whenever you came home during the war, Mother and I had to listen to Mr. Fraser this, or Mr. Fraser that. He could do no wrong in your eyes. Then when the war ended, and he went elsewhere, you mourned his loss as if he were a dead son."

"I admit I thought of him as such," Nathan said. "I had always longed for such a son."

"Do you think I didn't guess that, Father?" Tears streaked her cheeks. "But you didn't have that son, did you? You had a daughter."

Nathan drew her trembling body into his arms. "And I thank God every day for that daughter." He smiled tenderly. "I love you, my dearest child."

Caroline flung her arms around his neck, sobbing, and buried her head against his chest. "I know you do, Father. I'm so sorry. These past few days have been so stressful, worrying about losing Garrett, Calhoun's threats, and now the thought of this ridiculous marriage to Jed." She raised her head. "I can't even think sensibly anymore."

Nathan stepped back and looked deeply into her tear-filled eyes. "Do you actually believe I'd ever be a party to forcing you into a marriage you didn't want, my child? And when the time comes, I know Jed won't, either. He's too honorable a man."

"Isn't that the whole issue—his and his family's honor?" Caroline slumped down on a bale of hay. "At least now the secret's in the open. And Jed is right. I *have* denied Garrett a father. I've never considered his needs, only my own selfish ones to keep him to myself. So as long as Jed has agreed to my terms, I might as well marry him for Garrett's sake. I may not be able to bear the sight of Jed Fraser, but I know he'll be a good father to my son."

Nathan smiled kindly. "Do you really dislike him that much, honey?"

"I didn't at first; I was only being rude to him in the hope of driving him away. I just wish he'd go away and leave us alone."

"If that's your decision, my dear, I'll not interfere."

"You've interfered already, you old curmudgeon." She wiped away her tears and stood up. "Let's hitch Belle to the buckboard and find them. We've got a train to catch."

They were just preparing to leave when they spied Buffer approaching the barn, and within seconds Liberty appeared with the two riders on her back.

When they reached them, Garrett slid off the rear of the horse and ran up to them. "Mama! Granddad! Jed and I went fishing and he showed me how to spear a fish! And I did it!" He triumphantly held up a string with a small fish dangling from the end.

Jed dismounted. "He learns quickly." He handed Caroline several larger fish on a string.

She just looked at him with the same nonplussed expression as Nathan.

"What?" he asked in confusion.

"How thoughtful of you, Jed," Caroline said sweetly. "Now The Buffer won't have to hunt for something to eat while we're gone." She patted the dog's head. "Right, Buffer? And you thought he didn't like you."

Jed watched her saunter up to the house, swinging the fish by the string—and those damn hips of hers.

Okay, sweetheart, you've won this hand. But the next deal is mine.

CHAPTER
9

They boarded the train to Sacramento just as it was about to depart. Nathan sat down next to Garrett, leaving Caroline to share the opposite seat with Jed.

"I'm glad we made it," she said. "Father and I were worried that we wouldn't when we discovered Garrett was gone."

Nathan peered over the top of the newspaper he'd purchased when they boarded. "I wasn't the least bit worried."

"Honey, in the future I want you to tell me before running off like that," she said.

"I'll try to remember," Jed replied.

Garrett giggled. "She's talking to me, Jed."

Jed grinned. "I thought it was too good to be true."

"Mama, all we did was go fishing. What's wrong with that?"

She leaned over and squeezed Garrett's hand. I was just worried because I didn't know where you were. Next time you and Jed will have to take me with you. I've always been pretty good at fishing."

"All depends on what you're fishing for, missy," Nathan said. He winked at Jed and went back to reading.

Caroline forced back a smile. Somehow, her father always managed to calmly bring her back down to size whenever she tried to climb on her high horse. What would her life be like without him, or Garrett?

She glanced at Jed. He had leaned back his head, and his eyes were closed. He had promised he wouldn't let anything happen to any one of them, and she believed him. As much as he irritated her, it was comforting to have him around in a crisis.

He had said he wouldn't disrupt their lives, but what if he changed his mind and insisted they leave Napa to live near his family, or even worse, return to Virginia?

With a heavy sigh, she opened her book. Though she tried to read it, the narrowness of the seat made Jed's nearness impossible to ignore.

Every jolt or sway of the train caused his arm to press against her, or his thigh to brush against her leg. Her body tingled from every contact. And deep in her imagination, she fantasized about their naked bodies pressed close together.

The heat of a blush surged through her, doubled by the heat within the train car. She opened the window, then coughed when a cloud of choking dust swirled in.

She removed her gloves and hat, but that did

little to ease her discomfort, so she undid the top buttons of her gown. Then she settled back to resume reading, the clickety-clack of the rails a rhythmic drone in her ears. In a short time, her eyelids began to droop.

Deep in thought, Jed mused about his mixed feelings for Caroline. The woman annoyed him as much as she aroused him. He had no intention of forcing her into an unwanted marriage; that would be lunacy! He'd be punishing himself as much as her. He was a rover, and no more wanted to be chained down to the responsibility of a wife and child than Caroline wanted a husband to complicate her life.

But there was undeniably an intense physical awareness between them. The wisest thing to do, after this Calhoun situation was resolved, was to legalize Garrett as a Fraser, then get out of her life as quickly as he could.

Jed opened his eyes and saw that Caroline had fallen asleep. He reached over and closed the book that was on the verge of slipping off her lap.

Then he stared at her face. He'd been doing a lot of that since he first saw her. Serene in slumber, she looked at peace, but he could easily imagine what troubled thoughts lay beneath that tranquil façade.

Lowering his gaze, the seductive draw of the open buttons of her gown gave him access to the slim column of her neck. His groin tightened as he stared hungrily at the rounded cleavage of her breasts.

His gaze softened to tenderness when he forced it back to her face. Reaching out, he brushed aside the golden strands that clung to her cheek. They felt silky and incredibly tantalizing to his fingertips. He slipped his arm around her shoulders, drew her gently to his side, and tucked her head in the hollow of his shoulder.

Caroline slowly fought through the curtain of sleep until she became aware of a steady pounding beneath her ear. She opened her eyes, which widened with shock when she realized she'd been sleeping in Jed Fraser's arms, and the steady pounding was his heartbeat.

To her relief, the sleeping man didn't stir as she eased herself carefully out of his arms and sat up. Garrett and her father had dozed off in the seat opposite them.

Caroline looked at the timepiece pinned to her gown and saw she had only slept for a half hour.

Hot sunlight was blazing through the window, and the heat was like a vise. She got up and went outside to the observation platform for some fresh air.

The door on the attached car opened, and Vincent Calhoun stepped out onto the platform. His surprise upon seeing her appeared to be as great as hers.

"Why, Miss Collins, what an unexpected pleasure. May I join you?"

Without waiting for her reply, he stepped across the coupling that linked the two cars together. "I trust I find you in good health."

"Yes, indeed, Mr. Calhoun. No thanks to you."

Threats or no threats, she refused to cower in front of this man.

"I'm not certain I understand what you're referring to, Miss Collins."

"Please drop the false courtesy, Mr. Calhoun. It's ludicrous, considering your threat to me and my family. Tell me, sir, does it give you a sense of power to terrify an eight-year-old child?"

"Business is business, Miss Collins. The price for being successful, I suppose." He sighed with false contrition. "A man must do what a man must do. Nothing personal, of course."

"I suppose that's true when that man is a cheap embezzler like you. Nothing personal, of course."

His mouth slashed into a thin line of fury. She turned to leave, and he grabbed her arm. "Who do you think you're talking to, you little whore? Give your father a message for me: he'll be lucky if he has a shirt on his back when he leaves Napa. If he's still alive."

Caroline had had enough of it all: the threats, the sneers from Calhoun and Slatter, the ultimatums from Jed. She had had it with men trying to coerce her and wouldn't tolerate another minute of it.

She hauled off and slapped Calhoun across the face.

"You bitch!" he cursed and raised his arm to strike her just as the door opened.

"What in hell!" Jed exclaimed and made a move toward them, but stopped when Caroline yanked her arm from Calhoun's grasp.

"Nothing to be alarmed about, Mr. Fraser. Mr. Calhoun has just been amusing me with his delusions of grandeur." She brushed past Jed and went back inside.

Calhoun stepped back onto the other car.

"What's going on?" Jed demanded.

The lawyer turned around and shook a pointed finger at him. "Tell her she crossed the line. And she'll pay for it." He went back inside.

Dammit! It wasn't safe to close his eyes for a minute, Jed fumed. When he had awakened, Nathan and Garrett were asleep, but Caroline's seat was empty and he'd assumed she'd gone to the water closet. But when she hadn't returned after a reasonable time, he'd begun to feel uneasy and went looking for her. And sure as hell, he found her, all right. Smack-dab in the middle of a fight, if he ever saw one.

At least the air felt good out here. It was a reminder of how much he hated trains. Aside from being hot and stuffy, their open windows were an invitation to every speck of blowing dust. The seats were hard and narrow, and if that wasn't enough to bear, the constant clatter of the wheels was deafening when the windows were opened.

He yearned for the feel of a deck underfoot, for the cool ocean breeze carrying the fresh smell and spray of the sea. What the hell was he doing on a damn train?

He lit a cigarillo and thought of the scene he'd just interrupted between Caroline and Calhoun. What could she have said to cause that bastard to shout open threats with no attempt at subtlety? The situation was rapidly reaching a boiling point. If Leland Stanford refused to see them, he'd have to cart them all off to Clay's.

He dropped the cigarillo into the provided pail of sand and went back inside.

The sun had set by the time they reached the city. Jed registered them into a hotel that offered connecting rooms, with Caroline and Garrett in one room and he and Nathan in the other. Even though he felt certain Calhoun wouldn't try any of his hanky-panky in the city, Jed wasn't letting anyone out of his sight. He reached for the hotel key.

"Are you serious?" Caroline complained when he unlocked the door between their two rooms.

"Remember, I said there would be no locked doors between us, Caroline."

"We aren't married yet, Mr. Fraser," she said, and slammed the door in his face.

Nathan chuckled and shook his head. "That's my girl! I'm going downstairs to the bar and have me a tall glass of cold beer."

"I'd rather you wait until we all go down together, sir."

"Jed, my boy, you aren't trying to tell me what to do, are you?"

"Wouldn't think of it, sir. I just feel there's safety in numbers. After the incident between Calhoun and Caroline, you don't know what that bastard will try next."

Nathan nodded. "You're right. I should have known better. But I know my daughter, Jed; she won't consent to allow my grandson near a bar-room."

"I'm sure you can order a glass of beer in the dining room, sir."

Nathan sighed. "It just never tastes quite as good as when you belly up to the bar with your foot on the rail."

Caroline stood by the door and listened to the male voices from the next room. She smiled when she heard the sound of her father's laughter. In her own loneliness, she'd forgotten about the possibility of her father's. He enjoyed Jed's company so much. But was it Jed he enjoyed, or was it the memories Jed helped him to recall?

I guess we're both wishing for something we can't have.

She walked over and opened her suitcase, then sat on the bed in annoyance.

"What's wrong, Mama?" Garrett asked.

"Oh, I just packed the wrong dress." She pulled out a pale-blue satin gown from her luggage. "I intended to wear a fresh gown tomorrow when we meet with Mr. Stanford, but certainly not this one. My mind sure wasn't on my packing this morning."

"You look pretty in that dress, Mama."

"Thank you, honey, but it's a party gown. Too fancy for our business meeting tomorrow."

"What are you going to do?"

"I guess I'll have to wear the gown tonight and freshen and hang up the one I have on now. At least it will be more appropriate to wear tomorrow."

"Mama, what did you mean when you said to Jed that you aren't married yet?"

Caroline patted the bed beside her. "Come over here, honey."

Once he was seated, she slipped her arm around his shoulders and hugged him to her side. "Do you like Jed, Garrett?"

"I sure do. He's 'bout the best man, I know 'cepting Granddad. Granddad's the best."

She gave him an extra little squeeze for that.

"What would you think of Jed and me getting married?"

Garrett looked perplexed. "Isn't there a rule you have to love each other to get married? Like Granddad and Grandma did. Don't seem like you and Jed love each other, Mama; you're always fighting."

"Sometimes people marry because it's the best thing to do. And we think the best thing for us to do is get married."

"Why is that the best thing to do?"

"Well, Jed likes you just as much as you like him, and he wants to take care of you."

"But you, Granddad, and Buffer take good care of me, so why would Jed want to?"

Caroline took a deep breath. This was the hardest part to explain. "Honey, your father was killed in the war, and Jed is his brother. That's why he wants to take care of you."

"You mean, I'd have to go away from you and Granddad?" he said in panic.

"No, no, no. Jed would live with *us*—when he isn't at sea. You know he's a sailor, and he's gone most of the time."

"That's okay, then. If you marry him, does that mean you'll stop fighting with each other?"

She laughed and kissed him on the forehead. "I can't promise you that. But I promise I'll try. But no matter what Jed and I feel about each other, we both love *you* dearly just the same."

Well, that was the final nail in her coffin. Since Garrett had no objections, she'd go ahead and marry Jed.

Caroline stood up. "I better get dressed. You know how grumpy your grandfather gets when he's hungry. After our meeting with Mr. Stanford tomorrow, we'll go back home, pack some clothes, and then all go to meet Jed's family in Calistoga. That's where the wedding will be. You'll be meeting many uncles, aunts, and cousins you've never known. Isn't that exciting?"

"Yeah, but can Buffer come with us, too?" Garrett asked.

She laughed. "We'll ask Jed what he thinks."

CHAPTER 10

Jed had changed into his white naval uniform for dinner. Deeply tanned from his voyages at sea, his skin and dark hair were a devastating contrast against the white of his uniform. Caroline noticed the female stares that followed him as they were shown to their table. Apparently women were unable to ignore the tall, dark handsomeness of the Fraser men. Pity the poor women who had married his brothers.

"Mr. Fraser," a voice called out as they passed one of the tables.

"Captain Beningham," Jed acknowledged with a slight bow.

"Whatever are you doing in Sacramento?" Beningham asked.

"We're here on business, sir. You remember Captain Collins, of course. And this is his daughter, Caroline Collins, and his grandson, Garrett."

Beningham stood up. "Good evening, Miss Collins. It's a pleasure to meet you. The same to you, young man," he told Garrett. "And Nathan, how good to see you again. We must have a brandy together later and talk over those good times we had running Yankee blockades."

"I'll look forward to it," Nathan said.

"And my lovely dinner partner is my wife, Elizabeth."

After he finished the introductions, Beningham said to his wife, "If you recall, my dear, Mr. Fraser is the mate on my ship."

"I do remember, Benjamin; you speak of him so often. My husband is very impressed with you, Mr. Fraser."

"That's very kind of him, ma'am," Jed said.

"I certainly can agree with your husband's opinion, madam," Nathan said. "Mr. Fraser served on my ship during the war."

She laughed lightly. "Then you will indeed have much to talk about, Captain Collins."

Clearly uncomfortable, Jed quickly said, "We won't disturb your dinner any longer. It was a pleasure meeting you, Mrs. Beningham." He put a hand on the small of Caroline's back and gently steered her to their table.

"My, what a handsome couple they are," Elizabeth Beningham remarked.

"Yes, and I don't like it," Beningham said.

"Benjamin, why would you object?"

"He's the best first mate I've ever had, and I hate to lose him to a woman."

"Oh, you old walrus," she teased. "You've got salt water in your veins." She stole another glance at Jed as he assisted in seating Caroline. "Oh, how I envy her."

"Good Lord, Beth, he's half your age."

"Not that." She squeezed his hand. "Don't you remember how exciting it was to be young and in love?"

"Yes, I remember only too well." Beningham sighed as he looked at the couple across the room. "I don't like it. I don't like it one bit."

As they dined, an orchestra began playing, and Caroline listened with pleasure to the lilt of a Viennese waltz. Soon dancers began to swirl by.

As much as she loved music, she had never attended a formal ball. While her mother was alive, she'd play the piano and watch with a smile when her mother and father waltzed together around the room. Then her mother would play the piano while her father taught her the steps.

Caroline still spent long hours at the piano, one of the few pastimes, other than reading, that gave her great pleasure.

When they finished their meal, she sat swaying her head to the rhythm of the music. Her fingers seemed to itch for the feel of a keyboard.

"Granddad, why don't you and Mama dance together like you used to?" Garrett asked.

"You were so young then; how can you even remember, Garrett?" Nathan asked.

"I was six years old then. Grandma would play the piano, and you and Mama would dance. But the part I liked the best was when you and Grandma danced together. You always kissed her hand when you were through, and she'd always have that special smile when you did."

Nathan stood with a smile. "Would you do me the pleasure of having this waltz with me, honey?"

Caroline's eyes were misty. "I'd love to, Father."

Jed's gaze followed the couple as Nathan waltzed Caroline around the floor. He had never seen her look so happy; her eyes glowed with warmth as she smiled up at her father. *She has a beautiful smile when her heart's in it.* Unlike the forced ones that she usually offered to him.

And she had done something different with her hair. It was swept up to the crown of her head, with two gardenias pinned near the nape of her neck.

Her blue gown enhanced her eyes even more, and her shoulders and arms were bare and smooth. He didn't fail to notice the roundness of her breasts, slim waist, and curve of her hips, either.

"My mother sure is pretty, don't you think?" Garrett asked.

"Yes, she is," Jed said.

"Bet she's 'bout the beautifulest lady here. Don't you think?"

"I've never seen her look lovelier."

"Bet there's a lot of men here who would sure like to marry her."

"Probably are, Garrett."

"Bet they'd love her like Granddad and me do."

"I don't doubt you're right." *You little conniver*, Jed thought affectionately.

"You figure you could love my mama, Jed?"

The waltz ended, saving him from answering, and when Caroline and Nathan returned to the table, Jed stood up and pulled out Caroline's chair for her.

"Aren't you gonna ask Mama to dance same as Granddad did?" Garrett asked.

"Yes, Jed, aren't you?" she asked playfully.

Jed bowed politely. "Miss Caroline, may I have the pleasure of this waltz?"

She dipped in a curtsy. "I'd be honored, sir."

He took her hand and led her to the dance floor. His fingers tingled from the contact of his hand on her bare back. It felt warm . . . and disturbing.

"You dance well, Jed. Must have been all those cotillions you attended before the war."

"And you play the belle equally well, Caroline. What are you up to now?"

She laughed merrily as he twirled her around, her eyes glowing as brightly as the crystal chandeliers overhead.

"I'm enjoying myself. Why would you think otherwise?"

"It must be because those same gorgeous sapphire eyes that were slicing me to ribbons about twelve hours ago are now blinding me with their glow. Is this a new tactic to weaken my defenses?"

"Why, Jed Fraser, I'm wounded. I've never had the opportunity to waltz with a real orchestra in a ballroom, and I intend to enjoy every moment of it. Tonight I am Cinderella at the ball."

"And I will be delighted to be your prince. So hold on to your slippers, Cinderella."

She smiled with pleasure as they glided around the floor. Caroline waved at Garrett and her father as they whirled past their table, and Garrett waved back happily.

"Mama sure looks happy, doesn't she, Granddad? You think someday Jed'll love Mama like you loved Grandma?"

Nathan patted his hand. "I think there's a pretty good chance that will happen, son."

Caroline's face had softened in a tender smile when she saw her son's face as he watched them. Jed had seen it, too, and he drew her closer.

"Do you mind if we step outside for a few minutes?" she asked.

"Not at all." He waltzed her through the open door onto the terrace. "But I want to be able to keep Nathan and Garrett in sight. So what's on your mind, Cinderella?"

"I told Garrett we were considering getting married."

"I figured as much, from his conversation while you were dancing with your father." He chuckled. "The little fox is devious. Did you tell him about Andy?"

"Only that his father was your brother who was killed in the war, and we're marrying because you want to take care of him." Then she frowned.

"What is it, Caroline?"

"I should tell you that I know I don't have to go through with this marriage. Father told me this morning he would not be a party to forcing me into an unwanted marriage. He also believes when the time comes, you won't, either."

"So are you telling me you have no intention of marrying me?"

"No. At first the thought was abhorrent to me, but I thought about it throughout last night and realized that I was wrong. I was selfishly considering my needs above Garrett's. You and I may disagree about the method we've chosen, but one thing is clear to both of us: Garrett's need for a father's guidance is greater than any of our personal preferences."

"And you really do want to marry? You don't feel you are being coerced into doing it?"

"Yes, I really *do* want to marry. Obviously we'll have to work out an arrangement where we don't keep up this bickering. Garrett's concerned about that, and it wouldn't be good for him."

"You're willing to give up the happy 'home and hearth' you yearn for and marry a man who'll be at sea for ten or eleven months each year?"

"I intend to do whatever is best for Garrett, and if you do the same, I see no reason why a marriage between us won't work."

"Well, I've been doing some thinking about this situation, too. We could simply legalize Garrett as a Fraser without marrying."

"And how would that benefit Garrett? We both agree he needs a father's guidance. I think we're up to the challenge."

"Caroline, living in the same household for just one week appears to be a monumental challenge to us." Jed grinned. "My life hasn't been this lively since the war ended."

The remark brought a smile to Caroline's face.

"And what about that edict about the marriage bed?" he asked.

She blushed profusely. "I release you of your promise. But I would be grateful if you'd give me a little time to adjust to . . . to becoming a wife to you."

"Remember that I'm going back to sea in a few weeks. How much time do you think it will take for you to . . . adjust to the idea?"

She met his gaze boldly. "I think a lot will depend on how well you can convince me."

"Another challenge, Miss Caroline?"

"Afraid you're not *up* to it, Fraser?"

Jed didn't miss the innuendo and burst into laughter. "To think you're the one who warned *me* about jumping into water over my head! Honey, I hate to brag, but I've never had to *convince* any woman to go to bed with me."

She shrugged. "Even Napoleon met his Waterloo."

He eyed her incredulously. "You really are serious, aren't you?"

She nodded.

"Very well." He sighed tragically. "A man's gotta do what a man's gotta do."

Caroline broke into laughter. "Strangely enough, Vincent Calhoun said the same thing on the train. It was his excuse for his nefarious actions. Is 'the end justifies the means' the litany all men use as an excuse for their misconduct?"

"It's more of a battle cry, madam. But tell me, what did you say that might have raised his wrath?"

"Only that I wasn't afraid of him and will no

longer tolerate his threats to my family. Oh, and I slapped him in the face."

Jed arched a brow. "I *have* sensed a greater degree of . . . mettle on your part, Miss Collins."

"Mr. Fraser, I don't think you or Mr. Calhoun have any idea how much *mettle* I have. But hold on to your hat, sir, because both of you will soon find out. Shall we return to our table?"

His hand on her arm stopped her, and he pulled her into his arms. "Was that a battle cry I just heard?"

Her eyes flashed in amusement. "Take it any way you wish, sailor."

"A challenge, and now a battle cry! Well, as John Paul Jones shouted to his British foes during the Revolutionary War, 'I have not yet begun to fight.'"

He claimed her lips in a devastating kiss that left her breathless but wanting more. "Ready to call it quits now, before I turn up the heat?"

She hoped he didn't feel her trembling as she looked up at him with a teasing smile. "If that's the best you can do, Captain Jones, I'm afraid you're going to need a lifeboat."

Jed slipped a hand on the back of her neck as they went back inside. He had intended to get out of the marriage, but she had turned the tables on him.

Hold on to your slippers, Cinderella, because I'm the one who'll claim the final dance.

"Well, is the marriage still on?" Nathan asked, when they were seated.

"Of course," Caroline said.

Garrett grinned.

"After we meet with Stanford, we'll travel back home, pack some additional clothes for a longer span of time, then leave for Calistoga."

Jed said, "We'll be staying with Clay. He's the eldest of us out here."

Jed winked at Garrett. "You're going to like your Uncle Clay, Garrett, and the rest of your uncles. And your Aunt Lissy, our sister."

"And how about Garrett's cousins, Jed?" Caroline asked.

"There's been quite a few in the last few years, but most of them are babies. And the last I heard, Garth's wife, Rory is about due, unless she's had it already. And I also have a cousin—my Uncle Henry married shortly before he died. I've only met Rico once, but he's a great guy."

Later, as Caroline lay in bed thinking about the coming week, she began to feel a touch of excitement at the thought of seeing the Fraser family. She was especially curious to meet the women they had chosen for wives.

It would be interesting.

CHAPTER 11

Leland Stanford greeted them warmly in his office the following morning. For all Stanford had accomplished through the years, Caroline was surprised to discover that the former governor of California, and president and director of the Central Pacific Railroad from the time of its founding was only forty-five years old.

After an exchange of introductions, he asked, "Do I detect a Southern accent, Mr. Fraser?"

"Yes, sir, my family's home is located between the James and York rivers in Virginia."

"Beautiful state, I remember it well. I visited it often when I was young. I'm from New York, and I didn't move to California until fifty-two. I'm curious to know what the conditions are now in the South since the war is over. I imagine there was a lot of devastation?"

"Yes, sir. I think it will take several more years to restore parts of it."

"The Civil War was the worst event that has happened to this nation since its existence," Stanford said. "American fighting American. What a tragedy. But just as that war tore our nation apart, the railroad will unite it again. The United States of America—it's good to hear *that* again. Only this time we'll really *be* united—East and West, Atlantic to the Pacific."

"Why are you so confident, Governor Stanford? There's still so much bitterness," Caroline said.

"Miss Collins, just imagine what will result. Those on the East Coast will soon be able to enjoy the merchandise from the Orient more cheaply and more readily than they could before, and we here on the West Coast will have the same benefit from British and European ports. And now families that have been separated by distance for years will be able to be reunited for the cost of a train ticket."

"That's my family's intention exactly, sir," Jed said. "We're planning a family reunion in Virginia next year."

"Then you'll be able to enjoy the amenities of a transcontinental train. Many restaurants have followed the tracks across the country. Excellent overnight facilities are available in many towns on the route, where one can get a good night's sleep in clean and comfortable beds, or remain and enjoy local sights of interest before boarding the next train on a later day.

"The economy of this country will completely change. Freight can be shipped from one coast to the other in a few days, compared to the weeks or months it took by wagon or ship. People will be able to cross mountain ranges that once took time and risks by wagon or horseback. Thousands of miles of government-owned land will now be offered free to anyone willing to homestead it. And out of that will come the growth of towns, and towns will become cities.

"Territories, due to increased population, will begin to petition to become individual states in the union. Businesses will spring up in areas that were once barren, creating schools, churches, and law and order in their wake."

"But you're speaking mainly of the taming of the West, Governor Stanford. How will a devastated South benefit from a transcontinental railroad?" Caroline asked.

Jed said, "We sure could have benefited from a few more railroads during the war. That was one of the many advantages the Yankees had over us. They could move their troops and supplies quickly by trains."

"Exactly, Mr. Fraser. And now anything can be moved quickly from coast to coast by train. A fresh peach from Georgia can be in the hands of a chef in a Nevada restaurant a few days after it's picked. A coal company in Pennsylvania can ship coal to warm a San Francisco mansion, or a New York boutique can ship the latest imported Paris wedding gown to a bride to be in Nebraska. All in a matter of days.

"Florida oranges will become accessible in New Mexico," he continued. "California wine in St. Louis. The needs of an increased population will put a demand on construction, thus offering more employment opportunities and a demand for greater outputs from steel factories, cattle ranches, the corn growers of Iowa, or potato farmers of Idaho.

"Fresh Maine lobsters will make their way into a pot in Illinois; Louisiana shrimp an added flavor to a Montana barbecue.

"And just as important, my friends, with the train will come a continual migration of people both east and west, resulting in a blending of different races, cultures, religions. As a result, this country will become more united than it has ever been."

"I concede your sincerity, Governor Stanford, but there've been so many scandals relating to the building of it, and the expense was phenomenal. And the Lord only knows how many lives were lost. I'm not certain I believe the end justifies the means," Caroline said.

"There are many who agree with you, my dear. But have we not marveled at the causeways and viaducts of the early Romans, or the wonderment of the Egyptian pyramids, Inca temples, the China wall? All magnificent feats of engineering for their time—but achieved by the sacrifice of thousands of lives of slave laborers.

"Many hardworking men died in the building of the railroad, but stop to think about this: a farmer can drop dead from exertion while plowing his field, a lawman can be shot to death in the execution of his duty, or a cowboy trampled by cattle.

"The same is true of the men who perished building this railroad. Most of the men in our crews were no different from that farmer or lawman. They were men of free will, prepared to exchange a hard day's labor, or even risk their lives, to earn an honest dollar—God rest their souls."

"I suspect money had something to do with that accomplishment, sir," Jed said.

"Yes, indeed, young man. Since the beginning of time, man has been willing to sell his soul to possess it. I'll not deny my associates and I may be the worst of such scoundrels. We amassed personal wealth in the process. Did everything short of out-and-out murder. We cheated and lied, bent laws, broke rules, bribed governments, and trampled over our rivals. We swindled and extorted money from whomever and whenever we could. But it wasn't greed and money that *drove* us to build that railroad; it took a unified dream—and the vision to keep that dream alive. Without it, there would be no transcontinental railroad today.

"Skeptics claimed it was impossible to lay track through the Sierra and the Rocky Mountains. We proved them wrong. We tunneled through granite walls and forty-foot snowdrifts when we had to—and we did it. Laid track through the heat and waterless sands of alkali deserts when we had to—and we did it. We built bridges to span raging rivers and granite gorges when we had to." He slammed a clenched fist on his desk. *"And we did it!"*

Stanford leaned back in his chair with a satisfied smile.

"Two-thousand miles between here and Missouri. We headed east, the Union Pacific headed west, and we met in Utah. I shall never forget what a glorious day that was."

"What happened?" Garrett asked, held spellbound by the man's oratory.

"We drove in the final spike linking the two railroads, my boy. A monumental event this country will never know again."

"Wow," Garrett murmured with hushed wonderment.

"What's in store for you now, Leland?" Nathan asked. "Do you have another vision in mind for the country?"

"Now, I'd like to see us crisscross this whole state with our trunk lines, then start branching out more. Maybe even form another railroad company in another state."

"Leland, you referred to your railroad adding trunk lines, which is what brings us here today. Jed, will you explain our problem to him and what you believe Calhoun's intentions are?"

Stanford listened intently as Jed explained the whole situation. When he finished, they waited a few moments while the man remained deep in thought.

"If I understand correctly, Nathan," Stanford finally said, "even without Mr. Calhoun's involvement, you'd have no intention of giving the railroad an easement on your property."

"Not at this time, Leland. Jed told you my reason: it's too soon to cut down those trees; they'd be worthless to me. I can't afford that loss."

"Excuse me a minute," Stanford said and left the room.

He returned within minutes accompanied by a serious-looking young man with spectacles, who was carrying a folder. After introducing him, Stanford said, "Bob is the surveyor and engineer who laid out the trunk line in question. Mr. Collins has a few questions that perhaps you could answer, Bob."

"Of course, Mr. Stanford," the young man said. "How can I be of help, Mr. Collins?"

"Well, I'm told you've routed the track through a particular section of land that would create a serious problem for me. Is it possible a different route could be considered?"

The young man opened a diagram and laid it out on the table. "As you can see, this drawing represents the four properties involved. The black line of cross-hatches running through it represents the intended railroad track. This became difficult because of the various elevations involved. Note the deep drop here, a sharp rise at this point, even a river. These were all considerations which couldn't be ignored."

He withdrew another diagram and spread it out. "Now, here is a detailed quadrant of your property. It has many varying elevations, but the only area that comes nearest to the elevation of your adjacent neighbors is the one I've indicated. Sadly, it has a river that runs through it."

"And bisects my mill and a section of the trees that I'm concerned about," Nathan said.

"Bob, can this portion be rerouted enough to avoid damaging the mill, without avoiding extensive additional costs to the railroad?" Stanford asked.

The young engineer studied the details. "Because of the river, it's important we don't lower the elevation so that we don't end up with any track underwater."

"The river never overflows," Nathan declared.

"We still have to make it a consideration, due to the bridge we have to build to span it."

He picked up a pencil and began to write some figures on a sheet. After several minutes, he put aside the pencil.

"If my calculations are correct, we can angle in at the same elevation thirty feet to the east of the mill and be back on the original route. Shouldn't take more than a couple of extra rails."

Stanford slapped him on the back. "Well done, Bob. Make the necessary changes on the drawings."

"One thing, Mr. Stanford," Bob said as he prepared to leave. "This change will take out Building C on the drawing."

Nathan looked at the sketch. "That's the bunk-house."

"It's a lot easier to rebuild a bunkhouse than a mill, Nathan," Stanford said. "Just make sure there's no one in it when we come through, because nothing gets in the path of the Central Pacific Railroad. Right, young man?" he said to Garrett and tousled his hair.

Garrett laughed in delight. "Right, Mr. Stanford."

"That doesn't fully solve the problem. I can't afford to lose those trees," Nathan said.

"I've already figured what to do about that. I'll pay for the trees that you'll lose. But your crew will have to cut them down."

"What will you do with them if we do cut them down?"

"We have many uses for wood on the railroad. The main need is for fuel to keep those iron horses chugging along, and we also use it on the interior walls on the freight cars. I'll give you ten cents a running yard and hire your mill to trim them."

Nathan was at a loss for words, so Caroline asked, "Why are you doing this for us, Mr. Stanford?"

"I'm a man of vision, Caroline, and I figure if I decide to run for president one day, I'll be able to count on the four votes from the people in this room."

"Five votes if you count yourself, sir," Jed said.

Stanford snorted. "You don't think I'd vote for a crook like me, do you?" he said, causing them all to laugh.

"Speaking of crooks, sir," Jed said, "we still have Calhoun to worry about, and his threats to the Collins family."

"You don't have to worry about him, Mr. Fraser. I'll handle our Mr. Calhoun. I intend to offer him a position with the Central Pacific. And, of course, threaten to withdraw my financial support when he runs for governor if any one of you is harmed—even accidentally."

"But why in the name of sanity would you hire a man like him?" Jed asked. "He intended to swindle you."

"In my forty-five years, Mr. Fraser, I've learned a lesson that Mr. Calhoun is about to learn if he intends to succeed in politics: never try to swindle a swindler."

"It's no wonder why the man was so successful at bamboozling investors he spoke of; he's amazing, isn't he?" Caroline said when they were on the train to return home.

"We're talking millions and millions of dollars. I can accept the desperation they resorted to in order to build the railroad, but if what the papers imply is true, what they skimmed off the top is unconscionable," Jed said. "Still, the insight it took to see the future economic gains for this country is remarkable, considering how difficult the physical challenges were," Jed said.

"No doubt they had their own economic gains in that vision, too," Nathan said. "But I can't help liking that man. Always did, from the first time I met him."

"So after a few hours in his presence, Caroline, you *now* believe that the end justifies the means?" Jed said.

"I would never go as far as to say that," she said. "Except, of course, he did prove that theory, didn't he?"

He hugged her and kissed her on the cheek. "Well, the next thing on our agenda is our marriage. Let's hope the end will justify the means in *that* case.

"Tomorrow we leave for Calistoga."

CHAPTER 12

The train ground to a stop at the Calistoga depot with a final hissing puff of steam.

Caroline looked out the window and saw Clay and Garth Fraser. She would have recognized them anywhere. They were probably in their early thirties by now.

Her breath caught in her throat when she studied Clay. She'd always thought Andy had resembled Clay so much they could have passed as twins, but Clay had always exuded confidence, compared to Andy's shy nature.

As for Garth Fraser, his grin and good nature had probably broken the hearts of most of the girls between here and Virginia.

But they weren't boys anymore; time and a war had transformed them into men, which had only enhanced their handsomeness.

When they found out the truth about Garrett, would they feel as resentful toward her as Jed did?

"All set?" Jed asked.

She took a deep breath, then nodded.

He tucked a finger under her chin and grinned down at her. "Hey, Cinderella, trust me. They're not going to eat you," he said gently. He kissed her lightly, then took her hand.

"Don't forget Buffer back in the freight car," Garrett said. "There was no reason why that mean old conductor wouldn't let him stay with us."

"I think he had the other passengers' interests at heart, honey," Caroline said.

"Well, Buffer wouldn't have caused them no trouble. I'm still gonna write that Mr. Stanford and tell him what I think about his dumb rule."

She took Garrett by the hand and stepped out onto the observation platform with Jed. Smiling, the two men straightened up and walked toward them.

Caroline felt like an early Christian about to be fed to the lions.

After a series of handshakes and backslaps between the men, Jed slipped an arm around her shoulders and drew her to his side.

"Caroline, do these guys look familiar? My brothers—"

She interrupted him. "You're Clay, and you're Garth. How could I forget?"

The two men exchanged perplexed glances. "We've met before?" Clay asked. "Brother Garth, help me out here."

"Virginia?" Garth asked, clearly as confused as Clay.

"Well, certainly," Caroline said with a grin.

"While you're trying to figure it out, do you

remember the captain of the ship I was on during the war?"

"Captain Collins, of course," Clay said as they shook hands.

Garth shook Nathan's hand. "It's a pleasure to see you again, sir. Are you the captain of the ship Jed's on now?"

Nathan laughed. "No, I'm not, Garth. I retired shortly after the war ended."

Jed rested a hand on Garrett's shoulder. "And this young man is Caroline's son, Garrett."

"Glad to meet you, Garrett. Let us be the first to welcome you into the family," Garth said.

"Thank you. The pleasure is all mine." He grinned. "When we were on the train, Mama made me practice saying that."

"And let me assure you, Garrett, it's a pleasure to meet you, too."

"I remember now," Clay suddenly said. "Captain Collins had a daughter . . . Caroline!"

"Of course." Garth grinned. "Lady, have you changed!"

"You were just a skinny little kid then," Clay said with a warm chuckle.

Caroline began to relax. "I would like you to know, sir, I was fifteen when we left Virginia." She'd dreaded this meeting, but it seemed to be going well. They both were so charming. Of course Jed had been, too, until he found out the truth about Andy.

"Let's load up this luggage and get moving," Garth said. "There's a lot of anxious women waiting to meet their future sister-in-law."

When the train whistle sounded a departing toot, Garrett cried, "Buffer! The train's leaving with Buffer on it!" Then his panic changed to laughter as the barking dog came racing along the side of the train and into his open arms. Reunited, Garrett and Buffer scrambled into the bed of the wagon, and they all broke into laughter.

Clay climbed onto the seat of the wagon. "Figure that must be the last of the luggage? Jed can ride with me. Caroline and Captain Collins, climb in with Garth. I'm sure you'll be more comfortable in the buggy."

"You didn't mention in your wire that your intended bride had a son," Clay said as they drove to his home. "He's a cute kid."

"Yeah, he's great. And we get along great, too."

"What happened to his father?"

"He's dead."

"I thought maybe you were the father."

"Why would you think that?"

"Because the two of you kind of resemble each other, and his mother's the daughter of your former captain. Coincidence?"

"I haven't seen Captain Collins since the war ended. And I think I saw Caroline once when she was little. I ran into them in a restaurant several days ago."

He and his brothers had always been honest with one another, but Jed thought it would be wiser to tell them the truth about Garrett after he and Caroline were married.

"It must be tough for a kid to grow up without

a father or any brothers and sisters. We were pretty lucky, weren't we?" Clay said.

"You're damn right, Brother Clay."

"You and Caroline planning on starting a family right away?"

At least he could give him a straight-out answer on that question. "Not at this time, Clay. I've used up a week of my leave already. I wouldn't want Caroline to have a baby while I'm at sea."

"Pretty hard to plan it otherwise, Jed, without you figuring on staying home."

"I'm not ready to give up the sea just yet."

"Then what's the reason for getting married at this time? What kind of marriage is that: you at sea, your wife and children home?"

"Speaking of children, isn't Rory about due?" Jed asked.

"Overdue would be more like it," Clay said. "Where are you planning on setting up housekeeping?"

"Captain Collins owns property and a sawmill near Napa. Caroline has always lived with him, although there is a problem at this time. Some shyster named Calhoun, who is working for the railroad, threatened Caroline and her family."

"Good Lord, you mean their lives?"

"Yes, but I think it's been resolved. We spoke to Leland Stanford and he's promised to move him to Sacramento, where he'll be out of our hair."

"You're traveling in pretty big company there, Jed."

"Captain Collins knows him. I'll soon be going

back to sea, and my concern is for Caroline and her family."

"Sure you wouldn't want them to stay here with us? There's plenty of room."

"I'd sure have peace of mind if they did, but they're determined to stay where they are. Thanks for the offer, anyway."

A short time later when Garth turned the buggy off the main road, Caroline saw a sign with FRASER KEEP hanging over the door of a small cabin. The line below read Home of the Fraser Wines of California in smaller print.

"We sell some of our bottled wine and other related items to passersby," Garth said to his passengers.

"For instance?" Caroline asked.

"Wineglasses, and corkscrew handles we make out of a patch of oak growing here. We even sell small serviettes; those were Becky's idea. The girls cut them out of white linen, and Lissy, who's the best artist in the group, draws an outline of several grapes on a stalk—the same design we use on the label of the wine bottles. Then they all embroider the outline and put tatting on the edges in their spare time."

"Don't they all have young children to take care of? When do they find any spare time?" Caroline asked.

"They're all remarkable women, Caroline," Garth said. "They enjoy their lives, and they make certain the people they love enjoy life, too."

Caroline felt a stab of shame, knowing how she

had strived to make Jed's life as miserable as possible.

"I thought Colt and his family lived in New Mexico."

"They do, but Cassie does the serviettes in her free time and ships them to us. She's a working hand on their cattle ranch, the way our wives work in the vineyard planting and picking the grapes. Colt claims she can ride and rope as well as any man on the ranch. Rain or shine, she's out doing whatever the men are doing.

"Becky, Lissy, and Rory do the same here," Garth continued. "Becky worked side by side with Clay, planting the cuttings, followed by long hours in the blazing sun fighting and watering to keep them from dying, in order to keep his dream alive. When Lissy and Steve moved here to help, it was a godsend to them, then Rory and I joined them after we married. Of course Rory can't do much physically now, since she's in a family way, so she minds the children for the other women and works on the napkins."

"Sounds to me like it's working out well," Nathan said.

"Captain Collins, everybody has helped in some way to keep the vineyard operating. We all live right here, except for Colt and Cassie, of course."

In the same house! The thought was horrifying to her. All the possible noise and confusion flashed through her mind. How hard it must have been on those poor women, bearing their husbands' children in the midst of all that hard work and stress!

She realized how calm and easy her life had

been in having her loving parents to rely upon, how blessed she had been. She reached over and squeezed her father's hand. This dear man who had looked after her welfare her whole life had always seen to her safety, a roof over her head, and a hot meal in her stomach.

How blessed, indeed.

"For the sake of all our sanities, we all live under separate roofs, as does Paddy O'Grady, Rory's father," Garth said. "We have an eleven-month-old son named Danny and are expecting another baby any day.

"Lissy and Steve have a four-year-old son, Ted. He's about the only child who can run around here. Their other two children, Sarah and Rachel, are three and two respectively. Most of the rest of our children aren't even housebroken yet." He glanced askance at Caroline. "Still in diapers, that is.

"Clay has a three-year-old son, Jake, and a set of twins, Clint and Cody, born at the end of last year. Colt and Cassie have a two-year-old son named Jeb, and a daughter Samantha born a couple of months ago. I'm afraid none of them are old enough to be a playmate for Garrett."

"That's no problem, Garth. Garrett's used to being alone, as long as he has Buffer."

"Is that the dog you brought with you?"

Caroline nodded. "They're inseparable."

"You did amazingly well, Garth," Nathan said.

Garth flashed that devastating grin of his. "Just want you folks to know we grow more around here than just grapes."

"Did I understand you to say your wife's father lives here with you?"

"In his own house, of course. Wait until you meet Paddy O'Grady. The old-timer used to dig for gold. He's a great old guy and is like a grandfather to all the children."

"Fortunately, Garrett has a grandfather already," she said with a smile at her father. "But I guess it wouldn't hurt to have more than one."

"Colt and Cassie brought her father along, too. Jethro Braden's an ex-sheriff; turned the badge over to Colt when he retired. Jethro has a raft of interesting stories to tell about outlaws and Indians. Even the Apache chief Cochise, and that crazy Geronimo. You must have heard about them."

"Can't help it if you read a newspaper," Nathan said.

They reached the houses, which only could be described as a compound. Caroline only had time to glimpse several houses and a large rectangular building when the door of the biggest house burst open and several women and men rushed out the door.

Caroline gaped with awe when she saw the women. Not one among them appeared tired and worn out, as she had expected. On the contrary, they were beautiful. Downright ravishing, all of them!

A lovely blonde with incredible green eyes stepped forward and hugged her. "Welcome, Caroline! I'm Becky, Clay's wife. We're so excited you've come. This will be our first wedding at Fraser Keep."

Before Caroline could even respond, she was hugged and kissed by another woman. Her blue eyes warm with welcome, she said, "Hi, Caroline, I'm Cassie, Colt's wife." She was wearing jeans and boots and perched on her dark hair was a Stetson.

"So you must be Rory, Garth's wife," Caroline said to the other blond woman, who was clearly pregnant. "He told us all about you on the way here."

Her blue eyes flashed with devilment. "I hope he didn't tell *all* about me," Rory Fraser said, with as much of a hug as her swollen stomach would allow. She took the arm of the man standing beside her with bushy white hair and a wide Irish grin. "And this is my father, Paddy O'Grady."

"Pleased to meet you, darlin'," Paddy O'Grady said.

"A pleasure to meet you, Mr. O'Grady."

"It's Paddy, darlin', and don't you be forgettin' it," he said.

"I'm Jethro Braden," another of the men said. Dressed in Western gear like Cassie, he wouldn't have had to tell her he was Cassie's father.

Caroline turned to a couple who had stood back and broke into a smile at the sight of the petite, dark-haired woman who now stepped up and hugged her.

"Caroline, what a pleasure to see you again."

"Oh, Lissy, you're still as beautiful as I remembered," Caroline said.

"I can't believe you and Jed are getting married! How are you ever going to keep my big brother on land?"

"My mother tolerated it with my father, and I guess I will, too."

Lissy reached for the hand of the man beside her. "Caroline, this is my husband, Stephen Berg."

The tall, redheaded man hugged her. "I've looked forward to meeting you, Caroline."

Caroline took her father's arm. "And this handsome gentleman is my father, Nathan Collins."

Clay arrived with the wagon, and when Garrett jumped off and ran over to her, Caroline said proudly, "And this is my son, Garrett."

A flurry of squeals of pleasure and greetings followed as the women gushed over Garrett and greeted Jed.

Another Fraser came over and hugged her. "Welcome, Caroline. I'm Jed's brother, Colt."

"Yes, I remember you."

"So Jed's marrying a Reb. It's about time one of us did."

Jed slipped an arm around her shoulders. "You're barking up the wrong tree, Brother Colt. Caroline doesn't exactly walk around the house whistling 'Carry Me Back to Old Virginny.'"

"Ignore him, Caroline," Becky said. "Lissy's been very protective of her brothers, so we're dying to know the whole story of what these men were like when they were younger. Aren't we, ladies?"

"We sure are," Cassie said. "So let's get out of this sun and go inside for a glass of cool lemonade."

"Mr. Collins, rather then listen to the ladies' palaver, will you do us the pleasure of joinin' Jethro and me on me porch for a cool glass of *lemonade*?" Paddy winked at Nathan.

"Mr. O'Grady, I can't think of anything I'd rather do."

The three older men moved away, and Becky tucked Caroline's arm into her own. "Cassie's got the right idea. Let's go in and sit down."

"That's not fair," Lissy moaned. "I have to go and check to see if my children are still napping."

"Don't worry about it, honey. I'll check on the children," Steve said.

Jed picked up several pieces of the luggage. "I'll get Caroline settled in. Same bedroom I've used before, Becky?" he asked.

"No, take the two empty ones at the end of the hallway. Same ones Lissy and Steve used before their house was completed."

"Let me help you with those bags," Steve said, grabbing the remaining luggage.

"We'll unsaddle the horses and get rid of the buckboard and buggy," Clay called to them.

Jed and Steve took the luggage inside the house, and the women trouped in behind them.

Forgotten in all the excitement, Garrett looked around at the now deserted yard, which only moments before had been swarming with people.

He sat down in the shade of a nearby oak tree and put his arm around Buffer's neck.

"Sure has been nice meeting my aunts and uncles, wasn't it, Buffer? I'm anxious to meet my cousins, too."

The dog stretched out with his head on Garrett's lap.

CHAPTER
13

As soon as they finished with the horses and vehicles, Clay pulled out a bottle of wine and some glasses. "I've been saving this for a special occasion. Can't think of a better one than the last of us getting married."

Colt voiced the question foremost on all their minds. "Yeah, but did any of you notice the same thing that I did?"

"You mean how much Garrett resembles Jed?" Clay asked.

"Hell, yes," Garth agreed. "The kid looks more like a Fraser than my own son, Danny."

Colt winked at Clay. "You got a secret you want to confess, Brother Garth?"

The three men broke into laughter, then Clay sobered. "All joking aside, there's no doubt in my mind that Garrett is a Fraser. From what Jed said to me, it's clear he's not the boy's father, and I'm damn sure I'm not. So that leaves one of you."

Colt raised his hand in denial. "It's sure as hell not me."

The two men swung their attention to Garth.

"Hey, don't look at me," he said. "I never went near her. I had my hands full with those Forsyth twins. You guys remember that pair?"

"Who could forget them?" Colt said. "You don't think it could be Will, do you?"

"Em's always been the only woman Will's ever wanted," Garth said.

"Then it's *got* to be Jed," Colt declared.

After a pause, Clay asked softly, "What about Andy?"

Garth arched a brow. "Andy was only a kid. He hadn't figured out yet that his dick could be used for something besides peeing."

"Apparently he had, if he *is* the father," Colt remarked.

More convinced than ever, Clay asked, "Anyone remember what year Caroline's family left Virginia?"

"It had to be sixty or sixty-one," Colt said. "They got out before the war actually started, and Andy had turned eighteen by the time he went into the army. Remember, he'd been laid up with a broken leg and then a case of pneumonia before he could enlist."

"So he'd have been either seventeen or just turned eighteen when the Collinses left," Clay said. "So even if he'd only been seventeen, it's not as far-fetched as we think. You boys have short memories. Were any of us still virgins at that age?"

"Not as long as those Forsyth twins were around," Garth said.

Colt still harbored doubt. "I don't know. . . . He

never showed any interest in girls. He was quiet and always had his nose in a book."

Clay smiled. "Yeah, but remember how Mom always warned Lissy to look out for the quiet ones?"

That brought a sentimental smile to Garth. "He *was* the quiet one of us, all right, except when he was all fired up about becoming a minister after the war."

"So you figured it out."

They turned around to discover that Jed had joined them.

"You're saying Garrett *is* Andy's son?" Clay said.

Jed nodded.

"Well, I'll be damned," Garth said softly. "I'm happy for him. "I'm glad he at least had that before he died."

"He would have made a damn good father if given the chance," Colt said.

"Or a great preacher," Clay added. "But he didn't get the chance to prove it."

"Hey, we're getting too morbid here," Jed warned. "A wedding is supposed to be a happy occasion. What about it, fellas?"

"You're right." Clay filled their glasses. "Wait until you taste this wine. I've named it Becky."

Jed winked at the others. "Rather an unusual name for a wine, isn't it, Clay?"

"Jed, you have no idea how many of these *Beckys* we've had to taste since Clay became a vintner," Colt said. "What is this one now? Becky five or number six? Although I do have to say, this one's pretty good." He extended his glass for a refill.

"Yes, I think I have finally created perfection. Lusciously sweet, with just the hint of spice to give it elegance." Clay rolled his eyes and with a villainous twirl of the end of an imaginary mustache, he added, "And intended for my stock *only*."

Jed groaned. "Has he been this way for long?" he asked Colt. "What does Becky think?"

"She thinks he's been out in the sun picking grapes for too long."

They laughed, and Jed said, "I was hoping Rico could make it to the wedding."

"We wired him as soon as we got your telegram," Clay said. "He wired back and said it's pretty short notice, but he's hoping to get here in time."

"We can always hold off the ceremony for another day. I'm sure Caroline wouldn't object."

"Has she ever married, Jed?" Clay asked.

"No, she's remained with her parents from the time she left Virginia. Captain Collins retired when his wife died a couple of years ago, and Caroline had no idea our family lived so close. She assumed we all had remained in Virginia."

"I'm glad she didn't marry," Garth suddenly spoke up.

Clay nodded. "I understand what you mean. Had she married, we might never have known our nephew. Now, because of Brother Jed here, Garrett will be raised a Fraser, and we'll always have a part of Andy among us."

"Providence," Jed said with a nod. "Caroline believes very heavily in Providence. Have you seen The Buffer?"

"Isn't that the mongrel hound you brought with you?" Garth asked.

"Yes. Did he growl at you?"

"Dogs never growl at me," Garth replied.

"Well, I'll be damned," Jed grumbled.

"They love me on sight," Garth continued. "Same as horses do."

"That damn dog is my nemesis, but Caroline thinks there's something providential about him."

"Enough talk about dogs and horses. I was about to make a toast." Clay raised his glass. "Here's to Providence."

"To Providence," they echoed in accord.

The women sat around the kitchen table, drinking lemonade and eating cookies.

"Was it a long engagement, Caroline?" Rory asked. "When did Jed propose to you?"

"Three days ago," Caroline said.

"And how long has he been courting you?" Cassie asked. "With Jed at sea most of the time, it must have been for years."

"Well, I can't say you'd really call it courting," Caroline said, trying to stall. "You see, I was only fifteen when we left Virginia."

"You mean you've been sweethearts since you were fifteen?"

"Good heavens, no!"

"I didn't think so," Lissy said. "Jed was calling on Mary Belle Cameron then. Oh, how I disliked that girl! I was relieved that he went to sea before she could get her claws into him."

"I bet it started when he left here last year after his visit," Rory reflected. "Otherwise I'm sure he would have told our husbands. Am I right, Caroline?"

"No, it wasn't last year," Caroline said.

"These Fraser men don't walk easily to the preachers," Becky said. "I had to get Clay so drunk he didn't know what he was doing. And it took him four months before he finally admitted he loved me."

"If you think you had a hard time with Clay, you should have seen what I went through with Colt!" Cassie said. "I had to actually hold up a stagecoach and force him at gunpoint to get off of it when he was leaving me."

Rory started to laugh. "I had to steal Garth's map to a gold mine, or I might never have seen him again. And then it wasn't until we were on the verge of being killed by bandits that he admitted he loved me."

Lissy laughed. "Well, you all did pretty well for yourselves, if you ask me. Truth is, if it weren't for me eloping with Steve, you wouldn't be married to them now. Because that caused Clay and Garth to follow me to take me back home, and they ended up on the same wagon train as you, Becky. Then if Colt hadn't decided to follow *them* to California, he wouldn't have ended up in that town in New Mexico where he met you, Cassie. And if Garth hadn't decided to go off hunting for his Uncle Henry's gold mine while he was here in California, Rory, you would never have been able to steal the map from him."

"You're right, honey," Rory teased. "And look what

it got me?" She rubbed her swollen stomach. "The *pot* at the end of the rainbow."

Caroline couldn't help laughing with them, for despite their complaints, it was obvious these women worshipped the men they married.

Becky wiped the tears of laughter from her eyes. "So we all agree it wasn't easy getting that 'will you marry me' out of the darlings. So how long did he court *you*, Caroline, before you got it out of Jed—the mysterious and elusive brother who was always off visiting glamorous and exotic ports?"

"Well . . . ah . . ." Caroline hesitated to tell them the truth without them knowing the circumstances of the marriage. There was certainly no love or romance to Jed's proposal, but she couldn't lie to them since they were bound to find out the truth later.

"Go on, Caroline, how long?" Becky asked. "One year? Two years?"

"I guess you could say about three days."

"You've told us that Jed proposed to you three days ago," Lissy said. "But how long did he court you before he finally proposed marriage?"

Caroline cleared her throat and lowered her eyes. "I suppose you could say for six days."

When she finally got the courage to raise her eyes, they were all looking at her in disbelief, apparently waiting for her to continue.

"Things happened very swiftly between us."

"That's an understatement," Becky murmured.

"We were in San Francisco having breakfast when Jed walked into the dining room. As you probably know, he had served on my father's ship during the war, but they hadn't seen each other since it ended. He joined us for breakfast, and later my father invited him home to see the mill."

"Mill?" Becky asked.

"Our home and sawmill is near Napa. In the days that followed, one thing led to another, and he asked me to marry him."

"Oh, my God!" Rory exclaimed, clutching at her heart. "Six days! It's a miracle. I swear I'm going to have my baby right here."

"Are you serious?" Caroline cried, alarmed.

Rory giggled. "No, I'm just surprised. It's so romantic, Caroline. You've accomplished the impossible— only six days to get a proposal from a Fraser."

Lissy stood up. "What my darling sister-in-law is trying to say is that they're all green with envy." She leaned down, kissed her on the cheek, and hugged her. "I'm so happy for both of you, Caroline. Jed is a wonderful person; I know he'll be as great a husband and father as my other brothers turned out to be. I have to leave now to feed the children, so I'd appreciate if you women would delay any more discussion on the wedding until I get back. I don't want to miss anything."

"Oh, right," Becky said good-naturedly. "We'll scrub floors or wash diapers until you get back."

Laughing, Lissy disappeared through the door.

Cassie got up to leave. "My children will be waking soon. I'd better get back, too."

Rory joined her. "Yes, me, too. We'll see you later."

"I'll show you to your rooms, Caroline," Becky said.

"I hope we're not inconveniencing you."

"Not at all. We moved Jake's bed into the twins' room, so the two rooms at the end of the hall are for you. I emptied one of the drawers for you to use; will that be enough?"

"Oh, yes. I didn't bring much clothing because I have no idea how long Jed intends to stay."

Becky sat down on the edge of the bed. "Jed and your father can decide which one of them will take the other room here, and there's room at Paddy O'Grady's. Jethro's staying there, too—no crying babies. Cassie and Colt are staying with Lissy and Steve. It must be nice for you gals to still have fathers."

"Yes. I guess we just take them for granted."

"I adore Paddy," Becky said. "I've adopted him as a father."

Caroline smiled. "And I bet you and Rory spoil him."

"I can't help it; he's so lovable. Both my parents died when I was thirteen. My brother wasn't much older than me, but if it weren't for him, we'd both have ended up in an orphanage."

"Do you have any other brothers and sisters?"

"No, what about you?" Becky asked.

"I was an only child. Spoiled rotten, as Jed will be the first to agree."

Becky broke into a smile. "Are you saying you and Jed have had a lovers' quarrel after only six days of courting?"

"I have to admit, it wasn't only his fault. I'm just as much to blame."

"Honey, don't worry about it. Clay and I argued for four solid months, from Missouri to California. Would you believe we never exchange a cross word now?"

The cry of a baby sounded from another room, and Becky jumped to her feet. "Uh-oh, duty calls. It's feeding time for the twins. Come along and meet the little darlings."

When Becky handed her one of the infants, Caroline cooed, "Oh, how precious. How old is he?"

"Eight months."

"And which one is this?"

"That's Clint. He and Cody are identical twins. And this handsome guy is Jake, our three-year-old." Becky snuggled and kissed the little tot who had just climbed up on her lap.

"Your children are beautiful, Becky. I miss having a little one to snuggle. It seems like Garrett grew up so fast. The last eight years have passed so swiftly."

"Hang in there, honey, it won't be for long. If Jed is anything like his brothers, you'll probably be pregnant by the time he goes back to sea."

Caroline blushed. "I hope not, because he'll be gone in another three weeks. But speaking of children, I'd better see what Garrett's up to."

She hurried away. She didn't want to discuss the conditions of her marriage with these women; it was too easy to tell where their loyalties lay.

Outside, she heard the sound of talk and laughter coming from the barn, and she started over to it until she saw Garrett sitting under a nearby tree with Buffer and another large dog. She went over and sat down beside him.

"Where'd you meet this big fellow?" she asked, scratching the dog between the ears.

"My aunt who's gonna have a baby."

"That would be your Aunt Rory, honey."

"Aunt Rory told me the dog's name is Saddle. He's my Uncle Garth's dog."

"He seems like a nice dog."

"Mama, do dogs talk to each other?"

Caroline laughed lightly. "Wherever did you get such an idea, honey?"

"They bark, and maybe that's their talk. Just because we don't know what they're saying doesn't mean another dog doesn't. And I think Buffer and Saddle like each other, 'cause they didn't growl, they just barked and sniffed at each other a couple times, and then Saddle sat down beside us."

"Then I'd say they probably do like each other."

"Bet that barking was dog talk," Garrett declared. "Maybe Buffer invited him to sit with us."

"Maybe he did, honey."

Garrett's face screwed up in intense concentration. "You know, Mama, a dog's 'bout the best friend a kid could have, 'cepting his mom."

"Dads make good friends, too. Your granddad is my best friend."

"Can uncles and aunts be a best friend?"

"Many often are," she said.

"Well, I sure have a lot of aunts and uncles. So how can all of them be my *best* friend?"

"You're right, honey; you can only have *one* best friend."

"But what about the others who aren't?"

"They'll still be people you love."

"Will they still love me?"

"I think they already do, sweetheart." She leaned back against the tree and closed her eyes.

CHAPTER
14

Jed left the barn to go and unpack his seabag. His brothers had asked him to delay the wedding until their cousin Rico arrived and he knew Caroline wouldn't have a problem with that; she certainly wasn't looking forward to the event. But he wanted to inform her of it so it wouldn't come as a surprise to her.

As he walked to Clay's house, he saw Caroline and Garrett asleep under a tree. Buffer and Saddle were stretched out beside them like sentinels.

Jed sat down under an opposite tree in the clearing and stared at them. As if relieved of duty, the two dogs rose and padded away.

Had he read more into their departure than intended? Were the two dogs actually aware that the woman and child would now be his responsibility to protect for the rest of his life?

You're losing your mind, Fraser, when you start wondering what a dog is thinking.

His gaze fixed on Caroline's face, and he marveled again how peaceful she looked when she slept. No bitterness, no scornful glares to mar its loveliness.

He'd known from the morning after she'd told him about Andy that he wouldn't force her to marry him. That had been a hasty and ludicrous decision on his part. But she had stunned him by agreeing to marry him, and that astounding challenge to convince him to seduce her.

His gaze rested on her face again. She was delightful to be around when she wasn't angry at him, and he enjoyed her company to no end. Especially the way she constantly challenged him. No woman ever did that with him, and he found it a refreshing change.

It was a shame that due to the bad beginning between them, she'd probably never forgive him—and he couldn't forgive her for what she'd done to his family.

Funny that not one of his brothers had appeared disturbed by her action—or lack of action. Were they so elated to hear that Andy had fathered a child that they didn't realize that they might have never seen or known that child? That's what would have happened if the issue had been left to her.

He stood up. *Yes, you're beautiful and appealing, Caroline Collins, but beauty is only skin deep. Integrity is the real beauty in a woman . . . or man.*

Later, Clay took them on a tour of the building where they made the wine. He led them over to a large vat in the corner. "This is the press where we squeeze the grape juice."

"I thought the women stomped the grapes with their bare feet."

"We've let them do it a couple of times, because they enjoy it. It's hysterical—but slippery, and if they're pregnant we certainly don't want them to fall. That's why we generally use a press. The wine fermenting in those barrels that run along that whole wall over there is a claret we make from California grapes, which is our predominant crop. Jed, remember those grape cuttings you brought me from France two years ago? We harvested a small crop of them, and I've been experimenting with a white, drier wine than the claret."

"What actually causes the wine to ferment?" Caroline asked.

"The natural yeast in the skins of the grapes. The oak barrel adds to the flavor of the wine during the fermentation."

"Who makes the barrels for you?" Caroline asked.

"Believe it or not, Garth. He's great at it and seems to really enjoy it."

"We bottle it and store it in here, in the wine cave." Clay opened a door to reveal racks of sealed bottles. He lit a lantern, and they stepped inside.

"This actually is a cave!" Caroline exclaimed as she glanced around.

"Yes, it is," he said. "We keep the wine in here because the temperature is cool and stays constant. We framed the entrance, put a door on it, and *voilà!*"

"Remarkable," Nathan said.

"I discovered it when we first came here, and that's why I decided to build my house nearby."

"Well, this has been a fascinating tour, Clay," Nathan said. "I'm impressed with your vision and skill. I'm sure you didn't accomplish all this overnight."

"Clay always was the one among us who had vision, sir," Jed said. "Garth fixated on finding Uncle Henry's gold mine. Colt's dreams were to become a lawman, Andy a preacher. Will's love was Fraser Keep, and mine was the sea."

"Thankfully, I've had a lot of help from my family—physically and financially—and it's finally beginning to pay off. I've got a hunch that one day California wine is going to be as popular as the French and other European labels. And Fraser Keep wines will be right up there with them."

"I don't doubt that for a moment. I promised Paddy I'd play a game of chess, so I should be leaving," Nathan said. "My thanks again for the tour, Clay."

"I'll come with you, Father," Caroline said. "I want to see what Garrett's up to."

"You and Caroline have a quarrel?" Clay asked, as soon as they were alone.

"Why do you ask?"

"No body contact. No eye contact. And I could have cut the tension between you with a knife. I noticed it from the time you arrived today, despite a couple of feeble attempts by you to try and show affection toward her."

"It's just marriage jitters."

"Marriage jitters my ass, Jed. If you don't want to talk about it, fine—it's none of my business. But when the excitement dies down, don't think the others won't notice, too."

"We won't be around that long for them to no-tice."

"If that's the way you want it." Clay turned to leave.

"Hell, Clay, that's *not* the way I want it. The truth is . . . Caroline and I aren't in love. This is a marriage of convenience."

"You mean she's pregnant?"

"No, I haven't touched her. It's about Garrett."

Jed proceeded to tell him the whole truth about his relationship with Caroline and why he'd de-manded she marry him. When he finished, Clay was silent for a long moment before he finally spoke.

"That's not fair to Caroline, Jed. Or to you. You both deserve better."

"We're doing it for Garrett's sake. I love that kid, and I know I can be a good father to him."

"I'm sure you can, but what kind of husband will you be to Caroline?"

"Doesn't it bother you that she never tried to no-tify Andy that he had a son?"

Clay looked at him sadly. "Jed, Andy was dead be-fore any word would have reached him."

"At least Mom and Dad would have known about Garrett before they died."

"Perhaps, but does it really matter in the end? How could it have changed their lives in any way?"

"I would think knowing that the memory of Andy would live on in his son might have eased their pass-ing."

"Perhaps you're right. But their faith was so strong; I'm sure they were at peace knowing they would soon be joining Andy, and our nephews Joey and little Paul." He smiled gently. "You know Mom; had she lived, she probably would have fretted herself to death worrying they were up there without her to look after them."

"Garrett's a *Fraser*, Clay! If I hadn't run into them by chance in San Francisco, he never would have been raised as one."

"Aren't you forgetting about destiny, Brother Jed?"

"Destiny! Good God—do you think when Andy was born, he was destined to die on a battlefield in Gettysburg, Pennsylvania? Or sixteen-year-old Joey at Sharpsburg; or little Paul, burning up with fever in his crib? Every time there's no rhyme nor reason for what happens, we cry Destiny or Providence. Oh, yeah, and Fate. That's another word to fall back on when you don't have the answers."

"I believe in predetermined destiny," Clay said. "Garth was destined to find Uncle Henry's gold mine, or he wouldn't have; Becky picking me out of a wagon train of men because she needed a husband was destiny, or she would have picked a different one; Colt being on the same stagecoach as Cassie when it was held up was destiny; and your walking into a restaurant in San Francisco the same time Caroline was there was destiny.

"Providence is just another way of believing God is determining our destiny. Fate is where God and Destiny part company. Whether by choice or chance, our lives often lead us down a different path than He had planned for us. And that's when Fate gets involved.

Sometimes the result can be good, sometimes bad. But don't blame God for the outcome."

"So you believe it was Destiny that brought me and Caroline together after all these years?"

"Yes, but I think it was Garrett's destiny—not yours or Caroline's. He was destined to be raised a Fraser, no matter what path Andy, Caroline, or you may have chosen. And the final chapter hasn't been written yet for you. It's in the hands of Fate now, because the way I see it, you're marrying Caroline for all the wrong reasons. Are you sure you aren't forcing her into this marriage for something other than what you're claiming?"

"What the hell is that supposed to mean?"

"Maybe you care for her more than you're willing to admit—even to yourself—and using Garrett as an excuse to get her."

"That's bullshit. I'm a grown man. I know what I'm doing when it comes to women."

Clay grinned. "If you do, then you're the only man I know who's been able to figure it out."

"No matter what you think, Caroline and I agree it's the right thing to do for Garrett's sake."

"But what about love? You have to have that for a happy marriage, you know."

"We're both adults and understand what we have to do. We've worked out an agreement that shouldn't be too difficult to honor. I'll be at sea most of the time, anyway, so that will make it easier."

"Worked out an agreement? I can't believe I'm hearing this from you. You're not thinking straight, Jed."

"Garrett will legally have the name of Fraser. I felt it's a matter of family honor. I owe it to Andy."

"Yeah, that's great—but what's honorable about trying to delude Garrett into believing his parents are in love? And not only Garrett; you intend to do it to the whole family."

"What they don't know won't hurt them. I shouldn't have even told you."

"They already figured out Garrett is a Fraser. Nobody had to tell them."

"How did they react?"

"They think it's great that Andy had a son and that you'll be raising him. As far as the two of you getting married, they figure it's the icing on the cake. Of course, it hasn't entered their minds that you and Caroline aren't marrying for love."

"Then don't tell them differently, Clay. Keep it between you and me."

"I don't keep secrets from them, Jed. They're your brothers and sister, too. If we start keeping secrets from each other, before you know it, the truth gets out and results in bad feelings.

"Becky and I have no secrets between us. A good marriage is all about love and trust. That's the real *agreement* in marriage.

"The resemblance between you and Garrett is so remarkable, our wives are probably thinking you're the father. You think they won't question us? They'll be all over us with questions! You talk family honor from one side of your mouth, then tell us to lie to our wives from the other side of it. As long as you're determined to go through with this marriage, don't hide from the truth, Jed. That will catch up with you and start eating you alive."

Deflated, Jed walked to the door. "You're right; I should tell them the truth. I don't want any bad feelings between any of us."

Clay slapped him on the shoulder. "You know that Lissy and your brothers are behind you one hundred percent. But, Brother Jed, don't ever try to deceive those women we married. Together, they're a united force, and you wouldn't have a prayer."

Caroline found Garrett sitting on a fence railing watching Colt trim the bark off a log.

"There you are. I've been looking for you," she said.

"Mama, did you know Uncle Colt knows Kit Carson? He's been telling me 'bout the time Apache Indians surrounded their town, and him and Kit Carson faced off with them."

"That must have been exciting."

Colt grinned. "Things still aren't as settled in New Mexico as they are here in California."

"I understand you're a sheriff, Colt."

"Just a deputy now. I turned the job over to Jeff Braden, Cassie's brother. Sometimes I give him a hand on weekends when there's a big crowd in town. Cassie and I have our hands full running the ranch, especially since we've had children. Cassie can handle a horse better than most men, but I don't want her riding yet. She just had Sam a couple of months ago."

"That's too bad, cowboy, because I'm not stopping," Cassie said from the doorway.

He chuckled. "Riding or having babies, Cass?"

"Neither one, Colt Fraser. Caroline, come on inside where we can talk."

Caroline joined her in the kitchen where Cassie was rolling out a pie crust.

"You feel like peeling apples?" she asked. "I'm making pies for the barbecue tomorrow."

Grateful for having something useful to do, Caroline said, "I'd love to. I'm used to being the one *doing* the waiting on not being waited on."

"Then sit yourself down at the table. You've just been hired." Cassie put a bowl of apples down on the table and rooted through a kitchen drawer.

"This is Rory's kitchen, so I'm having a little trouble finding things. Aha, here's one!" She handed Caroline a paring knife.

"Where is Rory?"

"She's lying down. Her back's been bothering her. The poor dear had a rough time with her first pregnancy, and she'd barely gotten back on her feet when she got pregnant again. Danny's only eleven months old, and now this one's past due."

Cassie lowered her voice to a whisper. "She told me Garth wanted to abstain until she was healthy and back on her feet, but Rory said she wanted childbearing out of the way so she could enjoy her children while she was still young."

"I've totally forgotten what it was like to bear a child. I was sixteen when Garrett was born," Caroline said.

"So that would make you twenty-four now."

Caroline nodded. "How long have you been married, Cassie?"

"Three years. Colt and I were married in '66; Jeb was born the following year."

"Did you say Jeb or Jed?"

"Jeb," Cassie said. "One Jed in the family is enough. Our son's named after Colt's hero, General J.E.B. Stuart, his commanding officer during the late war until the general was killed."

Cassie waved the rolling pin in the air as if it were a saber. "'The greatest cavalry leader in the whole damn war—Reb or Yankee alike.' To quote Captain Colt Fraser, that is."

Smiling, Cassie lowered her arm. "Maybe General Stuart was as great as he said, but I wouldn't know. Living out here in the West, the war didn't really affect my life that much. We had to wage our own wars against Nature and marauding Indians. These men all have their heroes, but they don't realize how much greater heroes they themselves are—to the women who love them." She paused in deep thought.

"What are you thinking about right this minute, Cassie?"

Cassie's lips curled in a soft smile. "Colt."

"How did you meet?"

"He was heading out here to California when he was wounded during a stagecoach holdup. He had to spend a week in Arena Roja, waiting for the next stage to come through. Oh, that man was big and beautiful, and so cocky! He openly declared to me that by the time he left town, he'd have me in the hayloft." She laughed in remembrance. "And he did. Lord, how I love that man!"

"If I remember, Garth said your son Jeb was two years old," Caroline said.

"Yes, just last week. And Sam was two months old. They have identical birthdays except for the years."

"So you have two sons? I thought Garth said you had a son and daughter."

"We do, our daughter Samantha. But Garth's already hung the name Sam on her. Caroline, since the wedding's not until the day after tomorrow, your father wanted to take all of us to town for dinner tomorrow as an engagement celebration. But since poor Rory isn't feeling well, we thought it better to just spend a quiet day here."

"You mean a calm-before-the-storm kind of day?" Caroline teased.

"There's no such thing around here," Cassie said. "But I told him it would be easier on us if we stay here and celebrate. It's too difficult to bundle up all the children and take them to town, so we're going to have a barbecue here."

"That sounds like work, too," Caroline said.

"We have to eat anyway, and when we eat outside, the men do all the cooking. Becky and I are making pies, and Garth's ridden out to invite a few of the neighbors. I know Maggie Palmer will bring her specialty potato salad, and Helena Garson will bring her baked beans. Wait until you meet the Garsons; you'll love them. They came West on the same wagon train as Clay, Garth, and Becky.

"The rest of the cooking is up to the men, and

based on past experience, it will be beef roasted on a spit and potatoes roasted in the fire, apple pies, and Paddy will churn up some ice cream.

"We women will just sit around tomorrow and watch the men do all the work. I can't wait! So let's get those apples peeled, Miz Caroline."

That evening, long after Garrett had fallen asleep beside her, Caroline lay thinking about the Fraser family. If she were to believe them, in the beginning, Becky and Cassie had not liked the men they had ended up marrying. Yet they worshipped their husbands now. Could that happen to her and Jed, too? She couldn't imagine it; their bitterness toward each other went far beyond an initial wrong impression.

Tomorrow, she would find out what Rory had to say about her first meeting with Garth. She couldn't imagine not liking Garth; the man was so genuinely charming that it would be impossible not to. In truth, all the Fraser men were.

But unlike the other Fraser women, she wouldn't allow herself to fall victim to Jed's charm. It would only complicate the relationship between them even more.

CHAPTER
15

Caroline awoke to a deserted house. No adults, no infants—even Garrett and Buffer were gone. Bewildered, she went outside and saw a turkey and a ham roasting on a spit. Then she saw Rory sitting in front of her house surrounded by net-covered cribs.

"Good morning!" Rory called out.

"Good morning. Where is everyone?"

"Picking grapes." Rory pointed to the distant rows of grapes.

Everyone was down there, including the three older men. Becky's three-year-old and Lissy's four- and three-year-olds trailed at their mothers' feet as their mothers picked.

"How are you feeling this morning, Rory? Cassie said your back was bothering you yesterday?"

"If I sit quietly, I'm fine. But if I try to move around too much, it starts aching. So unfortunately I can't help this time because of my condition. And you, my dear, have been designated to watch me, just in case the baby decides to join us today. Since she's held off introducing herself this long, I prefer she continues to do so until after the wedding."

"Are you that certain the baby's a girl?" Caroline teased.

"No, I'm just hoping. I'd like to have a girl with dark hair that I can twist into long curls, and her daddy's brown eyes and thick lashes."

"Her mother's blond hair and blue eyes wouldn't be so bad, either."

Rory chuckled. "Now you sound just like Garth."

"So he's hoping for a girl, too?"

"He'll be happy with whatever it is. Garth loves children. He'll pick up any infant when it cries, just to be holding a little one in his arms. What about Jed? Will you be having children right away?"

So Jed hadn't spread the truth of their marriage among them. She was glad. She couldn't believe that any of them would be able to understand the arrangement they had.

"With Jed going back to sea in three weeks, I wouldn't want to consider it at this time. But he and Garrett get along famously, and Garrett adores him."

"It looks like the feeling's pretty mutual, honey."

Caroline glanced back down to the vineyard, where Garrett was picking the grapes off the lower growth of the bush, while Jed stood over him and picked from the higher vines. "They've become quite attached."

"I'll be honest with you, Caroline. We all figured because of the resemblance between them that Jed *was* Garrett's father. Garth told me the truth last night. The only thing we were aware of until then was that they had a brother Andy who was killed in the war."

"That's my fault, I'm afraid. I didn't know the Frasers had moved to California, much less the Napa Valley. We're practically neighbors."

She went over to a cradle and picked up one of the infants who had started to cry. "Now, which one is this little darling?"

"That's Sam, Cassie's and Colt's daughter. She's just a couple of months old."

"I'll never be able to remember all these little faces and names."

"Oh, it will come in time. I hope when Jed's at sea, you'll come and visit us often. The door's always open at Fraser Keep. Even though I was an only child, I feel the same as the rest of them do. We want to have our children grow up together. It creates a bond that will remain throughout their lives."

"So you were an only child, the same as I," Caroline said. "What about Cassie and Becky? I know Cassie has a brother. Any sisters?"

"She has a twin sister who lives in New Mexico with her father and brother. Becky has a married brother who lives in Sacramento."

"Do any of the Frasers ever talk of returning to Virginia?"

"I've never heard it mentioned, other than an intended visit next year. Lissy and Steve certainly don't intend to move elsewhere; they started the migration west. Becky once said Clay had intended to go back, often spoke wistfully about returning, but Garth had finding his uncle's gold mine on his mind.

Colt wanted to be a lawman and came West for that reason; he said the carpetbaggers got all the law-enforcement positions in the South after the war.

"I think calling this Fraser Keep after their ancestral home was the most revealing indication they were here to stay. I'm confident Garth would never leave."

"I think he would be contented anywhere, Rory, as long as you were there."

"I think it's true of all of them, Caroline. I do believe we've found our Garden of Eden."

"Looks like they're all headed back," Caroline said. She saw Garrett was straddled on Jed's shoulders.

"They've got to start thinking about setting up for the barbecue. Guess what? Becky's convinced Clay to let the women stomp the first load of the grapes as soon as the Garsons arrive. Their daughter, Etta, and her husband, Tom Davis, are coming with them, and Garth promised Etta we'd wait for her. Etta and Tom were on the same wagon train as Clay and Garth. Talk about interesting courtships! Have Becky tell you about Etta's and Tom's; it's fascinating."

The sound of Nathan's laughter carried to her ears, and Caroline smiled to see the three grandfathers putting their baskets of grapes onto a wagon.

"My father is certainly enjoying himself."

"So is mine . . . and Cassie's for that matter. I just spoke of the children growing up together, but it's also good for our fathers to have the companionship of men their own ages, as well as that of their young grandchildren."

"I guess I've never thought about that. But I can

see the wisdom of it." Caroline changed the subject. "I've heard Cassie's and Becky's stories about their courtships, and I'm eager to hear how you and Garth came to meet."

"In a hole-in-the-wall saloon in Buckman, right here in California. From the moment that big, beautiful man walked in the door, I was in love."

"I remember you said you stole his gold map," Caroline said as she rocked the infant in her arms.

Rory chuckled. "Well, I didn't actually steal it. Pop picked it up when it fell from Garth's pocket during a fight. He just neglected to give it back," she said with a twinkle in her eye. "So of course Garth followed us." She smiled in remembrance. "It proved to be quite an adventure for us to tell our children one day."

Garrett ran up to Caroline as soon as Jed lifted him off his shoulders. "Mama, I helped pick the grapes! It was fun."

"I saw you, sweetheart. It looked to me like you were doing a good job."

"Couldn't have done it without him," Jed said with a familiar rumple to the boy's hair. He walked over and kissed her on the cheek. "Good morning, Caroline."

The rest of the Frasers all offered her a cheerful greeting, then Colt said, "That cry sounds familiar."

He came over and took the infant out of Caroline's arms, and the baby stopped crying immediately. He winked at Caroline. "Her father's touch. You missed your daddy, didn't you, pudding?" he cooed to the infant.

"I think she missed her mama more; she's hungry." Cassie took the baby out of his arms and headed for her home.

Colt lifted his toddler son into his arms. "Come on, Tiger, you can help your daddy get the barbecue started."

As quickly as they had all descended on the spot, infants and parents disappeared in one direction or the other. Even the three grandfathers left, and Garrett ran off to join the two dogs, who had stretched out under a shade tree after an exhausting morning of overseeing the activity. Only Jed remained.

"Why didn't you wake me, Jed? You've all been working so hard, and I feel utterly useless."

"I figure you could use the sleep."

"Jed, if there's any hope for us to have a compatible relationship, don't try to do my thinking for me."

"My apologies. I know the stress you've been under leading up to this visit and I only had your interests at heart. So is this as bad as you anticipated?"

She felt contrite. "On the contrary. Your family has been so nice to me. It's not them I have a problem with; it's you."

"What have I done now?"

"Must you continuously subject me to demonstrations of affection in front of them?"

Jed appeared to be the soul of innocence. "What demonstrations are you talking about?"

"You're constantly touching or kissing me. Hovering over me protectively. Truly, Jed, it's not necessary, and you're wasting your time if you think you can break down my resistance."

"I'm only trying to act like an expectant groom."

"I wonder if you're fooling anyone."

"Maybe you're right. I'm acting too restrained."

He glanced into the open door of the barn and pulled her inside. Crushing her to him, his kiss was slow and sensuous as he explored her lips and recess of her mouth with an expertise that sent sensation spiraling through her and shivers running down her spine.

She was too breathless to resist when he swept her up and lowered her into a nearby pile of hay. He licked her lips and moved his hand to her breast.

"I'm *up* to a roll in the hay. What about you?" he murmured in her ear.

"Get off me, you big oaf!" She shoved him away, and he lay back, laughing as she adjusted her clothing and pulled strands of hay out of her hair.

"You aren't amusing, Jed."

"Relax, Cinderella," he said, getting to his feet and brushing himself off. "It was only a joke; you know I had no intention of making love."

"Anyone could have walked through that door. Did you stop to think about that?"

"So what? It would only have been one of my brothers. They don't shock that easy."

"See, that's the very thing I'm talking about. Nobody's watching us, so it's not necessary for you to kiss me."

His grin was roguish. "Now who's trying to do the thinking for the other one?" He pulled a piece of the hay out of her hair, then bent his head and kissed her lightly on the lips.

The man was hopeless. Utterly, incurably hopeless!

The butterflies were still fluttering in her stomach when she returned to the house on trembling legs.

Becky was feeding the twins, so she pressed out her blue gown to wear at the wedding, then pressed Jed's pants and shirt as well.

She had just finished when she heard Cassie call out, "The Garsons have arrived."

Becky had told her at great length about Howard and Helena Garson and their two sons and a daughter. Farmers from Ohio, the family had been on the same California-bound wagon train in '65. Despite the fact that the men had fought on opposite sides during the war, the Frasers and Garsons had formed a lasting friendship on that arduous and often treacherous journey.

Helena Garson greeted Caroline with a hearty bear hug and a booming greeting from the depths of her small stature. Howard doffed his hat and shyly offered his congratulations.

Then a dark-haired young lady carrying a babe in arms stepped forward. "Hi, Caroline, I'm their daughter Etta." Her bright blue eyes were as warm as her greeting. "And this is my husband, Tom," she said of the tall, redheaded man at her side. Neither one looked old enough to be married, much less have a baby. "And this little bundle in my arms is our daughter Melinda, whom I'm planning on marrying off someday to one of these handsome Frasers."

"You're a lucky little girl, sweetheart," Caroline

said to the tiny infant. "You'll have quite a number to choose from."

Several other families arrived in buckboards and wagons, and she soon lost track of names and who was married to whom. Bowls of salad and beans, baskets of fruits, breads, pies, and cakes were pulled from wagons and buckboards.

The barbecue had officially begun.

"Time to crush the grapes," Clay announced.

All of the younger women tied up their skirts, removed their shoes and stockings, then washed their feet in a bucket of hot, soapy water before being allowed to climb into the vat, whose bottom was covered several feet high with grapes. Jed lifted Garrett over the rim of the tub so he could join them.

At first Caroline slipped-slopped along and held cautiously to the side of the tub to keep from slipping, but soon she was stomping and laughing like the rest of the women.

She grabbed Garrett's hands and they hopped, skipped, and jumped together as the men whistled and clapped. Amid the cheering and shouts, the women linked elbows and danced around Garrett in the center of their circle.

"Granddad, look at us! We're squashing grapes!" Garrett yelled to Nathan. Caroline waved to her father, clapping and cheering among the men. She couldn't remember a time seeing him having such a good time.

Laughing, Caroline looked up and saw that Jed was grinning as he watched her and Garrett. Smiling, she waded over to him.

"Hey, sailor, I dare you to come in here," she said.

"Not on your life, lady."

"Well then, will you help me out of here?" she asked, extending her hand.

"I know what you've got in mind, and I'm not going to fall for it. Or should I say, fall *in* it?"

"Spoilsport." She laughed and sloshed away.

Finally, tired and splattered, the women climbed out to the cheers of a job well done from the spectators. They hosed off their legs and feet, then went inside the houses to change their splattered gowns.

Caroline finished cleaning up Garrett and sent him back outside, changed her own clothing, and went out to join the others. Long sheets of wood were being laid on sawhorses to be used as tables to hold the food.

A half dozen white tablecloths appeared from various houses to cover the tables, which within minutes were spread with food.

As Cassie had said, from the time the barbecue officially began, the men took over the tasks and the women sat in the shade, chatting and enjoying themselves.

The afternoon passed swiftly. The kind of afternoon Caroline had longed for: talking, laughing, and giggling with other women about recipes, children, and life in general—everything that had been missing for so long. She ate it up as hungrily as she did the food.

The men started playing "base ball," a game whose popularity was spreading rapidly across the nation. This time it was the women cheering and applauding the men. Cassie even emitted several whistles she had mastered from herding cattle.

The day turned into night, and soon a makeshift band had formed, and the dancing began. The air rang with clapping and foot-stomping to the rhythm of a fiddle, guitar, harmonica, and piano that had been wheeled out of the house. Caroline was whirled and twirled from partner to partner until she was exhausted and couldn't dance another step.

Then the crowd settled back and listened to Tom Davis's clear baritone as he sang familiar ballads like "Beautiful Dreamer" and "Annie Laurie." On these and many others, they all joined in and sang with him.

Throughout the day, much to Caroline's distress, Jed continued to put on an appearance of being a loving and devoted suitor to her. She didn't like putting up a false front to these people she had grown to care for.

The evening drew to an end, and when the makeshift band prepared to play their final selection, Tom Davis stepped forward.

"Ladies and gentlemen, in honor and appreciation to our hosts for their hospitality and friendship, we will close the evening with 'Dixie.'" That brought whistles and cheers from the Fraser men.

But rather than the rousing rendition they expected, Tom began to sing it slowly, haunting in its poignancy.

"'For I wish I was in the land of cotton, old times there are not forgotten, look away, look away, look away, Dixie Land.'"

Jed came over to her and reached for her hand. "I believe this is our dance, Miss Caroline."

As they stepped onto the dance floor the men had fashioned for the event, Caroline saw that his brothers had led their wives to the floor as well. Even Garth had his arms around Rory, swaying to the music.

"Do you miss your home, Jed?" she asked gently.

"I do at times like this."

He was silent and held her closely as they moved to the nostalgic ballad, which once had been a rallying cry of independence to them, now a reminder of a time and life that was gone forever.

Caroline felt a stirring in her heart that had nothing to do with physical desires or arousals. She closed her eyes and they finished the dance.

After the guests departed with their congratulations and good wishes for the nuptials the next day, Caroline sat down and sighed in contentment. If this day was an example of what her life would be like married to Jed Fraser, maybe it wasn't a mistake. Maybe the outlandish agreement would prove to be the right one for her as well as Garrett.

Jed picked up the sleeping boy and carried him into the house.

"Thank you, Jed," she said upon his return. "He's getting too big for me to carry anymore."

"He never opened his eyes," he assured her and went over to join his brothers.

One by one the women said good night, and with their husbands' help gathered up their children to return to their houses. Caroline watched these tall, rugged men tenderly pick up the tiny little bundles and carry them away.

"If Virginia could only see you now," she murmured with an affectionate smile.

A short time later as she prepared to call it a night, she paused in the doorway and looked back. The Fraser brothers had returned and were grouped around the fire talking together in low tones. She couldn't help wondering if she and Garrett were the topic of their conversation.

CHAPTER
16

After several hours of restlessly trying to fall asleep, Caroline slipped carefully out of bed to avoid waking Garrett beside her. Buffer raised his head, and she put a finger to her mouth to caution him to be quiet.

The house was in darkness, lit only by moonlight shining through the kitchen window. She stepped outside and closed the door softly behind her, then took a deep breath and sighed, missing the fragrance of her garden flowers at home.

"So you can't sleep, either," Jed said, stepping out of the shadows.

"I guess I miss my bed at home."

Jed ground out the cigarette he had been smoking. "Do you want to try my bed? Maybe that would help. I can move in with Garrett."

"I don't think the bed's the problem." She smiled. "Besides, where Garrett sleeps, so does Buffer. If you move in with him, I think his growling would disturb the whole household."

They started down the path leading to the vine-yard.

"It's been a long day," Jed said.

"Yes, the party was so nice. Everyone was so friendly, and they appeared to have a good time."

"Reminded me of home before the war."

"Your family's been so wonderful."

"Caroline, I had a talk with Clay last night and told him our reason for getting married. You'll be glad to know he didn't feel I should force you into marriage. He said it wouldn't be fair to either of us."

She stopped and turned to face him. "And what did you say?"

"I said I offered you a way out, but you decided against it."

"I see." She resumed walking again.

"Now that you've had more time to think about it, have you changed your mind? Twelve hours from now it will be too late to do so."

"My feelings and decision haven't changed." She paused again and looked at him. "Have yours?"

Jed chuckled. "Maybe my conscience, a little. My concern is still for Garrett's welfare, but my only reservation is whether or not you're doing it against your will."

"Six days ago, I would have said I was. Jed, I'm not so naïve that I'm unaware that many people marry for reasons other than love. I think our reason is a good one. We don't have to love each other. And with you at sea practically all the time, I don't fore-see any troubles. Do you?"

"No, I can't say I do. I think of Garrett as my son already, and I love and respect your father."

"I think the reason we're doubting ourselves is because we're surrounded by all these people whose love for each other oozes out of their pores," she said. "I feel as if we're being irreverent in marrying for any reason other than love."

"This whole situation is very complicated. I guess I have to trust my instincts."

"Some marry for money, others to gain power or prestige. Not everyone is fortunate to meet that one person with whom they want to spend the rest of their lives. It would be nice if it were true in our case, but often circumstances force marriage for a different reason."

They halted at a low stone wall, and he lifted her up so she could sit down.

"I think we're intelligent enough to make our arrangement work, Jed. Besides, when you're in port, we can always spend some time with your family. It's a good diversion."

"What do you know? Miz Caroline suggesting we spend time with those Fraser boys?"

"You're not going to let me forget that, are you? I suppose you repeated what I said about them to Clay."

"Not a word. They're sensitive. Besides, I don't think I could watch them falling over each other trying to prove you wrong."

She laughed, then studied him intently.

"What did I do now?" he asked. "I swear, I didn't say a word to Clay about that."

"I learned something about you tonight, Jed. It surprised me."

"I hesitate to ask what that might be," he said, amused.

"You're a man of many mixed qualities. In this past week there have been many occasions for me to witness your humor, and I certainly can't deny your intelligence. You have a fine mind and don't make hasty decisions. You seem to put a lot of thought into an issue before deciding it."

"Especially the one demanding we marry," he said sardonically.

She giggled. "I never meant to imply you were perfect, Fraser. You have an admirable quality of loyalty and honor, not only to your family, but to my father, for instance—putting yourself in the middle of his problem with Calhoun, or insisting on becoming a father to Garrett. Oh, I know you said that was for family honor, but now that I know you a little better, I think you're doing it for Andy as much as for Garrett. You're courageous; I've witnessed that when you saved my son's life, and you have patience. Particularly with Garrett when he's pesty."

He shook his head. "I never thought he was pesty, Caroline."

"To add to those qualities, I've admired your capacity for love, not only to your family but also to another man's child."

"You're making me sound like a pretty good guy, lady."

"You have some serious negatives, Jed. You're self-righteous, your cockiness is maddening, and you can be horribly nasty when you choose to be. That was evident when I had to bear the wrath of your anger about Andy.

"But tonight I discovered a new quality. And I like it. You're sentimental. I saw your heartache when you thought of your home. It touched me, because it showed to me a vulnerability I never suspected you possessed."

"So if I'm such a nice guy, how come we're always scrapping?"

"I think because from the beginning we've been attracted to each other—and it scares the daylights out of both of us."

Jed chuckled. "I think you're right, Miss Caroline.

"Be careful," he warned, when she started to get down. He reached to lift her down, but she started to slide and fell into his arms. Her cry of alarm faded into an indrawn breath, and for the course of several heartbeats their gazes locked in surprise.

Her treacherous body filled with anticipation as a sensuous intensity surged between them. Lowering his head, he took possession of her mouth. Restraint was washed away in the tide of passion that swept through her, bombarding her senses with a spiraling excitement that kept escalating and escalating until she thought she would explode.

The heated probe of his tongue sent a ripple down her spine. She drew a much-needed breath when he slid his mouth to her neck and trailed kisses along it, then reclaimed her lips as he lowered her feet to the ground.

Her trembling legs threatened to collapse as the

slide of his hand became an erotic seduction that
burned away any resistance as he shoved the robe off
her shoulders. For the briefest of seconds the sudden
chill of the night air dueled with the heat ravaging
her internally.

Then he reclaimed her lips, silencing any possible
protest as he lowered her to the ground. She had
never known such a consuming feeling of ecstasy; it
obliterated anything but the need for fulfillment.

Her only experience with sex had been with
Andy—two young people discovering their first rise
of passion. Now she felt the desire and fantasies of
a woman. Her deepest thoughts had fixated on this
moment from the first time she had looked into the
eyes of Jed Fraser.

Her cotton nightgown became a weak bar-
rier against the heat of his body, his hands, and his
mouth.

"Please, Jed," she moaned. "Please." Mercifully her
plea needed no explanation, and he continued the
exquisite assault.

He pulled the gown over her head and tossed it
aside; when he disrobed, she had a blurred impression of bronzed muscle.

Awareness throbbed from every place their naked
bodies touched. The brush of his bristled chin, his
moistened mouth on the swollen tips of her breasts,
the heat of his hands—caressing, stroking—became
an erotic torture. She moaned in rapture as they
sensitized her body, her heated blood surging to the
throbbing core of her being.

Then, swollen with his own need, he entered her.

The feel of his hot, pulsating organ within her drove her to fulfillment, and together, their bodies erupted with climactic release.

It took Caroline a long time to restore her breathing to normal. And with that came the realization.

She sat up. "Oh, my God! What did we just do?"

"It's called making love," Jed said.

"I'm not in love with you!" She grabbed her nightgown and got to her feet, then picked up her robe.

"You seemed to enjoy it, whatever you choose to call it," Jed said as he pulled on his jeans.

"It's exactly what I *didn't* want to happen. I thought I could trust you. I asked you to give me time to think about it."

Unabashed, he grinned. "I did. The trouble is, *I* got to thinking about it, too."

"Very amusing. You're enjoying this, aren't you?"

"I had the impression you did, too. Let me think, how long ago did you throw out that challenge? One day, or was it two whole days ago?"

She started to walk away, but he grabbed her arm and pulled her back. "Caroline, I didn't make love to you in the hope of winning any silly challenge; that was the farthest thing from my mind. I reacted to the moment, the same as you did. If I succeeded in anything, it was getting you to climb down from that pedestal you've put yourself on. You're not some paradigm of virtue, Caroline, you're a woman—a flesh-and-blood woman. And you just proved it to yourself and to me. *That's* why you're angry."

"Of course I'm angry with myself. Despite your accusation, I'm not that stone statue on a pedestal.

I *am* human; I *am* flesh and blood. I've fantasized about our being intimate from the time we've met, and I believed I had the strength to fight that desire. That's why I'm angry—I've betrayed *myself*. But I won't let it happen again."

"Honey, our making love was inevitable. And it *will* happen again. You've admitted our desire for each other; I've wanted you from the time I saw you sitting in that restaurant with that pert little nose of yours stuck up in the air. So why should we fight what we both feel?"

"Because I don't want to fall in love with you, Jed, and I know that will happen if we continue to be intimate! We could even end up having a child. And that would be a more irrevocable bond between us than the marriage of convenience we've planned."

"Do you think you're the only one with feelings? Surely you must realize that the same would happen to me. This is a two-sided sword we're holding, Caroline. Is the possibility of us falling in love, having a child, that repugnant to you?"

"You're married to the sea, Jed. I've vowed I'd never end up like my mother, waiting to see the man she loved once or twice a year. I will not *let* it happen to me."

"In a few hours it'll be dawn. You've got twelve hours to make up your mind," he said.

She yanked out of his grasp and strode away. Upon returning to the house, she closed her bedroom door harder than she intended.

Clay awoke and sat up in bed.

"What was that?" Becky asked beside him.

"Sounded like the door slamming in the next room. Probably a lovers' quarrel."

"You mean between Jed and Caroline?"

"Who else?"

"Why would they be up at this hour?"

"Why do you think?" Clay asked.

Becky considered the comment for a moment, then shook her head. "But you told me Jed said they weren't in love."

"That's what *he* said. But I took a longer look at them at that barbecue. They only *think* they're not attracted to each other."

Becky giggled. "And you think they might just have been practicing the honeymoon before the wedding?"

"Listen," he whispered when he heard the front door open and then the door to Jed's room closing. He lay back. "Reminds me of the old days in Virginia, when a couple of us would sneak out of the house at night for a tryst with the—"

"*Forsyth twins.*" Becky groaned. "Those two gals must have been quite a pair."

"Speaking of twins, ours are asleep right now, and so is Jake, or he would have crawled into bed with us by now." He rolled over on her. "Seems to me we're wasting a damn good opportunity."

Becky smiled and slipped her arms around his neck. "*You're* the one who's wasting it, Clay Fraser. I'm wondering if you'll ever stop talking."

When Caroline awoke, Garrett was already up. She dressed and then, hearing voices from the kitchen, went out to see what was going on.

Becky was putting the finishing touches on the wedding cake, and Cassie was sitting on a kitchen chair, holding her infant son on her lap.

"Hail, the bride cometh," Cassie greeted. "This is your wedding day, girl. I thought you'd be up at the crack of dawn."

"I practically was. I had trouble sleeping and didn't fall asleep until then."

"I know what you mean; I had the same problem," Becky agreed, stifling a smile.

"Where is everyone?"

"I can account for the whereabouts of Jake and the twins," Becky said. "They're in their bedroom."

"And Sam's asleep on the couch," Cassie said.

"Garrett must have gotten up when Jed did."

"Yes, they ate breakfast with Clay and me."

"Have you talked to Rory? I was wondering how she's feeling today."

"Lissy's with her now. Don't worry, honey. She'll hold out until the wedding's over. She told me she'll push that baby back in if she has to; she does not intend to miss this wedding."

"What would you like for breakfast, Caroline?" Becky asked. "This is your day, so you can pick what you want."

"A cup of coffee and a piece of toasted bread will do just fine. I'll get that myself; you've been busy enough this morning."

"I've been dying for the opportunity to attempt to make a wedding cake. Finally, I have the chance."

"Anything you make is successful, Becky. I'm the one who *attempts* to cook." Cassie arched a brow and grinned kittenishly. "Of course I have other talents. But I keep them between Colt and me."

"Not to interrupt your reverie, my dear, but I'm changing the subject. I hope Rico makes it here on time for the wedding," Becky said. "Rory will be disappointed if he doesn't."

"Are they that close?" Caroline asked. "I thought he was a Fraser cousin."

"He is, but Rico saved her life a couple of times, so she's very partial toward him."

"It's not hard to favor him," Becky said. "He's a real sweetheart."

"And almost as handsome as Colt," Cassie interjected.

"Who's almost as handsome as Clay," Becky added with a delightful giggle.

"And I can't believe any of them is as handsome as that cake, Becky," said Caroline. "It's beautiful. I don't know how I'll ever be able to repay all of you for making this such a special day for Jed and me . . . and Garrett. Speaking of him, I better go see what he's up to."

The clearing was deserted, so she went to the wine building and found Jed and Clay.

"Jed, where's Garrett?" she asked, after the morning greetings and Clay's reference to the big day.

"I thought he went back inside. He wanted to wake you, but I told him you needed your sleep."

"I'll check with my father; he may have gone there."

"I'll go with you," Jed said.

They hadn't taken more than a few steps when they saw Nathan coming down the road.

"Sir, have you seen Garrett?" Jed shouted.

"Not this morning," Nathan yelled back.

"What about you, Garth?" Jed asked, when Garth rode up and dismounted.

"No, I haven't seen him. He's not in the grape fields; I was just there. Did you try the barn?"

"We were about to."

Colt was mucking out the horse stalls when they entered and asked him.

"I saw him walking away about fifteen minutes ago. The two dogs were with him."

Caroline began to feel the tightening in her chest she always experienced whenever she worried about Garrett's safety.

"Which direction was he going, Colt?" Jed asked.

"East, toward the river."

"The river? How good a swimmer is he, Caroline?" Garth asked.

"He can't swim at all!" She hadn't missed the worried glances between Colt and Garth.

At that moment, Garth's dog Saddle came barking and racing up to him. Then the dog turned around and started to run back in the direction he'd just come from.

"Something's wrong." Garth jumped onto his horse and rode off, pursuing the dog.

Colt shouted to Clay, then ran into the barn. He put a bit and reins on a horse, then jumped on the animal's bare back. He goaded the animal to a gallop and they leaped a nearby fence in pursuit of Garth.

Jed mounted the horse he'd swiftly saddled, and

Clay tossed him a rifle. "Here, you might need this."
He shoved it into the rifle sling attached to the
saddle. An ex-cavalry man himself, Clay had his own
horse saddled before Jed was out of the barn, and
they followed the dust of the other two riders.

Cassie and Becky hurried outside, and Rory joined
them. "What's going on?" Becky asked.

Caroline spoke in stuttering gasps. "Garrett's missing . . . Garth's dog came back. The men all rode off."

"Which direction did they go?"

"Toward the river. Garrett can't swim."

The two women exchanged alarmed glances. "The
river has a swift and treacherous current. Even the
men don't swim in it," Cassie said.

"Oh, dear God!" Caroline cried.

Nathan had reached them and put an arm around
her quivering shoulders. "Honey, he may not have
gone near the river."

"Something serious has happened; I can feel it.
Buffer didn't come back here with Saddle. That
means he stayed with Garrett and might even have
been killed if they were attacked by a wild animal."

"We don't see too many wild animals, Caroline.
The area's pretty populated, and the animals have
moved on," Becky said. "Let's go inside and sit down.
There's nothing we can do until the men return."

"What happened?" Lissy asked, as she and Stephen
joined them, accompanied by the Garson family.
"Howard said he saw the men ride off in a hurry."

Cassie told them what had happened.

"Let's follow them," Stephen Berg suggested. "We
can hitch up the buckboard."

"We'd never catch them now, especially with a buckboard," Tom said.

"I can't stay here just waiting," Caroline said. "Stephen, will you take me to the river?" she pleaded.

"You bet."

CHAPTER
17

They followed the barking dogs that raced along the riverbank and led them to Garrett, clinging to the limb of a rotting tree caught in the river's current. Years of erosion had gouged away the earth, and the riverbank now rose several yards above the flowing water.

"Hold on, Garrett! We'll get you out of there," Garth shouted to the boy as Colt rode up and joined him.

"Our best bet is to get downstream." Garth grabbed the rope from his saddle. "I'll string a lifeline at the river bend. The river's narrowest there, and we can catch him as he passes." Garth rode off.

Jed and Clay rode up, and Colt told them, "Garth's going to string a lifeline at the river bend. We'll catch him there."

"How far is that?" Jed said.

"About three-quarters of a mile." Colt rode after Garth.

Jed dismounted and began to pull off his boots.

"God only knows how long he can hold on. I'm going to try and reach him."

"Jed, that current's too swift to get to him," Clay said. "He'll be past before you can even reach him."

"I'm a good swimmer, and I've swam in a lot worse places than this. Just have that rope strung by the time we get there." He dove into the water.

The current grabbed him, and Jed realized Clay had not exaggerated its force. The effort of fighting the river's attempt to drag him under slowed him down, and when he finally reached midstream, the tree trunk had passed. The current now aided his effort as it carried him faster downstream to catch the floating tree.

A few hard strokes enabled him to grab a limb of the trunk, and he got one arm around Garrett's waist.

The boy clutched him around the neck in panic, sending both their heads underwater, but Jed was able to hold on to the limb and resurface.

"Garrett, stop struggling," Jed yelled.

Coughing up river water, the boy was too frightened to know what he was doing and continued to thrash about.

Jed finally managed to get a firm grasp under the boy's arms to keep the youngster's head above water. Ahead, he could see the lifeline his brothers had made. Now it depended on muscle and timing.

Every second was critical by the time Garth and Colt reached the bend in the river, where the embankment was just a couple of feet above the water.

Garth tied one end of the rope around the saddle horn on his horse, then handed the other to Colt, who wrapped it several times around the trunk of a tree and knotted it firmly.

"I'm going to head for that tree over there," Garth said, pointing to a big willow across the river. He tossed aside his hat and led the horse to the water's edge.

"Good luck, Garth," Colt called out.

"Well, Boots, it's not the first time we've crossed a river," Garth said, patting the horse. "So let's give it a try."

The current caught them immediately, but the powerful horse didn't falter. Near midstream, Boots lost his footing and began to swim. Garth slid out of the saddle into the water and held on to the stirrup, paddling alongside it as the horse pulled him along. As soon as Boots touched bottom again, Garth swung back into the saddle.

Up on the bank, he stretched the rope until it was taut and wrapped it around the tree. Then grasping the rope as a guideline, he stepped back into the water.

Seeing Garrett and Jed approaching rapidly, Colt and Clay stepped into the water and worked their way along the rope. Just as the trunk hit the rope, Jed let go of the limb and grabbed the hand reaching out to him, while other hands snatched Garrett from his grasp. Jed quickly grabbed the rope with his now free hand and held on.

The driving force of the tree trunk snapped the taut rope in half, and one end of the rope fanned out to the opposite side with Garth clinging to it, while the other end swung toward shore with Colt and Clay each holding a hand of Garrett, and Jed clinging to the shirred end.

They had Garrett on his stomach and were pumping out the water from his lungs by the time Garth crossed back to them on Boots.

"He okay?" Garth asked, dismounting.

"He'll be fine. He was full of river water, but I think we got most of it out of him now," Colt said.

"He looks pretty pale," Garth said and walked over to Jed, who was sitting nearby, exhausted. "How are you doing, Brother Jed?"

"At this moment, I never want to see even a puddle of water again," Jed declared.

"I never expected to hear that from you," Clay said. "I think the ambulance has arrived." He nodded toward the buckboard rumbling toward them, with Howard Garson driving and Caroline and Stephen Berg seated beside him.

Caroline jumped off the buckboard as soon as it reached them and rushed over to Garrett, who was throwing up into the river.

When he sat up again, she hugged him fiercely. "Do you feel better now?"

"Kinda."

"Whatever were you doing in that water, Garrett?"

"Me, Buffer, and Saddle were just walking along the bank, skimming stones into the water."

"How did you end up in the water?" Clay asked.

"There was a mud slide, kinda like the one Grand-dad has at the sawmill—"

"Good Lord, Garrett! You didn't try to slide down it, did you?"

"Sure did. But it wasn't long like Granddad's. It was just a little one. I slid right into the water and couldn't get up. Then I started to float away and this big tree came along and almost banged me in the head. I grabbed a branch and held on 'til Jed swam out and got me."

Caroline glanced up at Jed in surprise. "That's the third time you've saved Garrett's life, Jed."

"So the little rascal's down to six more remaining."

"This is no joking matter, Jed," Caroline said. "I'm indebted to you."

"All my brothers helped."

Caroline looked around for the first time and saw their sodden clothing.

"Thank you. Thank you all. I'm eternally grateful to you men."

"We couldn't have done it without the dogs," Garth said. "That dog of yours stayed with the boy, which made it easy for us to locate him. Then Saddle went for help."

"See, Mama, dogs *do* talk to each other."

"I guess they do, sweetheart."

Jed lifted Garrett into the bed of the buckboard, and Caroline climbed up to the seat. The two dogs jumped up and joined Garrett in the bed. Then the other men mounted their horses.

As soon as they returned, the buckboard became

surrounded by the relieved people who had remained behind. Caroline noticed a minister's collar among them. The men all went to their homes to get out of their wet clothing, but Garrett remained behind to relate his harrowing experience until Caroline insisted he come into the house to clean up and change.

With the morning excitement behind them, the residents of Fraser Keep returned their attention to the anticipated event of the day.

With everyone's attention concentrated on the wedding preparations, only the two dogs noticed the rider approaching the house. They got up and wandered out to investigate.

Rory was in the middle of a sentence when she saw the rider. "Rico!" she shouted.

He waved and dismounted. "*¡Hola, mis primos y primas hermosas!*"

They all broke into wide smiles and gathered around him. Caroline stood back with Garrett, observing the family's welcome of the cousin they never knew existed until two years ago.

With his back to her, he was hard to distinguish from the other Fraser men; like them, he was long-legged, broad-shouldered, and slim-hipped.

When he turned toward her, Caroline saw that a dark mustache curved down below his lower lip. She thought he looked menacing, until she looked into the warmth of the most beautiful brown eyes she had ever seen on a man, tipped with long dark lashes that any woman would envy.

When he removed his hat, his straight dark hair hung almost to his shoulders.

"Rico, this is Caroline, who's about to become Mrs. Jed Fraser, and her son, Garrett," Rory said.

Rico's teeth glistened against the dark bronze of his Spanish ancestry. "It's a pleasure to meet you, Caroline," he said in perfect English. "And the same to you, Garrett. I know you will come to love this family as much as I have."

Rory said, "Rico not only saved me from being mauled by a bear but later prevented us from being murdered by a band of outlaws on that *Montaña del Diablo*. Mountain of the Devil!" she said dramatically.

"Mountain of the Devil!" Caroline shuddered. "Sounds frightening. I definitely want to hear that story."

Rico laughed. "I suggest you hear it from someone other than Rory. She tends to embellish it each time she repeats it."

"Well, I was there, darlin'," Paddy O'Grady said to Caroline. "And the lass is not exaggeratin'. We'd all have been killed up on that devil mountain had it not been for this lad." Paddy slapped him on the shoulder. "If you don't have a taste for the wine, laddie, I've a bit of Irish at me place." He winked at Rico, then sashayed away.

"I think Pop's been sampling that 'bit of Irish' already," Rory said.

Rico chuckled. "He's just having a good time. You know how much he enjoys it when the family gets together."

"Hey, Rico, come on over and join us," Garth called to him. "We're about to have a toast before Jed gives up his free life as a bachelor."

"Excuse me, Caroline; I've been summoned."

"He seems very nice," Caroline said when Rico left.

"He's wonderful," Rory said. "His mother is the same way—beautiful inside and out. We all adore her. Her brother is a priest, and Father Chavez married us. I wore Aunt Elena's wedding gown." Rory held out her hand to show Caroline her small gold wedding band. "Uncle Henry made the ring himself. Aunt Elena said she knew he would want it to be passed down in the family, so she gave it to Garth for us to pass on to our children."

"How thoughtful," Caroline said. "Is she still alive?"

"Oh, yes. So is Father Chavez. They live in Hope. Actually, the proper name of the town is *Tierra de Esperanza*—Land of Hope. But everyone just calls it Hope. Father Chavez runs a mission there, and married Garth and me there. That's also where Uncle Henry is buried.

"Listen, honey, I could talk about this all day, but aren't you supposed to get dressed for your wedding? That husband of mine has been pouring wine down Pastor Renfrew for the last couple of hours. He'll end up as tipsy as Pop if we don't get this wedding started."

"Hey, when is this wedding taking place?" Cassie asked, joining them. "Somebody's going to have to hold up Jed if his scheming brothers don't stop refilling his wineglass."

"That's all we need, a drunken groom," Becky declared, coming over in a snit. "So help me, I'll kick

Clay out of the house tonight if he pops the cork on another bottle."

Lissy came hurrying over to them. "Girls, don't you think we should start the wedding? I'm getting worried; the men are trying to get Jed drunk. Let's get you dressed, Caroline, and fast."

"Garrett," Becky said, "I'm putting you in charge of telling everybody to get inside and sit down. The wedding will be starting in ten minutes. Lissy, start playing the piano; that will attract their attention."

"What should I play?"

"How about a lively version of 'Dixie'?" Becky said. "That bunch of Johnny Rebs will snap to attention when they hear that."

"Or start crying in their beer," Cassie said with a droll glance.

"Now, let's get you dressed, Miss Caroline," Becky declared.

Within minutes, the three women had stripped off Caroline's gown and camisole, redressed her in clean undergarments, and pulled her blue gown over her head. Becky pinned Caroline's hair to the top of her head, and Rory tucked in several sprigs of lilies of the valley at the back of her head, then crowned it with a strip of white lace.

"We need something borrowed," Cassie said. "Becky, how about the string of pearls Clay bought you in San Francisco?"

"Perfect!" Becky raced out of the room and came back seconds later carrying a string of pearls.

Cassie gave Caroline a small nosegay of red poppies

and white lilies of the valley, trimmed in the same lace as that on her head.

"You look gorgeous, honey," Rory said.

"Now, as soon as Lissy starts the wedding march, you come out of this room," Becky instructed.

They kissed her on the cheek, then left to take seats next to their husbands.

At a nod from Becky, Lissy struck the chord and Caroline walked into the room.

She wanted to turn and run back when she became aware they were all staring at her, including Jed, who was standing up in front with the preacher. When she looked at her son, sitting next to her father, Garrett was grinning from ear to ear.

I'm doing this for your sake, sweetheart. That thought gave her the strength to take the remaining steps to Jed's side.

Lissy finished the song, sat down next to her husband, and the preacher began to speak.

Caroline found it hard to concentrate on what Pastor Renfrew was saying. Was she actually getting married? *Wake up, Caroline. This is not a dream.*

"Who giveth this woman to this man?" Pastor Renfrew asked.

Her father and Garrett stood up. "We do," they said in unison.

"Well then, who giveth this man to this woman?" the pastor asked, the question no doubt suggested by one of the partly inebriated Fraser men.

"We do," Jed's brothers called out from all sections of the room and followed it up with whistles, hoots, and applause. Caroline was certain she heard some women's voices, too.

At the proper time, Jed slipped a gold band on her finger with a tiny pearl inlaid on each side of a larger pearl in the center.

Surprised, she glanced up at him, and he said softly, "I bought it in Sacramento."

The preacher said, "And now, by the power invested in me, I pronounce you man and wife. You may kiss the bride."

And Jed had had enough to drink to do just that. It was long, it was passionate—and it curled her toes.

By the time he broke the kiss, her legs were trembling. Amid another round of whistles, hoots, and applause, he grinned as she stared at him in astonishment.

"Seems you missed the twelve-hour deadline, Mrs. Fraser."

CHAPTER
18

After all the congratulations to the newlyweds, the furniture was shoved against the walls and the carpet rolled up. Then with the applause of the assembly accompanying them, Jed led Caroline to the floor.

"You're a lovely bride, Mrs. Fraser. Are you enjoying your wedding waltz?" he asked as they danced.

"Yes, I am. I think I've danced more in these last few days than I have the rest of my life."

"I never would have suspected that. You're an excellent dancer, Caroline."

"I declare, sir, it must be due to the skill of my dancing partner."

"You're being very flirtatious, Mrs. Fraser."

"Fiddle-faddle, sir. What need would I have to flirt with my own husband? Especially on our wedding day."

"My very thought, madam."

"I do have a favor to ask of you, Jed."

"Ah-hah! The plot thickens."

"It's about our wedding night."

"You can't wait to get to it, either!"

"Please be serious, Jed. If you remember, last night we agreed not to be intimate again."

"I remember no such thing, Caroline. I *do* remember, though, that you released me of *any* previous agreements. What is the favor you want?"

"Please don't let your family know we won't be sharing the same bed tonight."

He began to reply hotly, and she said, "Let's discuss this outside."

Jed followed her out. "Why do you care what my family thinks if we don't sleep together tonight?"

"We're being so deceitful to all these people. They're all so in love . . . they *believe* in love, Jed. You and I are merely playing roles."

He tried to remain patient. "Caroline, we had this discussion last night; you're feeling guilty because we made love, and you enjoyed it. I can't see how that affects anyone here."

"So you don't think deceiving your family is wrong? I had hoped by now that you'd have enough common sense to acknowledge I'm right."

"You're wrong. Dead wrong. Why should a woman with your passion deny herself a God-given pleasure? That was His intention. So what are you trying to prove: God is wrong; you're right? I believe the world has already had one Blessed Virgin, Caroline."

"Oh, you have a nasty tongue, Jed Fraser."

"It's intentional. I'm trying to jolt you into facing reality."

"Well, you've failed miserably and have only succeeded in making me feel more upset. As for any future *God-given pleasures,* I'm standing by what I said last night. No marriage bed. No more intimacy."

She spun on her heel and went back inside.

The moment she entered, Clay grabbed her by the hand and led her to the dance floor. For the next hour she was passed from one brother to the other, until she finally plopped down exhausted next to Garrett and Rory on the couch.

"You must be pretty much done in, honey," Rory said.

"Totally. When is it proper for a bride to leave her wedding? This has been a strenuous day." She slipped her arm around Garrett's shoulders. "What about you, sweetheart? You about ready to go to bed?"

"Me and Aunt Rory are having a good time watching all of you dancing. It's like when I'd watch Granddad and Grandma, 'cept a lot noisier. Did you know, Mama, that Aunt Rory used to work in a saloon and it cost twenty-five cents to dance with her? She sure must have been a good dancer. That's how she met Uncle Garth."

Rory winked at Caroline. "And he was my best customer."

"And just think, Mama, if you charged twenty-five cents each dance tonight, you could have made a lot of money."

"Hey, that's *my* specialty, young man," Rory said.

"You and Uncle Garth sure did exciting things together. Working in a saloon, discovering gold, fighting off outlaws—nothing that exciting ever happens to me."

"What are you talking about, Garrett Fraser?" Rory declared. "Didn't you almost drown this morning?"

"My name's not Garrett Fra— That's right; my real name *is* Garrett Fraser. 'Specially since my mama's name is Fraser now, too. Is Granddad a Fraser now, too, Mama?"

"Only in spirit, son," Nathan said, patting him on the head in passing.

"Honey, I don't want to spoil your fun, but you should get to bed. We'll be leaving early tomorrow."

"Good night, love," Rory said. "Give Aunt Rory a kiss." She leaned forward, then suddenly clutched her stomach and gasped in pain.

"Rory, what's wrong?" Caroline asked.

"I think the baby's coming." She tried to get to her feet, then fell back again in pain.

"Garrett, run outside and get your Uncle Garth!"

Lissy and Cassie had noticed Rory's reaction and came hurrying over. "Is she in labor?"

Caroline nodded. "I think so."

"Why don't you ask me?" Rory cried. "I can guarantee I'm in labor. Laboring to get some help to get off this couch."

Garth rushed into the house, followed by all the men.

"Get that bunch of gawking males out of here!" Rory declared. Then she gasped in pain again. "Are you going to help me off this couch, Garth Fraser, or are you just going to stand there with your mouth open?"

Garth picked her up, and she slipped her arms around his neck, still in pain.

"Where are you going with her?" Becky said, when Garth headed for the door.

"I'm taking her home."

"Then what? You going to deliver that baby yourself? She can stay right here. Stephen, will you go for the doctor?"

"I'm halfway there," he said and ran out.

Helena and Etta came hurrying into the house. "Stephen just told me. Let's get her undressed and in bed."

"Put her in my bed," Caroline said. "Garrett can sleep with Jed tonight."

They all paused momentarily and looked at her with surprise, until Becky said, "I'll put some towels down." She hurried from the room.

"Danny—somebody take care of Danny," Rory cried out as Garth started to tote her away.

"Don't worry, honey," Cassie assured her. "We'll take care of him."

Paddy O'Grady came in, huffing and puffing. "Rory! Where's me Rory?"

"The baby's coming, Pop," Cassie said.

"God be with you, darlin'," he called out to her.

"Thanks, Pop," Rory yelled back before Garth kicked the bedroom door closed.

"Take your party outside, boys," Cassie announced. "There's a baby to be born here."

"What can we do to help?" Colt asked.

"Stay out of the way," she said.

One by one they filed out, until only the women and Garrett remained.

"Time for you to get into bed, Garrett," Caroline said.

"Can't I stay up until the baby is born?"

"That could take hours, honey. You can sleep in Jed's bed tonight."

"It's a good thing *somebody* is, since his bride won't be there," Cassie said.

It broke the tension among them, and they all laughed and relaxed.

Caroline didn't see any humor in the remark and took Garrett by the hand into the bedroom. "Get undressed, honey, and I'll be back to tuck you in."

He sat down on the bedside and took off his shoes and stockings. "My nightshirt's in the other room."

"You can sleep in your drawers tonight."

"Mama, how long does it take for a baby to be born?" he asked again as she pulled his shirt over his head.

"Some are born very quickly, and sometimes it can take hours—even days."

"I sure hope it doesn't take that long. Will Aunt Rory be okay, Mama?"

"I'm sure she will. And once she holds that baby in her arms, she'll forget all about the pain."

"How long did it take me to be born?" he asked as he crawled into bed and lay back.

"About twenty-four hours, you stubborn little dickens." She leaned over and kissed him on the cheek.

Garrett slipped his arms around her neck. "I'm sorry I took so long to be born."

Caroline smiled into his troubled face. "That's why you're so precious to me, sweetheart. The harder it is to get what you want, the more you cherish it when you finally get it."

"I love you, Mama."

"I love you, too," she said. "Pleasant dreams."

"Mama," he called out when she turned down the lamp. "Do you think it would be okay if Buffer slept on the bed?"

"Sure. I'll go and find him."

She didn't have to go far. As soon as she opened the door, the dog padded past her, jumped up on the foot of the bed, and stretched out at Garrett's feet.

The men had been busy in her absence. The carpet had been replaced and the furniture returned to its proper setting in the parlor. She glanced out the open door and saw that someone had built a campfire, and all the men were standing or sitting around it in small groups, talking—relaxed but considerably less festive. The wedding celebration had turned into a baby vigil. With the exception of Jed and Rico, the rest of the men had been through it before—most more than once—so this was nothing new to them.

Lissy, Cassie, and Etta were sitting around the kitchen table drinking coffee.

Caroline joined them. "How is Rory doing?"

Cassie shook her head. "Not good; she's in a lot of pain. Colt and I were here when she had Danny; she labored for forty-eight hours."

Lissy nodded. "The doctor said some women just aren't built for having a baby. She's so tiny; my heart aches for her."

"I hope Stephen gets back soon with the doctor, who can give her something to ease her suffering," Etta said.

"How long do you think it will be?" Caroline asked.

"It takes about an hour to get there and back."

Becky came out of the bedroom and sat down with them. "I can't take much more. She's in so much pain. We don't know what we can do for her, and she's so pale. I think she's losing the battle."

Becky jumped to her feet. "When is that doctor going to get here!"

Cassie poured her a cup of coffee. "You can probably use this."

"I'll go in with my mother," Etta said, and got up from the table. "Sit down and relax, Becky. You've been working hard for the last couple of days."

"How is Garth holding up?" Lissy asked.

Becky sat down at the table again. "He won't budge from her side. Every time she has a contraction, it's like someone drives a knife into him."

"Do you think one of my brothers could convince him to come out and have a cup of coffee or something stronger?" Lissy asked.

"When pigs fly," Becky said. "Rory's also bleeding."

"Staining or bleeding?" Caroline asked worriedly.

"It's beyond a stain. I don't remember any bleeding until my baby actually was delivered. Did any of you experience it before then?"

A long silence followed. Saying no would confirm the fear that they were trying so hard to repress. The knowledge that not all women survived was very real to every one of them.

Cassie went out to find Colt, needing the comfort of his arms around her.

"Becky, did you just call me?" Clay asked, suddenly appearing in the doorway. She shook her head. "Funny, I would have sworn it was you."

Unable to restrain her tears, Becky ran to him, and they withdrew to find a spot to be alone.

Lissy bolted to her feet. "I better check on the children," she said, trying to hold back her tears.

Alone with her grief, Caroline buried her head in her hands and swallowed her tears, the way she had always done in the past. She'd always sought some corner to escape to and hide from reality, in the hope her sorrow would go away.

She looked up, and Jed was standing in the kitchen doorway watching her. One look at him and her tears burst forth unrestrained. Caroline stood up and rushed into the comfort of his arms.

Word spread quickly among the people assembled. The grandfathers had already dozed off, and mercifully Paddy O'Grady had prematurely celebrated the birth of his grandchild by passing out. He lay on a blanket under a tree, snoring away peacefully, unaware that his daughter was fighting for her life.

By the time Stephen returned with the doctor, everyone was on pins and needles. The men were grouped in somber silence in the bedroom, along with the women, who had moved in to be near Rory.

"What are you men doing in here?" the doctor demanded. "You think it's a damn convention?"

"We came in to give Garth and Rory some moral support," Clay said.

The doctor raised his eyes heavenward. "God help me! Out of here, men and women alike," he ordered. "Mrs. Garson, will you please remain."

"I'm not going anywhere," Garth said.

His brothers squeezed his shoulder or tapped him on the back as they filed out.

"Hang in there, little sister," Clay said to Rory. "We know you can do it." Then he gave Garth a tap on the back and moved on.

"It would be easier if you left the room, too, Garth. At least while I examine your wife," the doctor said.

"Please let him stay, Doctor," Rory said weakly.

"It's not advisable, Mrs. Fraser, but very well. If that's what you wish."

"You know, we haven't eaten since morning," Becky said. "I bet the men are starved, and we've got a baked ham and the rest of that food that we prepared for the wedding dinner."

"Well, let's put it out and get some more coffee brewing. I doubt anyone is hungry, but it gives us something to do, instead of sitting on our hands," Cassie said.

The men had all moved outside for some fresh air when Dr. Meechem joined the women in the kitchen.

"I'm going to be honest with you, ladies. The

prognosis isn't good—she's only three-quarters dilated and losing blood."

"Why is she losing so much blood, Doctor?" Becky asked.

"The opening of her uterus is very small, and the uterus can only expand so far before it will rip. That's what's happening right now. The uterus rips every time the fetus tries to squeeze out, causing her to hemorrhage. If the infant isn't delivered soon, she will likely bleed to death."

"Dear God, no!" Caroline gasped.

Lissy and Etta began to sob softly.

"Dr. Meechem, isn't there something you can do?" a tearful Cassie asked. "Anything to prevent it? We can't just sit by and watch it happen!"

"I anticipated this might happen after I delivered her first child, so I've given her a drug to ease her pain and a medication to try and slow the hemorrhaging. But it can't stop the bleeding entirely. She's a courageous young woman with a strong will to survive. But the strength is flowing out of her. The longer she's in labor, the less chance she has."

Garth rinsed off the perspiration on Rory's brow with a cool cloth. "Did the medicine help, honey?" he asked.

"Yes, it doesn't hurt as much now," she said.

"You never were a very good liar, honey. Let it out. Scream, curse, rip the sheets. Do anything that will help. I've always heard that women scream when they're having babies."

She tried to smile gamely at him. "Fraser women

are like the men we married. We spit pain in the eye." A tear slid down her cheek, and he reached out and gently captured it with a finger. "I guess I'm not a very good Fraser woman. I just don't have it in me anymore."

"Honey, remember those bleak hours in the cave, when we knew those outlaws would kill us? I asked you why you came back, when you could have escaped to safety."

"And I told you I wouldn't want to live without you," she said weakly.

"That's how I feel now, baby. I don't want to go on without you. You've *got* to keep fighting. You can't give up."

"I just can't fight anymore, Garth. I tried, but I can't anymore."

"Yes, you can, baby. You're a fighter. You can't quit now. Think about Danny—he needs you as much as I do. Baby, you can do it, I know you can! You're tiny, but you're strong, love. You've got the grit to tough this out."

"It's been good between us, hasn't it?" she said, so low he could barely hear her. "I wouldn't trade a minute of it for a lifetime without you."

"You told me that then, too."

"You remember," she murmured.

He kissed her hand. "Every word you said that night."

"And I still mean every word of it."

"We *both* expected to die then, baby. It's different now. There are others besides me who need you. Do it for them, honey. For Danny. For our little girl. We all need your strength, now more than ever. You *have* to live, honey. You have to live for us and for our children."

"You're still certain our baby will be a girl."

"You bet, love. With blond hair and big, beautiful blue eyes just like her mother's."

"Garth!" she suddenly gasped, clutching his hand. "I love you." Then she closed her eyes.

"Doctor!" Garth cried in panic.

Helena rushed to the door. "Doctor, come quickly."

The doctor hurried to the bedside and listened to Rory's heartbeat, then took her pulse. "Garth, you must leave now."

Garth clasped Rory's hand between his own. "I'm not leaving her, Doctor."

"Mrs. Garson, I'll need your help," Dr. Meechem said. "Have any of the other women assisted in delivering a child?"

"Colt's wife is a rancher. She's had experience delivering foals and calves."

"That will have to do. Go tell her to sterilize her hands, and tell her to hurry. Every minute counts."

CHAPTER
19

As the evening wore on, one or the other of them would doze off for ten or fifteen minutes. Howard Garson and Tom Davis eventually retired to their tents. As close as the families were, the two men felt like intruders, witnessing the Frasers' grief.

Little was heard from the doctor or Helena and Cassie except for repeated requests for hot water, or an occasional "she's still alive," from one of them rushing between the kitchen and the bedroom.

The men remained outside, where they smoked and talked in low voices. Occasionally one or two would come in for a ham sandwich and a bite of salad; the coffeepot on the campfire was refilled as often as the one in the kitchen.

People spoke little during the vigil but their presence spoke volumes.

Mothers hugged their infants closer to their breasts when they nursed them. Husbands reached out just to touch their wives or kiss their foreheads in passing.

They were a united family, struggling with the

possible loss of one of their own. Every one among them had borne the loss of loved ones and knew the depth of despair and mourning. Faced once again with that dread, each of them handled it differently.

Some sought an answer to why one so young and vibrant might die. Others were engulfed in anguish by the thought of the suffering Rory had to bear before her final sleep. Many grieved for the infant who might never draw its first breath.

And all grieved for Garth, who would have to go on with only memories of the woman he cherished.

They all also grieved for their own loss—the dear friend, the loving sister-in-law who, if not laughing, always smiled. If not singing, always hummed. Nurturing all of them, as she did her own husband and child.

Dawn streaked the sky with rays of pink and gray by the time Nathan Collins and Jethro Braden walked wearily up the path to Paddy O'Grady's house. Paddy remained sleeping, and those passing wondered how they would explain to him what was happening.

Caroline woke with a start and looked at the clock. She had dozed off a half hour ago. She saw that Becky and Etta had done the same on the sofa and Rico on a nearby stuffed chair. She went out to the kitchen and put another kettle on the stove to boil.

Returning to the parlor, she sat on the piano stool and lightly struck a key or two with her finger, then began to play softly.

Rico opened his eyes and came over to her. "That is a beautiful melody you're playing, Caroline."

"Oh, Rico, I'm so sorry I woke you."

"Please don't stop. I've heard that song before, but I don't know its name."

"It's one of my favorites." She resumed playing. "It's called 'Liebestraum' or 'Dreams of Love.' It's written by a Hungarian composer named Franz Liszt."

"You play well, Caroline."

She smiled quietly. "I've always found it a good diversion when I'm lonely or feeling depressed. The haunting melody soothes me."

"How long have you played the piano?"

"Since I was twelve. We lived in Virginia then."

"Where the Frasers come from? Were you and Jed childhood sweethearts?"

"You're a romantic, Rico, but I'm afraid it was just the opposite. We lived in the same town, but I doubt most of the Frasers even knew my name. I only knew Andy well, the youngest brother."

"He was killed in the war. Is that right?"

"Yes. He's Garrett's father."

Funny, how easily she had said it—the deep secret she had harbored for almost nine years.

"I had no idea. Jed and Garrett resemble each other so much, I just assumed Jed was . . ."

Caroline smiled. "Everyone thinks the same when they see them together. I actually didn't meet Jed until a short time ago."

She started to play another soothing piece, and Rico listened in silence. When she finished, he said,

"That was as lovely as the first one. I've never heard it before."

"It's only a few years old. 'Ich Liebe Dich.' 'I Love Thee.' The composer, Edvard Grieg, was only twenty-two when he wrote it. The lyricist is Hans Christian Andersen."

"The same man who writes those children's fairy tales?"

She nodded. "He was sixty years old when he wrote the lyrics to this song."

"I learned much of my English when my mother read his stories to me. Will you play the song again, Caroline?"

She did, and when she finished, he stood up. "Thank you, Caroline. For a few minutes you have brought light into this house."

On his way out, Rico nodded to Jed, who had been standing in the doorway of the kitchen.

"Your bride is as talented as she is beautiful. Her music is a reflection of her soul. You have chosen wisely and well, Cousin Jed."

Jed had heard her play for Garrett a time or two, but only popular, lively songs like "Old Gray Mare" or "Little Brown Jug." He'd never guessed this side of Caroline existed. She was quite accomplished, playing classical selections from memory.

He suddenly was struck with a feeling of guilt. How many other things did he not know about her? She was a very private person. Who did she trust in life, other than her father? Even as a child, she had kept to herself.

He leaned against the doorframe to watch her. She

had been a relentless worker throughout the night, making sandwiches, brewing coffee, or putting kettles of water on the stove to boil. And her concern was heartfelt. Until now she had only shown affection for her father and son, protecting her vulnerability by never revealing this emotion to anyone else.

He'd been surprised by how well she had fit in with his family. Because of her strained relationship with him, he had expected she would be standoffish; instead, she had embraced his family and now shared the grief they were suffering.

His gaze rested on her face as she played. For a few stolen moments, she had found a release on the wings of the melody. As he had watched her smile and talk with Rico, he had wished it was him she was smiling at, chatting with so casually. Why couldn't they share the same casual companionship instead of the constant spatting between them?

The answer was clear, and it had nothing to do with her neglecting to inform the family of Garrett's birth or her resentment of an unwanted marriage. It was the sexual tension between them. No matter how much she tried to resist it, that desire was always there between them. And as long as she continued to deny that need, they could never resolve the problem between them. Any attempt on his part only led to raising her anger, or to her withdrawing even more from him.

We don't have to love each other—or even like each other . . . I don't foresee it to be "unbearable." Where in hell did she get damn fool ideas like that? And the pity of it was he had agreed!

Even now, with the crisis surrounding them, he wanted her, as he recalled how she felt in his arms, her moans of ecstasy, the taste of her, the scent of her, and the ultimate thrill of that incredible moment of climax.

Caroline suddenly stood up with a startled look. "Did you hear that?"

"Hear what?" Jed asked.

"It sounded like a baby crying."

"I've been hearing babies crying from the time we got here."

"But this came from there," she said and pointed to the bedroom Rory was in.

"Maybe Cassie's nursing Sam."

"I suppose you're right." Caroline sat down disconsolately. Then she jumped to her feet again. "Listen— there it is again. It sounds like the cry of a newborn!"

Jolted awake, Becky asked, "What? Newborn baby?"

"I think I heard a baby crying! It was very faint, but I'm sure it was coming from that bedroom."

Fully awake, Etta asked, "Do we dare knock on the door and ask?"

"I don't hear any baby crying," Jed said.

Becky put her ear to the door, then stepped away, shaking her head. "It's still quiet in there. I haven't heard a sound out of that room since the doctor entered it last night."

The women returned to their seats, and Jed went into the bedroom to check on Garrett. To his surprise, the boy was awake and sat up when Jed entered.

"Hey, what are you doing awake?" Jed asked.

"I've been thinking hard about something," Garrett said.

"What's bothering you, Garrett?" Jed sat down on the edge of the bed.

"I don't know what to call you."

The statement caught Jed by surprise. "What would you like to call me?"

"Mama told me before you were married that you and my father were brothers, and so you're my uncle. Should I call you Uncle Jed?"

"If that's what you want."

"But it don't seem right calling you Uncle Jed, the same as I do the others."

"Why not, Garrett?"

" 'Cause you're married to my mom now."

"Well then, I've got a good idea: why don't you call me by the name that I called my father?"

"What was that?" Garrett asked.

"Dad."

After a thoughtful moment, Garrett nodded. "Yeah, that's better than Uncle Jed. And you're gonna live with us all the time now, right?"

"I'm at sea most of the time, Garrett. But when I'm not, I'll live with you."

"I'm glad. Before you got married, Mama was afraid we'd have to go back to Virginia, where you used to live. I sure don't want to leave Granddad."

Jed grasped the boy's hand. Somehow, the hand felt smaller than it had before. "I promise you, Garrett, I will never take you away from your grandfather."

"Or Buffer?"

"Or Buffer," Jed said.

Garrett threw his arms around Jed's neck. "I'm glad Mama married you. I love you, Dad."

Jed felt his eyes moisten, and he hugged the youngster tighter. "And I love you, son. I love you."

Garrett lay back. "I bet I can go back to sleep now."

Jed stood up. "I bet you can, too." He bent down and kissed him on the cheek. "Good night, pal."

"Good night, Dad."

Jed's heart swelled with love, and he went outside and rejoined the men.

Exhausted, but too nervous to stay put, the three women were in the process of cleaning up the kitchen for breakfast when Dr. Meechem came out of the room. His shirtsleeves were rolled up to his elbows, and the front of his shirt was stained heavily with blood.

Fearing the worst, the three women stared numbly at him, waiting for him to speak.

"What does a man have to do around this house to get a cup of coffee?"

All three women jumped into motion, bumping into one another in an effort to serve him. He took a deep draught of the coffee, then shoved the cup to indicate he wanted it refilled.

Becky couldn't bear it. "Doctor . . . Rory . . . is she . . ."

"I've done all I can for her. From now on, it's between her and God."

"Is she still hemorrhaging?"

"She's bleeding, as to be expected after an operation, but the important thing for her is to remain still to avoid any more hemorrhaging."

"What kind of operation, Doctor?" Caroline asked.

"It's called a cesarean section. The baby is actually delivered through the abdomen, which spares the lives of mothers and infants. I observed several of them performed last year when I was in France, but this is the first one I've ever done. Rory will be able to bear more children with this procedure without jeopardizing her life."

"Oh, my God! I can't believe it," Becky cried. She sank down in a chair and, sobbing in relief, buried her head in her hands.

Caroline swallowed her own tears of joy and put a comforting hand on Becky's shoulder. "And the baby—"

"Is sleeping like a newborn," Dr. Meechem said. "A little levity there in an attempt to cheer you all up."

Becky lifted her head. "I don't understand. How can you deliver a baby through the abdomen, Doctor?"

"With the aid of two very efficient assistants. I'm sure they will explain it in detail to you soon. They're cleaning and padding Rory up now. I don't want to mislead you, ladies; she is still very weak from the loss of blood, and she'll be in bad pain for some time. But if she doesn't start hemorrhaging again or have any further complications, she has a good chance of making it. That little gal has a lot of grit." He cracked a tired smile. "Not much blood right now, but a lot of grit."

A tearful Etta ran outside to break the good news to the men.

"And Garth?" Becky asked.

"At one point I thought I would have to treat *him* before continuing the operation. A delivery room is no place for husbands."

"May we go in to see her now, Doctor?" Caroline asked.

"Give the ladies a few more minutes to finish cleaning up in there. You can well guess, it's pretty messy. You'll be needing a new mattress."

"It will be a pleasure, Doctor. How can we ever thank you?"

"I must say, I'm quite proud of myself. I might even write this up for medical journals, operating under the conditions I did. But she's not out of the woods yet—I can't emphasize enough that Rory must have *complete* bed rest for six to eight weeks. So please have your husbands go in there and haul Garth out of that room, or she'll never get any.

"I must go home and clean up since I have other patients to see, but I should be back in about four hours.

"I've given Rory a sedative to make her sleep, and it might be wise to move the baby into another room. I've examined the infant closely, and she appears to have survived the delivery without any harm. But the little tyke's had a pretty rough time of it, too, so she'll need her rest as well."

"Doctor, if you remove your shirt, I'll give you one

of Clay's to wear. And I'll see what I can do about soaking the blood out of the one you're wearing," Becky said.

He grinned. "Perhaps that would be wise. If Emily sees me like this, she'll think I've been shot. But you tell Clay I'm not settling for just a shirt. I expect a case of his best wine for all my hard work."

Becky left the room, and Dr. Meechem smiled at Caroline. "I understand that yesterday was your wedding day, Mrs. Fraser. I wish you good health and happiness. It's been my observation that it's easier to have happiness when you have good health."

"Thank you, Doctor, I'll keep that thought."

"If your husband is anything like his brothers, I know you will have a happy life. I'm very fond of this family."

"I suspected as much." She smiled.

"I've got a big investment in this family: I delivered most of their little tykes."

Becky returned with a clean shirt, and the doctor quickly changed into it.

"Thank you again, Dr. Meechem. We're eternally in your debt," Becky said.

"I won't let you forget it." He winked and departed.

CHAPTER
20

The Garsons left shortly after the doctor did. Helena was totally exhausted and intended to sleep around the clock. Heavily sedated, Rory continued to sleep, so Cassie and Lissy collected their children and went back home with their husbands.

Garth refused to sleep under a different roof than his wife and newborn daughter, so while Jed and Garth carried a sleeping Garrett and their luggage to Garth's house, Caroline and Becky cleaned up the connecting bedroom, changed the bedding, and moved the crib of eleven-month-old Danny into the room connected to his mother's, which he would be sharing with his father for the next couple of months.

Caroline was pleased with the new arrangement, because with Garth and Rory staying at Clay's house, she and Jed had complete privacy at Garth's—thus avoiding any curiosity or explanation why they didn't sleep together now that they were married.

Rory was awake and fully conscious when Jed and Caroline joined Clay and Becky for breakfast the following morning. Colt and Stephen rode into town to buy a replacement mattress, and when they returned, under Dr. Meechem's watchful eye and guidance, Garth carried his wife to the other bedroom while Jed and Clay toted the old mattress outside and burned it. Cassie, filling in for his mother, fed Danny, and Becky and Caroline scrubbed the floor of the room and put bedding on the new mattress.

Thirty minutes later Rory was tucked neatly back in bed and Dr. Meechem had departed, satisfied with her condition.

It was an amazing experience for Caroline. Everyone, in their own way, had chipped in to do their bit. Even the three grandfathers had taken over watching the children to free the women. And throughout the whole time there hadn't been a cross word or look between any of them.

Coupled with the previous evening's labor and a full day of scrubbing floors, changing beds, washing, and hanging out sheets and blankets to dry, Caroline was exhausted. The sight of Lissy and Cassie carrying in hot casseroles, freshly baked bread, and berry pies for the evening meal was a godsend, and she wanted to cry with joy.

After dinner and a few words of comfort to Rory and some coos at the baby, everyone left to go back to their homes.

It came as no surprise that the lights in all the houses were extinguished early that evening.

As soon as she put Garrett to bed, Caroline went outside and sat down on the stoop. The night air was refreshing, and for the first time in almost two days she thought about her marriage to Jed.

The screen door squeaked behind her, but Caroline didn't look up.

"I thought you were tired," Jed said and sat down beside her.

"I guess I'm overly tired. I suddenly don't feel sleepy. This air feels good though, doesn't it?" She turned to him with a smile and saw that he was studying her, his eyes hooded in pensiveness.

"Why are you staring at me like that?"

"You boggle my mind, Caroline."

She laughed lightly. "Am I that complicated to figure out? I thought you were an authority on women, Jed."

"I thought I was, too, until I met you. You scare me, lady."

"Is that good or bad?" she asked, amused.

Jed chuckled. "That's what scares me; I can't figure that out. It finally sank in that we're married. Man and wife! And we've taken a vow to love, honor, and obey each other until we die."

"Our marriage has been obscured by the events of the last couple of days," Caroline said.

"I know. But once we leave Fraser Keep, our lives will return to normal. Then in a couple of weeks I'll be out of your hair."

"Jed, what is there about the sea that causes you to want to leave here and your family? Clearly you all are very close, yet you've been content to sail away from them for most of each year."

"It's beginning to get harder every time, but the sea has always been in my blood."

"It must be salt water in your veins, not blood. If I had a family like yours, I could never consider leaving them."

"Colt isn't much different," he said. "In a couple of days he and Cassie will be going back to New Mexico."

"But they'll be returning for Christmas. Where will you be at Christmas, Jed? Singapore? Japan? At sea in the Mediterranean?" She shook her head. "I've longed for a sister or brother all my life. You don't realize how lucky you are, yet you are content to sail away on the next tide."

"Since it works to your benefit, that should please you, Caroline; you only have to tolerate me for one month a year."

"I suppose it should, but I doubt it will please Garrett. Have we both deceived ourselves about our actions being for his benefit? Rory's fight for life and Garth's raw anguish were so deep and powerful, I feel shame. I fear the shallowness of our actions was blasphemous, not only against their devotion, but in the eyes of God."

"So what is the answer for us, Caroline?"

"I was hoping you could tell me," Caroline said.

They sat in silence for a while, then she got up and went inside.

The following day, things returned to near normal at Fraser Keep.

Caroline became a nursemaid not only to Rory but

to all the other children while the rest of the adults were grooming the fields or harvesting grapes.

The color had begun to return to Rory's cheeks, and despite the pain, which she never complained about, she began to gain strength with every passing day. By the fourth day she was able to start nursing the baby, who she and Garth had named Hope.

To Garth, the fact that this infant and her mother had survived had been a sign of God's kindness and charity.

And the fact that he'd been given the yellow-haired daughter with her mother's blue eyes that he had hoped for was a sign of a benevolent God to Garth.

That the woman he loved more than life itself would no longer be put at risk if he made love to her, in Garth's eyes, meant that not only was He a very understanding God, but a *merciful* one, since in the throes of despair, he had prayed that if He spared Rory's life, he would practice abstinence rather than put her at such risk again.

Regrettably, the time had come when Jed and Caroline must depart. After kissing Danny good-bye, who was sitting next to his mother in bed, Caroline picked up Hope.

"I'm going to miss this little sweetheart," she said, kissing the tiny infant's cheek.

"We'll miss you. I wish you could stay."

Caroline laid the baby back in her crib. "We've been away from home for over a week, and my father has to get back to the mill."

Then she kissed and hugged Rory. "You stay in that bed, just as the doctor ordered. The next visit, I want to see you up and around."

"Will you come back for Christmas?" Rory asked eagerly.

"I would like that."

"And, Jed, I wish you a safe voyage," Rory said.

"Thank you, Rory. When I return, I expect you to be bouncing around as always, so listen to your doctor's orders. Don't try to rush things."

He put a hand on Caroline's back and steered her to the door. "I'll see you at Christmas," Caroline called back.

Colt was waiting in the wagon with Garrett and Nathan. Clay had the carriage harnessed, waiting for them.

Garth thanked her for all she had done for Rory, then hugged and kissed her. He shook hands with Jed as they said good-bye, then went inside to check on Rory and his children.

Saying good-bye to Paddy O'Grady and Jethro Braden was equally hard. And to the three women: Becky, Cassie, and Lissy, who stood back, holding their tots' hands and their infants in their arms. In this short time, they had become sisters.

Finally, amid shouted promises to see one another at Christmas, the wagon and carriage moved away.

When they reached town Caroline, Garrett, and Nathan boarded the train. She watched as Jed shook hands and said good-bye to his two brothers for another eleven months. The train whistle tooted, he climbed on board, and the train began to puff away.

When the cloud of steam cleared, she settled back in her seat.

She slept the rest of the ride back to Napa.

Tired and hungry, they decided to spend the night in town. After checking into the hotel, they freshened up to go down to the dining room for dinner.

When they were through, Caroline and Garrett left for the general store for several items she needed. Jed and Nathan went into the barroom to await their return.

"I received a letter from Leland Stanford while we were gone," Nathan said as he pulled the envelope out of his pocket. Leland said he spoke to Calhoun, and I can be assured there will be no further trouble." He chuckled. "It appears Calhoun is moving to Sacramento."

Their attention was drawn by loud laughter from four men who entered the bar; Ben Slatter was among them.

"Let's get out of here," Nathan said. "There's already no love lost between the two of you, and Slatter can be real mean when he's drunk."

They downed their drinks and got up to leave, but Slatter saw them. "Well, if it ain't my good friend, Mr. Fraser," he called. "You ain't runnin' out on me, are you?"

"Come on, Ben, settle down," the bartender said. "I don't want any trouble in my place."

"Then how come you let stinkin' Rebs in here?"

"The war's been over for four years, Ben, so let it go. I'll pour you a drink on the house."

"Naw, I've got a personal score to settle with Mr. Fraser."

"If you're gonna fight, take it outside. I don't want my place busted up."

"You've no cause for concern, sir," Jed said. "I have no intention of fighting this drunk."

When Jed turned to leave, one of Slatter's men put his foot out and tripped Jed, sending him stumbling into Slatter.

Before Jed could get his footing, Slatter punched him in the stomach. Jed doubled over, and Slatter delivered an uppercut to his chin. He fell backward and crashed into a table, which splintered and collapsed.

Dazed, Jed rolled aside when Slatter made a dive for him. The drunken bully landed on the floor, giving Jed a chance to get back on his feet.

Everyone scrambled to stay out of the way as the two men faced off. Jed landed a solid punch to Slatter's jaw before two of his friends grabbed his arms and held them to his sides while Slatter punched him several times in the stomach again. Jed's insides felt on fire as he struggled to free himself from their grasps.

Though Nathan tried to come to his aid, the third man shoved him back just as Caroline, Garrett, and Buffer appeared in the doorway.

"Don't you hurt them!" Garrett shouted. He rushed to their aid and began kicking at Slatter's leg while Caroline shouted for help.

"Get away from me, you little bastard." Slatter struck out with a backhand and knocked the child off his feet. With a feral growl, Buffer leaped at Slatter and got a hold of the bully's leg.

Cursing, Slatter tried to shake him off, and the two men holding Jed released him and headed for cover. The third man drew his pistol to shoot the dog. Seeing his intention, Jed dove and landed a punch on the man's chin. The gun went flying and slid across the floor to the feet of the tall man in the doorway. Sheriff Randy Newman entered the barroom, followed by Caroline.

"Call off Buffer, Garrett, or I'll have to shoot him," the sheriff warned.

"Buffer, stop!" Garrett cried. "Come here."

The dog released his hold on Slatter's leg and trotted over to Garrett, who knelt down and petted him.

"All right, somebody want to tell me what happened here?" Sheriff Newman asked.

"I want that dog shot," Slatter demanded. "Look what he did to me."

"I don't see any blood," the sheriff said. "But I'll see to it that they buy you a new pair of pants. Who started this, Charley?" he asked the bartender.

"Well, Ben had a little too much to drink. He and his boys were beating up on Mr. Fraser here."

"Is that right, Ben? Did you start this fight?"

"He certainly did, Sheriff," Nathan said. "Jed and I were peacefully leaving when Ben and his men attacked him."

"Four against one, was it?" the sheriff said. "Those odds don't seem quite fair. You can forget about buying him a new pair of pants, Miss Collins."

"It's Mrs. Fraser now, Sheriff," Jed said. "We were married earlier this week."

"Congratulations, Mr. Fraser, and best wishes to you, Caroline. You want to sign a complaint against Slatter?" the sheriff asked.

"No," Jed said. "I'll settle this with him when he's sober."

"All right—let's go, Ben. You can sleep it off in a cell. As for you three," the sheriff said to Slatter's accomplices, "if I hear of the three of you ganging up on one man again, you'll all find yourselves in a cell for the next thirty days." He left with his prisoner in tow.

Caroline went over to check Jed's injuries. "You look in pretty bad shape. I think we better get you to a doctor."

"I'll be okay; I'm just a little sore. Let's get out of here."

"Congratulations, folks," Charley called out as they departed.

Jed turned down any offers to help him upstairs, but his ribs were on fire, and he was bleeding from a cut above the eye.

Caroline took him to her room and had him sit down. She fetched a basin of water and a cloth, gently cleansed the wound, then leaned over him for a closer examination.

"It looks like it could use a couple of stitches."

"I'll be fine in the morning."

"I can't believe you and my father were engaging in a barroom brawl," she scolded.

"We were leaving without saying a word," Nathan said. "Then Slatter attacked Jed."

"And them bad guys held down Dad's arms while that mean old Mr. Slatter punched him," Garrett added.

"Jed, this wound definitely needs stitching," Caroline maintained. "I can do it with a needle and thread, or would you rather have a doctor take care of it?"

"It don't hurt that bad," Garrett piped up. "Mama sewed up my knee when I fell on a rock once. Now there's only a little scar. See?" He pulled up his trousers and showed Jed. "It only hurt for a little while. You're bigger than me, so it probably won't hurt you as much."

"Garrett had a very deep cut," Caroline said, "and it would have taken a long time to heal without stitches. Furthermore, I did an excellent job."

" 'Cept for the scar," Garrett said, managing to squeeze in the last word.

"Father, I think it will be wiser if you take Garrett and Buffer to your room while I finish this."

"Come along, my lad. I'll tell you about the time the *Virginia Lady* almost ran aground in a fog."

"Yes, I like that story and want to hear it again," Garrett said as Nathan led him away.

"Caroline, I'm fine," Jed declared. "I'll get out of here so you can go to bed. You haven't had much sleep in the last few days."

"I intend to, as soon as I'm through here. Go sit on the bed while I get my sewing box."

"You pack a sewing box when you go away?"

"Of course. What if I have to sew on a button or sew up somebody's face? I'll right back."

He hobbled over to the bed and sat down

painfully. His ribs were aching, and he felt them gingerly to see if any of them were cracked. From what he could tell, none appeared to be broken.

Caroline returned and saw him. "What's wrong with your ribs?"

"I must have hurt them when that table I fell on broke. Slatter kept hitting me in the stomach."

"If your ribs are hurting you, then obviously there's something wrong." As soon as she finished stitching his wound, she said, "Let's get that shirt off so I can check them out."

She reached to assist him, but her nearness was starting to awaken desire in him.

"I told you I'm all right. I'm getting the hell out of here," he lashed out. He bolted to his feet, but fell back from the pain.

"Jed, why are you being so unpleasant? Denying you're in pain? I'm only trying to help you."

He sighed in defeat. "Okay, get it over with." He struggled to remove his shirt.

"I'll be glad to pull it off over your head." She stepped between his legs and began to work the shirt over his head.

He closed his eyes, the provocative fragrance that was Caroline invading his senses. The tantalizing strokes of her fingertips were like heated strokes to his throbbing groin, and he groaned.

"I'm sorry. Does it hurt when I touch you?" she asked, skimming her fingers along the side of his torso.

"Yes," he snapped and opened his eyes. "You damn well know it hurts wherever you touch me—and I'm *not* referring to any sore ribs."

"I can't believe you have sex on your mind when you're in such pain," she declared and began to wind a narrow white strip around his ribs. The brush of her hair against his naked flesh felt like velvet as she worked. "I'm just trying to soothe the pain in your ribs."

"By creating a worse one in my groin," he groaned.

Ignoring him, she finished the task and tied the ends in a knot. "That should help you get through the night, but you really should see a doctor. He could give you something for your pain."

"So could you, Caroline, if you chose to do so."

She raised her head, and for several seconds they gazed into each other's eyes. Then he reached out and wove his fingers into the thick silkiness of her hair and slowly drew her head down to his. Once again he tasted the sweetness of her lips that parted beneath the pressure of his.

The kiss was deep and passionate, with the leisurely proficiency of the expert that he was. The deepening pressure of his lips aroused her own passion, and recalling those wondrous moments in his arms, she was tempted to surrender.

But her reasons to reject him were as valid now as they were before they married. She must not succumb to the seduction of the kiss or the excitement surging through her. She must not surrender.

She pulled away and raised her head. "No, Jed. Let me go."

He dropped his hand away. "You know I want you, Caroline."

"I believe you. But I won't become your whore for a month in this port, Jed."

"If all I wanted was a whore *in this port* I could have one, Caroline."

"For God's sake, Jed, what else do you want from me? I married you; I was intimate with you. Do you expect me to please you at your beck and call until you put on your sailor suit and sail off? You once told me your love of the sea wasn't fair to a wife; I thought you meant that. I saw my mother's loneliness, her tears when Father would leave, the nights when she paced the floor, missing him, needing him the way you claim you need me now.

"Each time you touch me or kiss me makes me want you, too. And I told you I won't knowingly choose the pain my mother lived with."

"Fine. I'm not going to beg you for something we both want, Caroline."

She managed to hold back her tears until he was out of the room.

CHAPTER
21

Caroline and Jed had barely spoken on the ride home the following morning; Nathan had the good sense to stay out of the obvious quarrel between them; and all three adults had been content to let Garrett chatter away.

"Feeling any better this morning, Jed?" Nathan asked as they ate breakfast.

"A little sore."

"Hot springs are good for soothing aches and pains, and we have one on our land. I've been in it often when my rheumatism kicks up. Ever try one before?"

"No," Jed said, "but I've heard about them."

"They're great. Caroline, why don't you take him there? I have to go to the mill, or I'd go with him myself. You coming with me, Garrett?"

"No, I think I'll go with Mama and Jed today to the hot spring." He turned to Jed. "It's not so hot. I stuck my finger in it, and it didn't burn."

"If it burned, Garrett, a person couldn't climb into it," Caroline said.

"Then why do they call it a *hot* spring?"

"Besides being warm, it has a different source than the cold river water," she replied with her usual patience with him. "Father, I hate the thought of you driving to the mill alone. There's no telling if Mr. Calhoun will live up to his promise."

"Calhoun's not stupid. I'm sure Leland Stanford made him a valuable enough proposition that he won't jeopardize it. I'll be back in time for dinner."

"As soon as I clean up the dishes we can go," Caroline said to Jed.

"I'll help you."

"That's not necessary; I'm used to doing it myself. But, Garrett, you help me clear the table."

"How come we don't have a table and chairs in the kitchen like my aunts do?"

"I guess your grandmother liked eating in the dining room."

"If we had a table in the kitchen, we wouldn't have to carry all these dishes back after we eat."

"But think of what Buffer would miss out on if we did," Caroline pointed out, when a half-eaten biscuit fell from a plate to the floor and Buffer went over and gobbled it up immediately.

"Thank you, sweetheart," she said to Garrett when the dining-room table had been cleared. "Now stay close to the house because we'll be driving Jed to the spring."

"I will, Mama. Let's go, Buffer," Garrett said. Boy and dog disappeared out of the house.

"He's some kid," Jed said.

Caroline smiled. "I wish I had his energy."

She began to wash the dishes, and Jed picked up a dish towel and began to dry them. Caroline suddenly stopped with her hands in the soapy water and looked at him. "He's worth it, isn't he, Jed? I mean, were we blinded by our love for him that we made a mistake in what we did?"

"It's too late for regrets now, Caroline."

She swallowed hard, and asked as calmly as she could, "But do you regret it, Jed?"

He gave her a narrow, measured glance. "No regrets. What about you?"

She felt a rush of relief. "I told you at Fraser Keep I'm ashamed of our shallowness toward each other. We've been acting more like children than responsible adults by allowing the issue of intimacy to overshadow the real purpose for marrying.

"But I *did* marry you for Garrett's sake, Jed; and I believe you did, too. I wouldn't hesitate to do it again."

She lowered her head and tried to concentrate on the plate she was washing. "I thought that maybe after last night . . . that is, our conversation . . . you might regret—"

"Caroline, you just said it; the reason we married was to put his needs above our personal feelings. Last night was about our personal needs as a man and woman. Not Garrett's."

"And the trouble is that we allowed bitterness to creep into our relationship the way it has."

"How can you expect it not to?" he said. "It *began* in bitterness, and both of us tend to fall back on that whenever we disagree on any topic."

"But must we, Jed? Even if we disagree on something, does it have to end up with a quarrel?"

"Many of the issues we've clashed on could have been resolved without quarreling. But there were lines drawn between us, and we accepted them, or they would never have existed."

She smiled shyly. "Ever hear of an armistice, Admiral Fraser?"

"You offering one, Miz Caroline?"

"I'm willing to try. Can't we at least agree to keep bitterness out of arguments?"

"So you figure this so-called armistice won't end the fights, only make them less . . . retaliatory."

She laughed, and he grinned. "Do we seal this agreement with a kiss or a handshake?"

She offered him a sudsy hand.

"Mama! Mama!" Garrett shouted, rushing into the kitchen. "Buffer and I thought of a great idea!"

She grinned at Jed, who was trying to hold back from laughing. "And what is that great idea you and Buffer thought of?"

"As long as we're going to that hot spring, why don't we have a picnic? Don't you think that's a good idea, Dad?"

Jed cleared his throat. "Well, ah . . . I always like picnics."

"Garrett, go down to the chicken coop and see if there's any eggs. I'll boil a few to take on the picnic."

"Yippee!" Garrett exclaimed. "Come on, Buffer. We're going on a picnic!"

The hot spring was set in a protective grove of oak and willow bordered on three sides by a granite wall. Caroline removed Jed's boots and stockings, then helped him off with his shirt and unwrapped the bandage from around his ribs. He slipped off his jeans, waded into the therapeutic water, and sat down in it.

"How does it feel?" Garrett asked.

"It's great," Jed said.

Caroline removed her boots and stockings and sat down on the edge of the pond to soak her feet. "Oh, this is heaven," she said.

"Why don't you come in and join me, Garrett?" Jed asked.

"It's too much like taking a bath."

"What's wrong with that?"

"Mama made me take a bath when we got home."

"And Heaven forbid you take one again," Caroline said.

"Granddad told me if I take too many baths, I'll shrink up into a prune. Is that true, Mama?"

"Of course not, honey. You know your grandfather loves to tease you."

"Well, all I can say," Jed said, "is that I hadn't realized what I've been missing all these years."

"Is it better than swimming in the ocean?" Garrett asked.

"This isn't water you'd normally swim in, Garrett."

"I think it looks dumb just to sit there in the water."

"It's a lot better than clinging to a branch in a

raging river, pal." Jed winked at Caroline, then closed his eyes and relaxed.

After a long pause, when he opened them again, Garrett and Buffer were off chasing a butterfly, and Caroline sat on the edge of the pool deep in thought. The summer breeze tugged gently at her hair, and she raised a hand and brushed it off her cheek. It was like watching a painting come to life, and he regretted he wasn't an artist to capture the moment on canvas.

"Penny for your thoughts," he said.

"I was just thinking what a beautiful day this is. The last couple of weeks have been so hectic, filled with noisy trains and crowds of people."

"I know what you mean. Its stillness is what I love about the sea."

"I cherish moments like this when there is peace and quiet, perhaps an occasional chirp of a bird. Nature at her loveliest. I'd never be content living in a city."

"From what I recall about Virginia, you didn't attend many balls and cotillions, either."

"I do prefer solitude."

"Did you really enjoy the visit with my family?"

"Oh yes. Your brothers are wonderful, but I enjoyed the female companionship even more. It was something I never had, except for my mother. And your brothers' wives all have such individual personalities, there was never a chance to be bored."

She stood up. "I think you've been in that water long enough. You don't want to wrinkle up into a prune, do you?" With a grin, she grabbed a towel as he climbed out of the water. "There's a river nearby if you want to rinse those minerals off you."

"No, I'll do that when we get back."

"Do you want me to wrap your ribs again?"

"I don't think it will be necessary. I can move my arms pretty well now without any pain."

He stretched out on his stomach on a blanket and closed his eyes. "The sun feels good."

She took the opportunity to study him unobserved. Ruffled by the wind, his dark hair glistened in the sunshine. His long body was perfectly proportioned. His whole upper torso was bronzed, and his broad, muscular shoulders tapered down to a narrow waist and slim hips. His wet, clinging underwear outlined strong thighs and long, muscular legs.

A woman could certainly be angry at this man, but she could never ignore him. He had a quality that grabbed you, no matter how hard you fought it. She was proof of that.

"Jed, I'd like to tell you about Andy and me."

She waited for his response, but after several seconds, she went over and examined him. He had fallen asleep. Here she had finally built up the courage to tell all to him—and he fell asleep!

She went back and sat down in the shade.

Caroline was almost on the verge of dozing off herself when Garrett came chasing up to her.

"Look, Mama, I found a four-leaf clover."

"That's wonderful, honey. They say it's supposed to bring you good luck."

"Do you think it will be lucky enough to keep Dad from leaving?"

"Sweetheart, you can't hope for the impossible. It will only cause you disappointment. Help me unpack our lunch, then we'll wake Jed."

"Will you be glad when he leaves, Mama?" Garrett asked as they laid out the food on a bright red-and-white-checked tablecloth.

Jed awoke and became aware of the low voices. Hearing Garrett ask Caroline about him leaving, Jed strained to hear her answer.

"No, Garrett, I'll be as sorry when he leaves as you will. But we knew from the beginning that was his intention, and we can't expect him to change his plans for us. He's done enough as it is. I'm sure he would have preferred to spend more time with his family on his leave."

"Just the same, I'm gonna wish on my four-leaf clover he doesn't leave."

"Go over and wake him, honey. We're ready to eat."

Jed was amazed how good his ribs felt, and even managed to pull on his trousers before joining them.

Caroline had done her usual superb, last-minute preparation of a picnic lunch. As Jed leaned back against a tree, he reflected on how easily she rose to the challenge of anything asked of her. It reminded him of his mother.

It had been six years since his parents had passed on, and often when he was at sea, on watch during the night, his thoughts would stray to them. He had been out of the country when they had died, and he had missed seeing them laid to rest. And death was such a final ending that if you missed seeing them laid to that final rest, you expected them to walk through the door at any time.

Deep in thought, he was unaware he was fingering the narrow beaded string bracelet that his mother had given him for luck the first time he went to sea.

"Why do you wear that?" Garrett asked.

"I'm sorry; what did you say?" Jed asked, jolted back to the conversation.

"Why do you wear that bracelet on your wrist?"

"My mother made it for me." He held out his wrist for Garrett to have a closer look at it.

"What does the writing say?"

"It spells my name: Jedemiah."

"How come your mother gave you such a long name?"

"I guess it was as close to being bibical as my dad would allow."

"Why did your mother want a biblical name, Jed?" Caroline asked. "Your brothers don't have them."

"If Mom had her way, her first four sons would have been named Matthew, Mark, Luke, and John, Dad said no way, anymore than he'd allow his sons to be named Bubba or Billy Bob." He chuckled in memory. "Dad had very strong convictions about some things, but by the time I was born he was willing to make a compromise. Mom liked the name Jeremiah from the Bible. Dad hated *Jer*, but did like Jed. It would have made me very happy if they'd stopped there, but Mom held firm for an end to the name. My father liked *diah*; my mother wanted *miah*." So Mom won and they settled on *miah*. And the compromise resulted in my being christened Jedemiah. A source of endless teasing by my brothers when we were younger."

"How come you named me Garrett, Mama?"

"That was your grandmother's maiden name before she married your grandfather."

"I thought Grandma's name was Emily. That's what Granddad always called her."

"It was. Garrett was her last name."

"Then why did you call it her maiden name? That sounds like it means a girl."

"It is: an unmarried girl is referred to as a maiden."

"Well, Grandma's mom and dad had the same last name, and they're married. I thought if a girl's not married, she's called Miss."

Caroline grinned. "That, too."

"So why are there two different words that mean the same thing? That sure is dumb," Garrett said with disgust.

"It sure is, isn't it?" Her blue eyes sparkled with mirth as they met Jed's.

"I guess we should think about packing up and getting back home."

CHAPTER 22

Early the following morning they all climbed into the buckboard and headed for Napa. Jed told them he needed a few items, not mentioning that a horse for Garrett was among them. It would only start an argument with Caroline. But this was a serious issue with Jed. Garrett would soon be nine years old, and it wasn't right that he had never sat a saddle. By the time he and his brothers were that age, they could leap short fences and ford shallow streams on horseback, and he only had less than two weeks to teach Garrett how to ride.

When they reached Napa, they separated. Caroline wanted to shop for a new dress, Nathan had business at the bank, and Garrett chose to accompany Jed.

"Where are we going, Dad?" he asked.

"To the livery. It's the best place to start for what I have in mind."

"What do you have in mind?"

"I'll tell you when I'm sure I can get what I want."

Burt Thomas, the livery owner, told him of a nearby farmer who had the very size horse he was looking for.

"Name's Bill Callahan," Burt said. "Saw him pass by this morning. If he's still in town, you'll most likely find him at the grain store."

"Thanks, Burt."

"Congratulations on your marriage, Mr. Fraser. Miz Collins is a mighty fine lady. You're a lucky man."

"I think so, too. And the name's Jed."

"So will you be living here, or somewhere else?"

"I'm a sailor. My ship will be sailing in a couple of weeks."

"Heard tell the whole family was moving out."

"Who started that rumor?" Jed asked.

Burt shrugged. "I heard it from Tony, the barber. He claimed Vincent Calhoun was bragging about it last time he came in for a haircut. Said he was buying up Nathan's property."

"Mr. Calhoun is mistaken. In fact, I'm told that it's Calhoun who is leaving Napa. Nathan Collins is not selling out, and Caroline and Garrett will remain with him while I'm at sea. Now I'd better try and find this Bill Callahan. Nice talking to you, Burt."

"If you have any luck, I've got an old saddle that would be perfect for what you have in mind. Knew if I held on to it long enough, it would come to some good."

Jed joined Garrett and Buffer outside. "Garrett, do you know who Bill Callahan is?"

"Sure. That's him loading that wagon in front of the grain store."

"I have to talk to him a minute, so don't wander off." Jed went over to the tall, thin man, and introduced himself.

"So you're the fella what married Miz Caroline," Callahan said.

"Yes, I am. And I'm told that you have a pony for sale."

"He's not really a pony, just the runt of the litter. By now he oughta be full grown, but he ain't."

"Is he sickly?" Jed asked.

"Don't seem to be. He's frisky and eats good. Just don't grow very much."

"He sounds like the very thing I'm looking for. I want to get Garrett started on riding. Is the horse gentle?"

"Oh, yeah. And he don't shy away from folks at all."

"How much are you asking for him?"

"Well, since he don't seem to be growing much bigger, I'm only asking twenty-five dollars. I always figured he wouldn't be good for much more than pulling a plow."

"Then you've got yourself a sale, Mr. Callahan."

"If we're gonna be neighbors, my name's Bill."

"And mine's Jed." The two men shook hands.

"Well, Jed, my farm's just a couple miles south of town."

"We'll swing by your place as soon as we finish here in town."

Callahan climbed up on the wagon. "Nathan knows where it is. I'll be expectin' you."

Jed was elated. He went back and bought the

saddle and necessary reins from Burt and carried them to the buckboard.

"What's the saddle for, Dad?" Garrett asked. "Don't you like the one we have?"

"I think we could use another one. Should we see what your mother's up to?"

They went to the small boutique in town. When they entered, Caroline was in front of a mirror studying the pale-green dress she had on. His gaze clung to her as the dress tightened across the curve of her breasts as she turned and stretched in an effort to see her back.

"It looks great from where I'm standing," he said.

She swung around in surprise, then with outstretched arms, she twirled around and laughed gaily. "What do you think of it?"

"Gorgeous, Cinderella," he said.

Caroline blushed at the glow of desire in his eyes.

She felt heated blood surge through her and knew it was part of the hold he had on her.

After all the past lonely years, she liked being openly desirable in his eyes. She was discovering the excitement of being desired by an attractive man, one who made her tremble just by the way he looked at her.

She shook her head. "I really don't need a new dress."

"Caroline, buy it," Jed said.

"But I really . . ."

Their gazes clung in an unspoken message, the way they had done at Fraser Keep the night she was playing the piano.

"Buy the dress, Caroline," he said softly.

"All right," she said to the woman, "I'll take it."

By the time she changed her clothes and went to pay for the gown, Celeste told her that Jed had already paid for it.

"You are most fortunate to have such a handsome husband, Caroline, and a generous one, too. Ooh, la, la! I should be that lucky." She started to wrap up a pair of jeweled pumps that matched the dress.

"I'm not buying the shoes, Celeste."

"Your husband bought them," Celeste said. "And these elbow-length gloves. He has impeccable taste." She glanced at the ring on Caroline's finger. "Yes, indeed, *chérie*. Impeccable taste."

"If you don't mind, Celeste, I'll pick up the packages when we're ready to leave town."

Once outside, there was no sign of Jed and Garrett. She saw her father just leaving the bank and hurried over to him.

"Have you seen Jed and Garrett?"

"Yes, he asked to borrow the buckboard because he had an important errand to run and told me we should finish our shopping and wait for him at the diner."

"Are you sure that Garrett's with him?"

"Yes, they rode out of here about ten minutes ago. I had to give him directions to Bill Callahan's farm."

"What in the world would he be going there for?"

"He didn't volunteer, so I didn't ask. I try to stay out of people's personal business."

"Since when, you old meddler?" She slipped her arm through his. "We might as well go have a cup of coffee until they get back."

An hour later, still waiting at the diner, Caroline wondered, "Why do you suppose they went to Bill Callahan's farm?"

"My dear, I haven't the faintest idea. But I suspect we'll find out soon, because they're back." Nathan nodded toward the door that Garrett had just burst through with his usual enthusiasm.

Caroline couldn't help smiling at his trying to contain himself.

"What is it, honey?" she asked, hugging him when he sat down beside her.

"Mama, I'm 'bout the luckiest kid in the world. I bet no kid is happier than me."

"Aren't you going to make us happy, too, by telling us what's making you so happy?"

"Can't right now. I promised Dad I wouldn't say a word 'til after we eat."

Caroline looked at Jed, who said, "I bought him a going-away gift. Something to remind him of me while I'm gone."

"How sweet. Is that dress you bought me for the same reason?"

"Just the opposite. The dress is something to remind me of you while I'm gone."

"Well, thank you. It was very generous of you."

"I hope I have the chance to see you in it again before I leave." The cocky look in his eyes said more than any words could.

"Let's order our lunch and get out of here," Nathan declared. "I've sat here so long in this wooden booth that my rear end is getting sore, and I can't wait to see what all the mystery is about.

"It seems like we've all been busy this morning. I filled out papers to have the ownership of my property and sawmill transferred into your name, Caroline, with the provision it will pass on to Garrett at your discretion."

"Father, why? It's yours. There was no need for you to do that."

"There's too much talk," Garrett declared. "Let's hurry up and eat so we can get out of here."

"Too much talk—coming from the world's greatest nonstop talker?" Caroline teased. "But you're right, Father, I'm just as curious to find out about this big surprise, so let's hurry up and finish our meal."

Later, as Caroline approached their buckboard, she stared at the buckskin horse tied to the rear of it.

"What is that?" she asked.

"That's Runt," Garrett exclaimed. "Dad bought him for me."

"What do we need him for?" she asked.

"To teach Garrett how to ride a horse, of course."

Her annoyed glance reflected her feelings as she climbed into the carriage. "I think you should have discussed it with me before you made such a decision."

"It would appear, Jed, my daughter is ready to leave," Nathan said and sat down beside her.

"Caroline, where are the packages from the boutique?" Jed asked.

"I told Celeste we would pick them up when we left town."

"I thought I would tie them to Runt's saddle so they wouldn't get crushed."

"You consider just about everything, Mr. Fraser—except what you *should* be considering," she added.

"Granddad, are they having another fight again?" Garrett asked.

"We are merely disagreeing. Isn't that right, Jed?"

"Seems like a fight to me, if you're going to sit there looking uppish with your arms folded across your chest all the way back to the house."

He climbed in and took the reins, and Garrett sat down next to Jed. Buffer squeezed into the front at Garrett's feet.

"Are you sure you feel up to driving?" Nathan asked. "How do your ribs feel?"

"They're fine, just a little sore. That hot spring did wonders. I'm glad you thought of it."

After a quick stop at the boutique, they headed for home.

"Will you teach me how to ride right away?" Garrett asked.

"You have to learn how to take care of a horse before you start thinking about riding one," Jed advised him. "You begin by being the only one who does anything for him. That will gain his trust. You must see that he's fed and that there's water in his trough. You muck out his stall, hose him down, and curry his mane. And you talk to him while you do it."

"You mean he'll understand what I say, just like Buffer does?"

"Not really. It gets him used to the sound of your voice. A horse isn't as smart as a dog, Garrett. I don't think any domesticated animal is, when it comes to being sensitive to human moods and routines.

"With a horse, it's total trust. Once that's established between you, they'll run until they drop dead if you're riding them. That's why it's essential that you learn the extent of their strength and endurance, so that you don't abuse that trust.

"Runt may not be the size of a full-grown horse, but he'll have the power and heart of one. He'll want to run, so you have to teach him signals he'll respond to, Garrett."

"What kind of signals?"

"How to veer right, or left, or straight ahead. When you want him to stop, to go. When you want him to gallop or just trot. It's all done with the right pressure of your legs and the tension on the reins. That's the way you talk to them when you're in the saddle."

Awestruck, Garrett asked, "Where'd you learn so much about horses, Dad?"

"Growing up in Virginia, we had a stable of horses. My parents had seven children and we all rode—your aunt Lissy can handle a horse as well as a man. There were a couple of horses that were used just for plowing, and we'd often race our horses at county fairs."

"Did you ever win?"

"A time or two."

"Which one of my uncles is the best rider?" Garrett asked.

Jed thought for a few moments, then said, "They're all pretty good, but I guess I'd have to say your uncle Garth. There's nothing that crazy brother of mine can't do on a horse. And your uncle Colt was in General Stuart's cavalry during the war. There wasn't a cavalry unit on either side of the war that could equal them."

Garrett reached over and patted Jed's leg. "Bet you can ride as good as any of them, Dad."

That's what he's always needed, Caroline thought. The anger had slowly eased from her as she'd listened and watched them together. As close as her father and her son were, Jed was bringing to Garrett's life the precious shared moments between a father and young son. Teaching him skills that a mother would never think to do, would never know how to do.

And Garrett was absorbing them like they were sustenance.

She smiled. He had even started to copy Jed's stance, the way Jed leaned his head when he was engrossed in a conversation. Every day, he absorbed something from Jed that became part of his growth toward manhood.

He needed the balance of a man's forthright answers and observations of life, as opposed to her nuanced answers that avoided unpleasantness and hurt feelings. Jed was teaching Garrett how to be a man.

CHAPTER
23

"I bet this feels good on such a hot day, Runt," Garrett said as he wet down his horse.

After several days of higher than normal temperatures, they had all come to the river to cool off.

Nathan grinned as he listened to the young boy talking to the horse. For the past few days, Garrett had cared diligently and devotedly for the horse. Whenever he was missing, they knew he and Buffer could be found in the barn.

After a refreshing swim, the men lay down to dry off in the sunshine and gave Caroline a chance to protect her modesty while splashing in the water.

"Dad, I've been thinking 'bout something since we came back home," Garrett said.

"Uh-huh," Jed murmured, on the border of dozing off.

"It's about Rico."

"Uh-huh."

"If he's your cousin, how come he's a different color than the rest of us?"

"My aunt Elena, who is Rico's mother, is Spanish,

so Rico is a mixture of Spanish and white blood. That's why he's darker than us."

"Is he my cousin, too, like my other cousins?"

"He's actually my cousin, and my brothers' and Lissy's cousin."

"Well, how come he's a cousin to all of you, but not mine?"

"He is, in a way. You understand that Lissy's and my brothers' children are your cousins, right?"

"Right."

Jed nodded. "Good. That makes them your first cousins."

"But there's a lot of them. How can they all be the first one?"

"That's what it's called if it's a child of your aunt or uncle."

"Which uncle?" Garrett asked.

"Any of your uncles." From the blank look on the boy's face, Jed knew he'd just confused him. "I guess we'll have to back up a bit. My father had a brother, my uncle Henry. And Uncle Henry had a son named Rico. That makes Rico my cousin, because he's the son of my uncle."

"Your *first* cousin."

"Absolutely right! My first cousin. And just like Rico is my cousin, because he is the son of *my* uncle Henry, you are a cousin to all the children of *your* father's sister and brothers: Jake, Clint, and Cody; Jeb and Sam; Danny; Ted, Sarah, and Rachel."

"You forgot Baby Hope, Dad," Garrett said.

"Of course, Baby Hope," Jed replied, trying to keep a hold on his patience. "They're all your *first* cousins. But since Rico is *my* first cousin, he's your *second* cousin."

Garrett reflected for a long moment. "I don't understand. Rico's older than my other cousins. Right? So how come he's not my *first* cousin, if he's the oldest one?"

Jed closed his eyes. He wasn't sure he was ready for fatherhood. Maybe fatherhood was something a man had to be gradually conditioned to rather than having it thrust upon him.

"No, Garrett. It has nothing to do with age. It's about generations." He sighed deeply. "Let's start over. Your grandfather was born before your father. Your father was born before you. And then you were born. So that's three generations. Right?"

"Okay," Garrett agreed. "What's a generation?"

"What are the two of you talking about so seriously?" Caroline asked, sitting down and joining them.

"Caroline! I'm glad you're here." Jed got to his feet. "I have to go and hitch up the buckboard. Garrett has a question he wants you to explain."

He hurried away.

The day finally arrived when Jed felt it was time to introduce Garrett to a saddle. Fortunately the horse was already saddle broken so there was only the need to do the same to the intended rider.

Caroline and Nathan stood back and watched. Trembling with excitement, Garrett waited as Jed led out Liberty and Runt.

"Now, Garrett, the first thing you have to know about mounting a horse is that you always do it from the left side of the horse. You gather both reins together loosely in your left hand, grasp the saddle horn with the same hand, then raise your left leg and put your foot into the stirrup. Then you swing your right leg over the horse and slip your foot into that stirrup. But you don't hesitate between these steps; it's all done in the same movement.

"I'll demonstrate what I just said. The only difference will be that I'll do it slowly." He went over to Liberty and gathered the reins, then grasped the saddle horn. "Do you see what I did?" he asked. Garrett nodded. "I'll do it one more time."

When he finished, he said, "Now let me see you do that with Runt. At first you might need to grab the saddle horn with both hands; that will give you a stronger lift to pull yourself up."

Caroline held her breath as Garrett followed Jed's instructions. He looked so small, even next to the little horse.

A half hour later, Garrett had succeeded in swinging himself on and off the horse without mishap.

With Jed astride Liberty and Garrett on Runt, she watched nervously as Jed demonstrated how to hold the reins and coordinate leg movements with them to indicate direction and speed to the horse.

When Jed was satisfied with Garrett's progress, he dismounted, leaving Garrett on his own. "Let's see you ride down to that pine clump and back again."

"Are you sure he's ready to ride alone?" Caroline asked worriedly.

"Of course. Frasers are born knowing how to ride."

Garrett passed the test with flying colors to the

applause of his mother and grandfather. Dismounting, he rushed into her open arms and flung his arms around her neck.

"I did it, Mama! I rode Runt all alone. I can ride a horse!"

Hugging him, she glanced up and saw Jed grinning as he watched them, unaware of the tears of happiness sliding down her cheeks.

Garrett scrambled away and remounted Runt. "Come on, Buffer," he shouted.

"Keep it slow, son," Jed shouted to the departing rider.

"And stay in sight," Caroline called out.

Nathan came over and shook Jed's hand. "Well done, Jed. You're a good instructor."

"I had a good student." He glanced at the distant rider wheeling his horse around to return and smiled with pride. "He's a Fraser, all right."

Caroline could feel his sense of pride in her own heart. She slipped away and returned to the house. Seeing how thrilled Garrett was warmed her heart, but riding a horse was also dangerous. He could be seriously injured if he fell off it.

Why did Jed have to do this so close to the time he was leaving? Had he discussed it with her, she could have explained her reservations and recommendations. Garrett would be a year older by the time Jed returned, and at the speed he was growing, it would have made a big difference in his size and maturity.

Her father came into the room and sat down at the table. "He did well, didn't he, honey?"

She looked up and smiled. "Yes, he did, but it's

another thing I have to worry about. Now that he can ride, it could be opening up a Pandora's box if Garrett starts disobeying the rules Jed established."

"Aren't you being pessimistic, honey? There's no reason to think that he'll do that. Garrett usually obeys what he's told to do."

"I hope you're right. I just wish Jed had discussed his intentions with me. 'Frasers are born knowing how to ride.' Does he actually believe that? It's ludicrous."

Nathan reached across the table and squeezed her hand. "Caroline, from the beginning you've convinced yourself Jed is a threat in some way. It goes deeper than that, doesn't it, honey? What's wrong, Caroline?"

"I'm afraid of losing Garrett, Father. He worships Jed."

"Do you resent that?"

"No, I'm . . . I'm hurt by it. He once came to me for answers, but now he seeks advice from Jed."

"Because right now Jed is a novelty to him, honey. In time he'll turn back to you, and you'll be able to scoff at these fears."

Caroline leaned on her elbow and cupped her head in her hands. "I'm not sure, Father. One minute I'm grateful he's around, and the next he does an impulsive thing like this and I want to curse the day he came into our lives."

"Are you in love with Jed, Caroline?" Nathan asked gently.

She raised her head, her expression tortured. "I wish I knew. I feel something for him, but can I call it love?"

"Well, I think you should decide soon, because he'll be gone in another week. If you love him, you're wasting precious time when you could be together."

Caroline got to her feet. "I'm going to take the buggy and ride over to the mill. I've neglected my bookwork."

"You're riding over alone?"

"I've done it plenty of times before, and the ride there and back will give me time to think about my situation with Jed. Where are they now?"

"They rode off to the river to go swimming."

"I guess it didn't occur to either of them to ask me to go along." She walked to the door. "I'll be back in time for supper."

"Where's Caroline?" Jed asked when they returned home.

"She rode over to the mill to catch up on some of her ledger work," Nathan said.

Jed glanced up at the darkened clouds overhead. "How long has she been gone? It looks like we're in for quite a storm."

"Caroline said she'd be home for dinner."

An hour later, when the distant rumbling had grown more severe, Jed had begun to pace the floor. "I'd have thought she'd be home by now."

"Frankly, I did, too. Caroline's got more common sense than to let herself be caught in a downpour," Nathan said.

"Maybe I'll ride out and meet her. Is there any possibility she'd take a shortcut home?"

"The trail is the shortest route home," Nathan said.

"Maybe she's run into a problem with the buggy. I'm going to saddle up Liberty and check it out."

"There's a couple of rain slickers in the barn. It might be wise to take them with you in case you don't make it back before the rain hits."

"Thanks. Hopefully we'll meet up on the trail."

Jed quickly saddled Liberty, stuffed the slickers into the saddlebags, and took off on a gallop.

Absorbed in her work, Caroline let the hours slip by. Now, as the rumble of thunder announced the approaching storm, she went to the window and saw she had better leave if she intended to get home before the storm struck.

She closed the ledger books and gathered them up to take home to finish them, then carried them outside and tucked them away in the carriage where they would remain dry. Then she quickly reharnessed Belle to the buggy.

The skeleton crew at the mill waved to her as they hurried to the comfort of the bunkhouse for the evening.

Caroline ran back inside to get some papers she needed and reached to extinguish the oil lamp. She jumped back as a rifle blast shattered the window glass, and the oil lamp at her fingertips fell over. A narrow stream of oil and flame slithered across the desktop, then raced down a table leg to the floor and began to consume a wooden chair.

The smoke that was swiftly filling the small cabin

stung her eyes, and she tripped on a chair and fell to the floor. She began to crawl on her hands and knees toward the door, when a pair of strong arms suddenly snatched her up and carried her outside.

"Caroline, were you shot?" Jed asked.

"No," she managed to gasp through her coughs.

Several of the men had come outside when they heard the gun blast, and they ran over to the cabin at the sight of the flames.

"Let's get that hose working before this spreads," the foreman, Pete Dodge, shouted.

A couple of the men came running with buckets in hand and began to throw water on the burning building, while several others strung a hose into the river and began to pump water onto the roof and walls of the mill to wet it down.

"It's too late to save the office," Dodge shouted. "Some of you men spread a fire break with dirt to keep the fire from spreading to the trees."

Jed was struggling to move the buggy, but Belle, who had smelled the smoke, was rearing in a frenzy to break lose. He finally managed to control her enough to get to the river, away from the burning building.

He grabbed a scarf of Caroline's lying on the seat and dunked it in the water, then raced back to the compound and handed the scarf to her. "Tie this over your nose and mouth."

The air was thick with smoke, but fortunately there was no wind to scatter the sparks into the trees. Despite the valiant effort of the limited men, though, patches of fire had crept to the shrub and brush near several trees and their bark had begun to burn.

Caroline felt near to exhaustion when, like an answered prayer, the sky opened up with a downpour. Within minutes the fires all fizzled out, and the men tossed shovels of dirt and mud over the ashes that fought to survive.

Despite the downpour, they formed teams and sawed down the trees that had been burning in case any sparks remained. As lumbermen, they knew what a few sparks fanned by the wind could do to a forest.

When they were finally confident that all was secure, they looked around at the damage. Only sodden ashes remained of the office and nearby privy, but the two main structures, the mill and bunkhouse, were unscathed.

Suddenly a rifle cracked, and Jed shoved Caroline to the ground and threw his body across her as a bullet whizzed by from some nearby foliage. Pete Dodge drew his Colt and returned the shot. The bullet found its mark, and they heard the sound of the concealed shooter falling to the ground.

They approached cautiously.

"It's Bomber!" Caroline exclaimed. "Oh, my God! We shot an innocent man?"

Pete Dodge knelt down and examined his gun, then shook his head.

"Bomber, did you fire the shot?"

The man nodded. "But why did you try to kill me?" Caroline asked, stunned.

"Your fault," he managed to gasp. "Yours and your

Reb husband's. All this would be mine. Calhoun promised . . . if I'd help drive you out."

"Did you tamper with the axle of the buggy, too?" Jed asked.

"Yeah. Meant to scare the boss."

"What about the accident when you were blowing stumps?" Jed asked, trying to tie up all the loose ends.

"Did that on purpose. Didn't put up warning flag, and knew when to light the fuse so the kid wouldn't get hurt."

The dying man's voice was fading, and Caroline had to lean over to hear him.

"Then he left . . . told me the deal was off."

"You mean Calhoun?" Jed asked.

Bomber nodded. "He laughed when I told him I'd tell the sheriff."

"But why did you even get mixed up with him, Bomber? You've worked for my father for years. He liked you, trusted you."

"Tired of working for other men. Wanted my own . . ." His voice trailed off as he closed his eyes.

"He's gone," Pete said.

Caroline stared into space, shocked and confused, until Jed slipped an arm around her shoulders and led her to the buggy. He put one of the slickers on her, seated her, then went back to the other men.

"Did Bomber have any relatives that should be informed?" Jed asked.

"None that we know of," Pete said. "He was a loner. Kept to himself and never spoke much to anyone."

"Then you might as well bury him. Since we all

witnessed what happened, and heard him confess to it, there shouldn't be any problem with the sheriff.

"I'm taking Caroline home now. On behalf of the Collins family, thank you, men, for the great job you did. I know Nathan will come tomorrow to thank you himself.

"Since you're the foreman, Pete, I'll leave it to your discretion what you want done here. But if these were my men, I'd sure as hell figure they've earned a rest," Jed added with a grin as he tied Liberty to the back of the carriage.

Pete laughed. "I had the same thought in mind."

Jed shook their hands and thanked them again, then drove away.

They were about halfway home when the sky darkened, and the rain and wind increased violently. Soon the torrential rain made visibility impossible.

Jed had to shout to be heard above the howling wind. "Is there any place nearby where we can take shelter?"

Caroline shook her head. "N-none th-that I kn-know of." She was shivering so badly, her teeth were chattering.

A back wheel hit a rut and was sucked down into a muddy sinkhole. Jed jumped out of the carriage to check it out.

He'd been at sea during hurricanes, and although this storm wasn't quite as severe, he didn't even attempt to harness Liberty for some extra horsepower; the wisest thing they could do was to find some shelter and get out of the path of the wind.

He lifted Caroline out of the carriage and carried

her into the trees lining the path. Then he slogged back in the mud to the carriage and returned with the two horses.

The trees did little to protect them from the rain, but at least they were out of the force of the wind. He looked around at the dead and fallen branches lying on the ground, and thought of an idea.

He tied the ends of Liberty's reins around one of the big branches and propped it up high enough against a tree to form some cover below it. By the time he added two more branches, he had enough of a lean-to for both of them to crawl under. It was a crude shelter, but it warded off the rain.

He took off his slicker, shook it out as best he could, and spread it on the ground. Then he peeled off Caroline's and shook it out as well, and proceeded to pull off her boots and stockings.

"Wh-what a-are y-you d-doing?" she protested, when he started to unbutton her shirt.

"Getting you out of these wet clothes before you catch pneumonia."

He stripped off her shirt and skirt. Her camisole was just as wet, so despite her attempt to ward off his hands, he pulled it off and tossed it aside.

"D-don't e-e-even th-th-think it, Fra-fraser," she ordered through her chattering teeth when he reached for the waistband of her bloomers.

"This is no time for modesty, Caroline." He yanked them down her legs and pulled them off her ankles.

"Now lie down." His firm hand forced her back. For several minutes he rubbed her legs and feet vigorously, then her arms and shoulders. "Turn over." She continued to shiver, and he rubbed her back.

"D-don't tr-ry t-to t-tell m-me y-you ar-ren't en-enjoy-ing th-this," she accused when he did the same to the cheeks of her rear end.

"I shall think of this moment very fondly some night when I'm standing a lonely watch at sea." He couldn't resist giving that little butt of hers a tender swat. "Are you feeling any warmer, darlin'?"

"N-not mu-much."

"Funny, I'm beginning to feel a lot warmer."

Jed stripped off his clothes and rolled her over. Then gathering her in his arms, he held her tightly against him, and pulled her rain slicker over them.

The heat of their bodies melded, and soon he felt her relax and her shivering cease.

"Thank you, Jed. I feel much better now."

"Since it's still raining, there's no sense in moving yet. When we do, we'll have to leave the carriage since it's stuck in the mud. Do you think you can handle Liberty?"

"I can give it a try. What about you? You'll have to ride Belle bareback."

"I'll manage."

She giggled. "That's right, Frasers are born knowing how to ride a horse."

"You are one ungrateful woman, Miss Caroline. Didn't I just sacrifice my body heat to warm you up?"

"And loved every minute of it," she joshed back. "Speaking of riding, Jed, thank you for what you did for Garrett. He's so thrilled with Runt. I dreaded the time when he'd ask me to let him ride a horse, but now he's been taught well."

"He's doing great. You don't have to worry."

"Thanks to you. You're always right, Jed. I mean that sincerely. I seem to make the wrong decisions so often with him."

"No, you don't. Honey, you've done a great job raising the boy. But he's growing up, so you have to start giving him a little longer rein."

She nodded thoughtfully. After a while she said, "Jed, it could rain the rest of the night. We can't stay here like this."

"We'll give it another fifteen minutes and then try our luck."

She looked up at him and laughed. "What difference will fifteen minutes make in the storm?" Their mouths were so close, they were almost touching.

"Which storm are you referring to, Caroline?" he whispered. "The one outside, or the one in here?"

He trailed a string of kisses down the column of her neck.

She closed her eyes against the passion his kiss aroused.

"I should have the strength to resist you, Jed—but it feels too good."

"More reason not to resist then, sweetheart."

He shifted her to her back, then slowly caressed the fullness of her breasts, down her body to the curve of her hips. He lowered his head, and his mouth closed over one breast as his hand cupped its mate.

"You're right again, Jed," she murmured as sweet,

sweet sensation washed through her. And he demonstrated just what a difference fifteen minutes could make in a storm.

She lay breathless, her heart pounding in her ears. Her body still tingled with sensation from Jed's lovemaking. She was finally glad she had succumbed to his seduction, and was even ready for him again.

She was wrong to think she could deny him, or herself. When he left, at least she would have these moments to remember, not just a fantasy.

Somehow, sometime in these past weeks, she had fallen in love with him. Though it was exactly what she had feared, it no longer mattered. They still had another week together.

Jed suddenly lifted his head. "Listen."

Caroline held her breath for several seconds. "I don't hear anything."

"That's what I mean. The wind has stopped." He got up and stood outside their shelter to listen, and her gaze devoured his nakedness. It was the first time she'd really had the opportunity of seeing him completely naked, and his perfectly proportioned physique was beautiful. Quite beautiful, indeed.

"The rain's down to a drizzle, so I think we can try to head home now," he said.

Caroline nodded and reached for her clothes.

CHAPTER
24

The day was sunny, hot, and humid, with a bit of breeze. Rico Fraser dismounted, tied his horse to a hitching post, and removed his hat.

His cousin Jed and lovely bride Caroline had said they lived near Napa. Now his pursuit of the four men who had raped and murdered his mother had led him to that town. Until these animals were brought to justice, though, there was no time for pleasure.

His dark-eyed gaze swept the street and paused at the hitching post in front of the saloon where four horses were tethered, a large gray one among them. He was certain these were the ones he was following.

Rico walked casually down the street. There weren't many people out in the hot noonday sun, and when he was certain no one observed him, he picked up the right rear leg of the gray horse and examined its hoof. There was a loose nail on the boot—the track he had been following for the past five days.

Rico checked the chamber of the Colt on his hip, then reholstered it and entered the saloon. He went up to the bar and ordered a beer.

It wasn't difficult to determine that the four, loud-mouthed drunkards at the end of the bar were his quarry. His blood simmered at the thought of these vile savages violating and murdering his mother.

Rico clutched his glass to keep from striking out at the big-mouthed speaker who appeared to be their leader. He had to remain cool-headed and memorize each of their faces. Then he would seek his revenge individually.

The one nearest him turned his head and saw Rico at the end of the bar.

"Hey, Charley, since when do you serve breeds at your bar?"

"I serve anyone who's got the two bits to pay for it," Charley said. "And I have'ta say, I ain't seen *your* money on the bar, Ben."

Ben snorted and pulled a chain from his pocket. "How about this? It oughta be worth a couple of beers."

The bartender picked it up and studied the necklace. A small golden cross dangled from the center of it.

Rico gripped the bar when he saw the chain his mother always wore around her neck. His father had made the tiny cross out of gold.

"Where'd you get it?"

The man's face settled into a smirk. "From a ad-mirer. If you get what I mean."

The remark brought some laughs and hoots from his companions.

Charley put it down on the counter. "All right, but just one more round."

"I don't like drinking alongside this half-breed."

"Knock it off, Ben. He's not hurting anybody. It's a hot day, and he wants a cool beer same as you," Charley said.

"Yeah, well, we don't need any half-breeds in our town. Let one in and before ya know it, town's full of them. Ain't that right, boys?"

His companions backed him up with words and nods.

"Hey, breed," he called to Rico, "you got a hot little sister who wants to spread her legs for old Ben here?" He elbowed the man next to him. "The last one we had was worthless. Right, Kansas? Laid there praying the whole time—"

"While you were raping her!" Rico finished, unable to hold his temper for another moment. "You rotten son of a bitch!" Rico threw the contents of his glass in Ben's face, then delivered a punch that sent the drunk reeling backward and crashing into a table. He picked up his mother's necklace and put it in his pocket.

"Dammit, Slatter, I figured this would happen," the bartender shouted. "Every time you come in here, you start a fight and break up the place."

Slatter staggered to his feet and wiped the blood away from his split lip with the back of his hand. "Nobody gets away with hitting Ben Slatter," he snarled. "Hold him, boys."

Before Rico could back up to draw, two of the men pounced on him. Rico managed to free himself

from one and threw a punch before the other two
succeeded in pinning back his arms.

One of the bar's patrons slipped out the door and
ran toward the sheriff's office.

Enraged, Slatter drove punch after punch into
Rico while his companions held the defenseless man.
Blood seeped from his nose and a cut over his eye.
When they finally released his arms, he collapsed to
the floor, which made the rest of his body an easy
target for brutal kicks from Slatter's boots.

"Kansas, flatten his gun hand on the floor," Slatter
ordered when the brute finished the merciless beating. Then he took his pistol and smashed the handle
against Rico's hand. "That should slow him up for a
while."

He knelt down and smirked in Rico's face. "Next
time, *amigo*, drink from the horse trough. And make
sure it's not in any town that I'm in."

With his last conscious breath, Rico raised his
head enough to spit blood and spittle into the bully's
face. Then mercifully, he passed out.

Slatter turned red with rage. "Drag him outside,"
he ordered. "Eddie, get the rope from my saddle. I'm
gonna hang the bastard as a lesson to any other breed
who comes to this town."

"You're insane, Slatter," Charley shouted as two
of them grabbed Rico by the arms and dragged him
across the floor. "Eddie, Curly, listen to me. You help
hang that man and you'll end up sitting in a peniten-
tiary for years."

"Don't pay him no mind, boys," Slatter said. "It's
all his fault for serving the breed to begin with."

Within minutes they had Rico's hands tied behind his back. Slatter slung a rope over a tree branch and slipped the noose around the unconscious man's neck.

The few citizens who were out in the hot sun stopped and watched with curiosity. None had ever witnessed a hanging.

"What did the man do?" one of them asked.

"He raped and murdered a old lady," Slatter said. "Then tried to blame it on me."

"Ain't this the sheriff's problem?" another asked.

"We ain't waiting for the sheriff. He's got too soft a heart. He'd probably let the bastard go. But we saw what the breed did, didn't we, boys? Okay, lift him up on the back of my horse," Slatter ordered.

"That's enough, Slatter," a voice declared. "Take that noose off him, Kansas."

The confused and inebriated cowboy looked at his leader, then back to Sheriff Newman's grim countenance.

"I warned you fellows, I won't put up with any more troublemaking. All four of you come with me, and I'll lock you up until you sober up."

"We'll do that, Sheriff, right after we hang the breed," Slatter said. He drew his gun. "Just stay out of this, Sheriff. Boys, keep him covered 'til I finish."

"You hang a man in my town, Slatter, and California won't be big enough for you to hide from me," Newman said. "You boys figure it's worth getting killed so Slatter can have his way? You know I can take a couple of you down with me if I have to, and I don't want to shoot any of you. So do what I said and take that noose off that man, Kansas," the sheriff said calmly.

"You heard what he said, boys," Charley said from the doorway of the saloon, his raised rifle pointed at them.

"Don't make no sense, Ben, for us to get killed over some half-breed," Kansas said.

"He's right, boss," Eddie agreed. "Ain't that so, Curly?" he asked his brother.

"Eddie and Curly, your folks are good, hardworking people," the sheriff said. "I know them well, and I'd sure hate to have to gun down any of their sons. So I'm giving you boys a chance. Put those guns back in the holsters before it's too late. I can see that boy on that horse is bleeding pretty bad. He needs medical attention and could die while we waste time standing here."

Eddie and Curly nodded and slipped their pistols back in the holsters. "You coming, Kansas?"

"Reckon so."

"What about you, Ben?"

"You bunch of yeller cowards," Slatter snarled in disgust and holstered his weapon.

"Will a couple of you folks tote this man to the doctor's office while I lock up these men?" Sheriff Newman asked.

Two of the spectators lifted Rico down and carried him away, while the sheriff herded the other four men to the jailhouse.

"I keep telling you, boys, I don't like your odds when you're picking on people," the sheriff lectured. "Four on one just ain't right."

"Dad, you figure the horses will like this corral when we're done?" Garrett asked.

"I know they will," Jed said. "It's out in the fresh air where they're able to run, instead of being cooped up in a stall all day. There's a few trees for shade, plenty of clover and brush to chew on, and a trough to drink from."

"Do we have to put them back in their stalls at night?"

"Not when the weather's good. Just if there's a bad storm or one of them is sick. Other than that, this corral will be home to them. The only thing you'll have to do is spread a few bales of hay around for them to eat."

"And we won't have to muck out stalls!" Garret exclaimed.

"Right. But you should dig a hole and bury their spoor a couple of times a week. That will help to keep the flies away."

"This is 'bout the greatest idea we ever had, Dad. 'Cept when you taught me how to ride Runt."

Jed ruffled his hair. "We'll have to repaint the corral every couple of years. Nothing looks better than a bright white fence around a corral with the green grass and the horses racing around in it. Back home when I was growing up, I used to sit on top of a hill and look down on the corral. Watching the mares and their frisky colts racing across it was a beautiful sight."

Garrett's eyes were filled with sympathy. "Do you miss Virginia very much, Dad?"

"Only when something like this stirs up a memory."

"Do you think this will feel like home to you someday?"

"My memories of home are growing up with my family around me. My memories of here will be watching you growing up with your family around you. Only I'll be part of that family, too."

Jed stood up. "There, that's the final stroke." They put their paintbrushes down and stepped back to admire it. Jed folded his arms across his chest. "What do you think, partner?"

Folding his arms across his chest, Garrett struck the same pose. "I think it looks good, pal."

They grinned at each other and shook hands.

"When can we bring the horses out?" Garrett asked.

"Tomorrow. We'll give the paint a good chance to dry."

Nathan and Caroline drove up just then, returning from the mill.

"Wow!" she exclaimed.

"Do you like it, Mama? Don't you think it's beautiful?"

"It certainly is."

"Dad wanted to paint it white so it looks like the ones in Virginia, and not like them run-down old ones in town."

"Then that's what we'll always do," Caroline agreed.

"How are things coming along at the mill?" Jed asked.

"I think when we're finished, it will be better than

it was before. They've got the privy up and painted, and the men have most of the office framed in. It's larger than the previous one; it even has a little extra room for storage and supplies."

"Did you paint the privy red and white like Dad said?" Garrett asked.

"You bet we did," Caroline said, amused. "Especially the bright-red door on the front of it. No one will ever mistake it for anything else now."

"Who's that riding up the drive?" Nathan asked.

Caroline shaded her eyes. "Looks like Sheriff Newman. He must have heard about our trouble at the mill."

The sheriff rode over. "Howdy, folks."

"Randy," Nathan said. "We didn't expect you to ride all the way out here. I was planning on riding in to Napa in the morning."

"It goes with my job, folks. Who told you already?"

"We were there, Sheriff," Caroline said. "I'm the one he tried to kill."

"Ben Slatter tried to kill you?" Newman asked.

"I don't think we're talking about the same thing," Jed said. "You didn't ride out here to ask about the incident at the mill yesterday, did you?"

"No, I didn't. I came about the incident in town today."

"Sounds like we're talking in circles. Let's go up to the house and discuss all this," Nathan advised.

Once they were settled inside, Caroline brought out lemonade and a cake she had baked that morning.

"I'd like to know what happened at the mill if it involves the law," the sheriff said.

"Well, Sheriff, I had gone to the mill to work on the ledgers. As I was preparing to leave, someone fired a shot at me through the office window," she began.

The sheriff listened silently as she related the whole incident.

"And you have the names of the other six men who witnessed Bomber's confession and death?"

Nathan got the list of the men's names from his study, and Newman folded it neatly and put it in his shirt pocket. "Since I'm so close now, I'll ride over to your mill and speak briefly to these men. I can't see why there would be any future problem over the incident."

"Thank you, Randy," Nathan said. "Now, why did you ride out here today?"

"On an equally unpleasant matter. Jed, do you have a cousin named Rico Fraser?"

"Yes, I do. What about him?" Jed asked.

"There's a young man in town who claims to be your cousin. Seems he had a confrontation with Ben Slatter and his gang. They beat him up pretty brutally and were about to hang him when I got there."

Jed jumped to his feet. "Hang him!"

"Slatter did a real job on him. Don't remember ever seeing a man in such shape. Doc Rivers stitched up what he could but said the fellow's pretty busted up. Couple broken ribs, broken nose. Might lose an eye, too. Doc's not sure about that. And Slatter busted up the man's right hand with the handle of his Colt."

"Is he going to make it?" Jed asked.

"Doc ain't making any promises right now."

"Oh, dear God!" Caroline exclaimed.

"Jed, would you mind riding into town to make sure it's your cousin?"

"You bet I will."

"I'll come with you, Jed," Caroline said.

Within minutes they were headed for town.

"I've got him pretty heavily sedated," the doctor said. "He's been slipping in and out of consciousness for the last few hours."

Rico's face was so badly swollen that it would have been difficult to identify him if it weren't for his hat and boots in the corner of the room. Caroline recognized them at once.

"Caroline, I've got a couple of telegrams to send," Jed said. "I don't know how to contact my Aunt Elena, but I'm sure my brothers will know."

"Is Elena the young man's mother?" the doctor asked.

"Yes," Jed said. He saw the sudden shift of expression on the doctor's face. "What about her, Doctor?"

"In one of his lucid moments, your cousin said that he followed Slatter and his gang here to kill them. They had raped and killed his mother."

Caroline gasped and choked back a sob.

Jed lowered his head in despair. "Guess I better send those telegrams."

"I'll stay here in case Rico wakes up," she said.

The doctor followed Jed out of the room.

"It might be worth your time to talk to Charley Walters. He and several of the men in the bar witnessed the whole thing."

"Witnessed," Jed said contemptuously. "But they didn't step forward to help a man being beaten to death. They were the same way when that bunch was beating me up."

"Don't condemn Charley, Mr. Fraser. He's a fair and honest man. And he stepped out against their drawn weapons to help the sheriff when they were about to string up your cousin."

"Then I guess I owe him my thanks for that."

The sheriff had returned to town by the time Jed left the telegraph office. "Was the victim your cousin, Mr. Fraser?"

"Yes. I just sent telegrams to our family and to Father Chavez, Rico's uncle in Hope. What do you intend to do with those bastards who beat him up?"

"I figure on letting them out after they sleep off their drunk. I don't have anything legal to hold them on. I sent a telegram to the marshal. If what your cousin says is true and they murdered his mother, it'll be the marshal's job to settle it."

"You're a generous fellow, Sheriff Newman. If I were in your boots, and had a conscienceless bastard like Ben Slatter harassing anyone who gets in his path, the town wouldn't be big enough for both of us."

"You think I'm not doing my job, Mr. Fraser?"

"Locking a man up to sleep off a drunk is not

protecting the people in this town. How many more times do you figure on letting this crazed man harm someone before you do something about it? The man is a rapist and murderer, and you're releasing him if you don't hear from the marshal? My brother's a lawman—and if someone like Slatter showed up in his town, the man wouldn't have lasted ten minutes."

Jed spun on his heel and headed back to the doctor's office.

CHAPTER 25

Once again Caroline found herself and Jed on a vigil for a beloved family member. As she sat at Rico's bedside holding his hand, she thought of Jed's family. When one of them suffered a crisis, they became a single body, with a unified purpose and one huge beating heart of love. One's pain or torment became their pain; one's laughter became their joy.

Clay's return wire to Jed had expressed that attitude succinctly. "We're on our way."

No message laden with questions of who, what, where, why, or when. Four simple words of assurance: "We're on our way."

The hours passed slowly through the night. Rico slipped in and out of consciousness, his pain so severe the doctor kept him as tranquilized as he could.

One time while Jed and the doctor had stepped into the other room, Rico had become agitated and kept calling out for the chain.

"Rico, you must remain still," she pleaded.

"Chain," he repeated. "Pocket."

She went over to where his trousers hung on a peg on the wall, and in a pocket she discovered a thin gold chain with a cross dangling from it.

She returned to the bedside and slipped the chain into his hand. A peace seemed to come over him, and he quieted. They sat the rest of the night, their hands linked together by a slim chain clasped between their fingers.

Toward morning Rico's bouts of unconsciousness drifted into slumber, and longer stretches of alertness prevailed. His fever had not increased, which was a favorable sign, but his pain did—which the doctor said was to be expected.

With the continued oppressive heat, and his ribs bound tightly, Rico was becoming increasingly restless and uncomfortable. Once again the doctor gave him a thorough check, and assured that there was nothing broken other then his nose, right hand, and several ribs, he permitted Rico to sit up in bed.

At first it made him dizzy, but gradually his head began to clear.

Caroline bathed his neck and shoulders with cool towels, which helped to ease the discomfort of the heat. The doctor removed the patch he had put on Rico's eye, and decided the eye itself did not appear to have been injured, which was another hopeful sign.

"You have a remarkable power of recovery, young man. Yesterday I wouldn't have given you a fifty-fifty chance to survive. So don't overdo it; healing takes time."

"What of my hand, Doctor? That is my greatest concern."

"It was smashed, and bones were broken. Fingers are not like the toes on your feet; they must be reset or they will be deformed. I hesitate to try to do it now, because it's excruciating."

"I would prefer you try, Doctor. What is a little more pain than I feel already?"

"Very well, if that is your wish. I can give you some laudanum, but it will still be painful for you. Jed, I'll need your help in holding him down."

"I can't watch this," Caroline said. She hurried from the room and went outside in the hopes of shutting out any sound.

Nathan and Garrett arrived early and accompanied her to the diner for breakfast until the doctor finished setting Rico's fingers. When Jed finally joined them, she was relieved to hear that Rico was sleeping quietly.

"So what do you boys intend to do about Slatter?" Nathan asked. "Charley told me the sheriff released him and his gang this morning."

"We'll talk it over. I know what Colt and Garth would want to do, but Clay is the steadying force in the family, so we'll see. I imagine they'll be coming in on the morning train."

"I know what family honor means to you, Jed. But consider whether it's worth possibly going to prison for years," Nathan said.

To Jed's disappointment, his brothers weren't on the train, and the next one wasn't due until later that evening. Since Rico appeared to be out of any foreseeable danger, Jed suggested Caroline go home and get some rest.

"What about you? You've been awake all night, too," she said, as they sat in the diner lingering over a cup of coffee, while Nathan and Garrett made a short visit with Rico.

"I want to wait for my brothers." He reached over and squeezed her hand. "Thank you, Caroline."

"For what?" she asked.

"For being such a wall of strength to my family."

"It's Garrett's and my family, too," she said gently. She got to her feet. "Here come Father and Garrett. I don't suppose you have any idea when you'll be home?"

"Not at this time." Jed kissed her on the forehead. "Thanks again for everything, Caroline."

She blurted out, "You know those men are dangerous, Jed. Will you promise me that none of you will do anything that could get you hurt?"

"I can't make any such promise, Caroline."

She sighed. "I didn't think so." She left and Nathan drove them home. Caroline slept all the way.

Later that day, Jed was standing alone at the bar when Slatter and his henchmen came in. For a change, they were sober.

"Will you look who's here, boys," Slatter said.

"Why don't you go back to your jail cell, Slatter, where you belong and leave decent people to their enjoyment?" Jed said.

"Heard tell that half-breed we beat up is supposed

to be a cousin of yours. Someone in your family dip his fingers into the honey pot of some señorita, Fraser?"

"Yes, Rico's my cousin. And I don't like what you did to him, or my aunt. I'm going to have to beat the hell out of you."

Slatter burst into laughter. "Little old you is gonna beat the hell out of us? Hear that, boys?"

"Your hearing must be as worthless as your brain, Slatter. I said beat *you* up—not them."

Slatter poked Kansas with his elbow. "Hear that, Kansas? You boys can stop shivering. The stupid Reb is just gonna beat me up," he said, and pounded the bar laughing.

The other three men joined in his laughter.

"And what do you think my boys are gonna do? Stand by and just watch you?"

"If they're smart, they'll get the hell out of here now, while they can still walk," Garth said, rising to his feet from a nearby table.

"Who the hell are you?" Slatter asked.

"Name's Fraser. Garth Fraser."

"You a cousin to that half-breed, too?"

"I have a cousin Rico, if that's who you're referring to," Garth said.

"What a coincidence," Colt said, rising to his feet from a different table. "I have a cousin Rico, too. Could be it's the same fellow. Tell me, Mr. Slatter, are you and those flunkies of yours the same ones who go around ganging up on a man?"

"Or raping and murdering helpless women," Clay

said from the other side of the room. The four men's eyes swung to him as he rose to his feet. "Because we all have the same Aunt Elena, too."

"No more four-to-one odds now, Slatter," Jed said. "They're pretty even, aren't they?"

"Who are you guys?" Slatter snarled.

"Name's Clay Fraser."

"Colt Fraser. You've met my brother Garth and Jed already. Tell me, do those henchmen of yours have names? I always like to know a fella's name when I'm about to beat the hell out of him."

Slatter looked around at the four Frasers, then reached for his gun on his hip. Before he could draw it, Colt's had cleared the holster.

"Don't even think it, you son of a bitch. Nothing would give me more pleasure than putting a bullet right between your eyes."

"Gentlemen, please take your fight to the street," Charley said. "I can't afford to keep repairing the place after you guys bust it up."

Garth grabbed the shirtfront of Kansas and slammed him against the bar. "What is your name, sir?" he asked the bartender, as Kansas struggled to free himself.

"Charley," the bartender replied.

"Well, Charley, we have no intention of busting up your bar. But this piece of shit is another matter." His punch sent Kansas sprawling backward over the bar, knocking Charley off his feet in the collision.

"He's all mine," Jed yelled, when Clay reached for Slatter.

Clay shoved him at Jed as if the man was a bag

of potatoes. "Then take the bastard; he stinks like hell." Then he reached for Eddie, who had already begun to whimper before Clay's fist smashed into his nose.

Colt beckoned a finger to Curly, who had started to back away. "Ever hear of 'Do unto others as you would have others do unto you'?" Colt's punch sent the coward sprawling to the floor. He picked Curly up by the belt and dragged him outside.

After several more punches, Garth dragged Kansas out and tossed him next to Curly.

A whimpering Eddie was crawling on his hands and knees to try and escape being hit again. Clay's kick to his rear end sent Eddie flying out the door, and he landed on the other two men, just as Jed's punch to Slatter's gut, followed by an uppercut to the jaw, sent their leader staggering into the pile-up.

Garth turned to Clay in disgust. "Hell, Brother Clay, you told us we came here for a fight."

Clay turned to the crowd of people who had gathered to watch. "Take a good look at them, folks. There's the pile of shit you all let beat up defenseless victims. Why the hell didn't some of you step in and prevent it?"

The sheriff stepped through the crowd and stared down at the gang. "I've warned you fellows for the last time about getting likkered up and fighting. Get on your horses and ride out of here. If you step foot in this town again, I'll shoot you on sight."

"We ain't drunk, and we didn't start this fight," Slatter shouted. "These Frasers did."

Garth said innocently, "Our mama raised us never

to hit a woman." Then he grinned. "You need any help in hauling these ladies out of here?"

The Frasers left, taking Rico to see him safely back to his home and the healing hands of the nuns who would see to his recovery.

While Jed was upstairs saying good night to Garrett, Caroline roamed the house restlessly. Tomorrow Jed would leave, departing from their lives for a long time; tomorrow this emotional seesaw would be over and her life would settle back to normal.

In the past thirty days, she felt she had lived a lifetime. The fear of having her secret exposed, regret for the marriage, and hatred . . . had she really believed she hated him?

There had been laughter, sadness, tears, heartache. Moments of jealousy, moments of resentment.

She had known extreme joy when her son's life had been spared, and the low of despair she felt now, knowing she had to endure Jed's departure. And what single word could ever describe those moments making love in his arms? Ecstasy? Rapture?

Now that the time had come for him to leave, the time she had once wanted so desperately, she didn't know how she would get through it.

But one thing remained before they parted. She had to tell him the truth about Andy.

Caroline sat down at the piano to calm herself. She only needed to get through one more night of pretending his leaving didn't matter to her. One more night of pretending that the next eleven months wouldn't be an eternity to her.

She knew when he came downstairs; she could feel his presence in the room. He didn't speak, and she continued playing as she fought back the rise of tears.

"I've never told you how beautifully you play, Caroline."

When had he come so close?

"Thank you," she responded woodenly.

"That's a beautiful piece you're playing."

"It's by Mozart. He's one of my favorite composers."

"I'm going to miss hearing you play."

Suddenly she couldn't take it anymore, and she bolted to her feet and ran outside through the garden door.

Jed followed her. "What's wrong, Caroline? Are you angry with me?"

She spun to face him, treacherous tears betraying her and sliding down her cheeks. "Yes, I'm angry with you. And with myself. I'm angry at life, Jed. It's as if we've lived a lifetime in these past few weeks, and now we're faced with the reality that nothing in our future will ever equal them!"

He gently took hold of her shoulders. "You speak as if we have no more future together. There will always be something for us to look forward to—just as there will always be sorrow, and joy to weather that sorrow. And there will always be hope, Caroline."

She sniffled. "And what are your hopes, Jed? Riches? Good health? Happiness?"

"I can't predict what life will bring, but I know that hope is eternal—the guiding belief that tomorrow will be better than today, and today is better than yesterday."

"Yesterday." She sighed. "Jed, I've been trying to tell you about one of my yesterdays—but somehow, something always interrupted me."

"What is it?"

"I want to tell you the truth about Andy. Until I do, it will always hover in the background."

They sat down on a garden bench. "Andy and I were never lovers in the true sense of the word," she began. "We had spoken a few words occasionally or nodded casually in passing, but that was the extent of it.

"Then one day I was reading by the pond near our home, when Andy walked by. He stopped and asked me what I was reading, and before you know it, we were chatting away about school, books, music, the likelihood of an impending war between the states.

"Soon we became close friends. We'd exchange books or talk about our futures. He encouraged me to go on with my music and told me he wanted to enter a seminary to become a clergyman, but feared his father would expect him to go to a military academy like his brothers.

"Then one day I burst into tears when I told him that my father insisted we go to California before the war broke out. I was crying about having to be separated from my father, and also from Andy, the only true friend I'd ever known.

"He put his arm around me to console me, and for some reason he kissed me. No boy had ever kissed me before, and I don't think he had kissed any other girl, either. It was all very tentative, both of us experimenting with something we'd never experienced before. The kissing led to petting, and the petting led to . . . you know what."

She took a deep breath. "We both were so naïve and inexperienced. The next day we were too embarrassed to even look at each other when he apologized, and we pledged to write to each other. It was the last time we ever spoke. The following day my mother and I sailed for California.

"When I realized I was pregnant, I decided to wait until the baby was born. I wrote to him then, but he never responded." Her voice dropped to a whisper. "Now I know why."

Caroline took another shuddering breath. "Still I'm eternally grateful that I have Garrett!" She closed her eyes, and Jed gently brushed a teardrop from her cheek.

Caroline gasped and opened her eyes when he cupped her neck with his warm palm and then lowered his head to hers, so close their breaths mingled.

"Thank you for telling me, Caroline."

The air was charged with the tension building between them. She could feel the draw of his compelling dark gaze, the desire in his eyes generating the same rising passion in her.

Now that she was in love with him, she desired him with an even greater intensity. Her common sense told her to run because he would be leaving in the morning, while her body ached with the need to feel his touch once more, if only for one night.

Her quickened breath matched the rhythm of his. "Is this a mistake, Jed?"

"This moment is ours to share, Caroline. Tomorrow it will be too late. Are we to let this moment pass?"

She trembled as passion surged through her, making the feminine chamber of her loins ache. The overpowering demand of his kiss drained the breath from her, and she gasped when he trailed quick kisses down the column of her neck, then reclaimed her lips.

Their bodies would not accept denial.

He swept her up in his arms and carried her up the stairs to his room, where they rapidly undressed each other. Then he picked her up and, sliding her slowly down his naked body, he lowered her to the bed, then covered her with his body as he drove his tongue past her lips and pulled her tighter into the circle of his arms, crushing her breasts against his bare chest. The heat from his body coursed through her as it had in the storm.

Lowering his head, he began to tease her turgid nipples with his tongue, the warmth of his thigh between her own an ecstatic sensation against the junction of her legs.

"Do you want me to stop, Caroline?" he panted.

"What do you think?" she murmured breathlessly. She slid her arms around his neck and drew his head down to hers, parting his lips with her kiss.

The kiss was hot with passion. Then he lifted her arms to trail a string of kisses up one and down the other, then shifted to the hollow of her throat, then down to her breasts.

Rapturous sensation filled her as his mouth and hands found every pleasure spot on her body. He slowly trailed his hand down the sensitive plane of her stomach and cupped the spot where, only seconds before, his thigh had reigned with a friction that had threatened to drive her to madness.

She couldn't bear another moment of it and cried out as her body began to implode with tremors of climax. He swiftly, entered her, thrusting deep to fill her with his own release. Afterward, when her breathing returned to normal, she rolled onto her side and snuggled her head in the hollow between his chest and shoulder.

"Why can't I resist you? The moment you touch me, I give in to the thrill of it," she said softly, lightly running her fingers along the corded brawn of his shoulder.

She placed a kiss in the dark hair on his chest, feeling euphoric, as if she was floating on air.

Then the arousing touch of his lips on her breast brought her back down to earth, and she clutched his head to press it even closer, as he began to take her soaring once again.

CHAPTER
26

Caroline was waiting the next morning when Jed came downstairs wearing his uniform and carrying his seabag. "Guess I'm all set," he said.

"Father and Garrett are waiting on the wagon." She handed him a round covered tin. "I made some sugar cookies and Scottish shortbread. I thought you'd enjoy them with your coffee in the evening."

"Thank you. That was real thoughtful of you, Caroline." He put the tin in his seabag and retied it.

When Buffer trotted over to him, Jed squatted down and scratched him behind his ears. "You're in charge again, pal. We both love them, so I'm depending on you to take care of them while I'm gone."

Heartache filled Caroline's breast. As much as she wanted to admit her love to him, foolish pride kept her from telling him. He was too much a gentleman to laugh at her and would only be embarrassed if she suddenly blurted out her real feelings for him.

Besides, why divulge them when he was leaving? A lot could change in both their lives in the next eleven months.

He stood up and came over to her. "I'm glad we have these few moments to be alone, Caroline. There's a lot I have to say to you."

Her heartbeat quickened. Was it too much to hope he would tell her what she yearned to hear? What she was too afraid to admit to him? Then she could shout her feelings to the world.

"Caroline, while I'm gone if you need anything—help, money, or whatever—get word to Fraser Keep. My brothers will come at once. Will you promise to do that?"

"Yes, I promise," she said, disappointed. It was not what she was hoping to hear.

"Cassie told me that as soon as Sam's a couple of months older, she'll come and spend a few weeks with you."

Caroline smiled. "Colt might not agree to that arrangement. Don't worry about us, Jed; we'll be fine. The problem with Calhoun's been resolved. Besides, it's not as if Garrett and I will be alone; my father's with us."

"Garrett's getting older, Caroline. He's more curious about things, and it can get him into serious problems if he gets careless. Look what's happened to him just this past month."

"We'll be fine. I have Father and Buffer to help keep an eye on him. And we don't have any raging rivers nearby. The other accidents were all caused by Vincent Calhoun."

He held her shoulders and smiled down at her. "Then take care of yourself, Miss Caroline," he said tenderly. "You've been a good sport putting up with me the past month. I've invaded your home and disrupted your life."

"Didn't you once say that we all have some choices in our own fate? We just can't change the mistakes we make when we do."

"Such as?" he asked.

"Your marrying me for the sake of your family honor, instead of for love."

"I'm not complaining; nor do I regret it. Do you?"

"I'm not sure. Maybe Clay was right. Without love, Jed, you'll never experience the total happiness that your brothers know."

"Are you that unhappy already, Caroline?"

"I'd be lying if I didn't admit that I'd like to have married for love."

"Hey, you two," Nathan yelled from outside, "if we're going to catch that train, we better get moving."

Jed didn't budge. "That's a hell of a topic to bring up," he said. "Why the issue of love now?"

Caroline concealed her feelings under a wooden smile. "You're right. It's water over the dam now, isn't it?"

She walked out the door, and Jed picked up his seabag and followed.

The train ride to San Francisco was considerably quieter than their previous one. Nathan did his best to try and cheer up Garrett, but it was useless.

Caroline sat in silence, staring out the window. Jed doubted if she was even aware of what she was looking at. Her actions were perplexing. She had gone into this marriage with her eyes wide open, and he had given her several opportunities to call off the wedding.

Her unexpected comment about wishing she had married for love almost knocked the legs out from under him. Caroline was not an easy woman to figure out, but she sure as hell was a fascinating one.

He stole another glance at her. She was so beautiful—exquisite would be closer. And yet, so sad. He wanted to kiss her until he brought the smile back to her face, the laughter to her eyes.

And Lord knows he didn't want to leave her. More and more lately, he had been thinking about what it would be like to look up and not see her. Not to hear the sound of her light laughter, catch her lavender scent, not be able to simply reach out and touch her or kiss the smooth softness of her cheek.

He tried not to think about what it would be like not to be able to make love to her. Last night had gone far beyond ordinary satisfaction. It had been an emotional release as much as a physical one. He had made *love* to her! If he recognized it, surely she must have, too.

He knew if he told her, though, she would withdraw completely from him. She wanted no such relationship with a man who wasn't the "home and hearth" type.

Why was the love for a woman so great that it could drive a man to forsake his lifetime goals and dreams? Take his brothers, for instance. Clay, the visionary, with his creative and imaginative mind, had always thought far beyond the moment at hand;

Colt, who had always aspired to become a lawman, had abandoned the opportunity for the life
of a rancher; and Garth, the romantic roamer with
dreams of finding gold at the end of the rainbow, was
now content fashioning wine barrels.

Well, not him. The *sea* had always been his love.
And once he was back at sea, with the deck of the
Belle beneath his feet, any such thought would be
banished.

Caroline deserved the happiness she sought, so
he wouldn't pursue her. He'd give her the peace and
quiet she enjoyed and not complicate her life anymore. She needed time, and his leaving would give
her that time.

Going to sea was the biggest favor he could do for
her.

But, he vowed, somehow, some way, he would
make her love him—because he would *not* release
her from their marriage. When he returned, he'd
convince her to forsake that damn agreement of
a marriage in name only. They were husband and
wife—and it was time she damn well knew it.

Saying good-bye would be difficult, but as Caroline had pointed out, reuniting again made the moments together that much more precious. If he'd
learned anything in his twenty-seven years, it was
that you had to swallow the bitter with the sweet.

Perhaps this separation was the very thing needed
to convince her of that.

When they reached San Francisco, they went directly
to the pier, where preparations were in progress for

their departure. Captain Beningham was shouting orders from the bridge, and an occasional late arrival raced up the gangplank.

"Sir, if you need anything, contact my brothers. They'll be happy to help in any way they can."

"I know, Jed. Clay told me the same thing before he left."

"Take care of our family, sir."

"I will, son," Nathan said as the two men shook hands. "And God's speed and good health. Come back to us, Jed. Come back to us."

"I will, sir."

Nathan stepped aside, and Jed hunkered down on his haunches. Sobbing, Garrett rushed into his arms.

"Why do you have to go away, Dad? Stay with us. *Please* stay with us."

"I can't do that, Garrett. I made a commitment to Captain Beningham before I even met you."

"But Captain Beningham is a nice man. I bet he'd let you stay if you ask him."

"It's too late to do that, Garrett."

"Do you love to go to sea more than you love Mama and me?"

"I love the two of you more than anything on this earth, Garrett."

"Then stay. Please don't go away. I promise not to ask you any more dumb questions if you stay."

"I would never want you to do that. Tell you what. While I'm gone, make a list of questions you have, and I'll answer all of them when I get back." Jed pulled him closer in a tight hug. "I love you, son."

Jed kissed him, then stood up. Garrett ran sobbing

into Nathan's arms, who had moved back to give them some privacy.

"I guess this is good-bye," Jed said to Caroline.

"I've never been very good with good-byes, Jed, so I'll just wish you a safe journey."

"I read in the paper that the Suez Canal is completed, and they expect to have traffic on it by November. If that's true, it would cut a lot of miles off the voyage. I could be home sooner than we planned," he said, trying to be heard above the loud blast of the ship's horn.

Then he pulled her closer. "Take care of yourself and Garrett. I'll post a letter to you from the first port we dock at."

He slipped the beaded bracelet off his wrist and slid it on hers. "This will remind you of me." A longer and louder horn blast sounded as he lowered his head and kissed her. "I love you, Caroline." Then he turned away.

"I couldn't hear you—what did you say?" she called. But he was already halfway up the gangplank.

She remained on the dock and watched his tall figure walk up the gangplank. They would be strangers again when he returned. Her heart skipped a beat when he hesitated at the top. Then he stepped onto the ship, looked back, and waved. A couple of crewmen immediately raised the plank and secured it firmly to the side of the ship.

Tears streaked Garrett's cheeks as he continued to wave.

She knew what he was feeling; she'd felt the same heartache at his age when her father went off to sea.

Now she could relate to how her mother must have felt, and she wondered if the ache would ever go away. How many times would she have to stand on a pier and say good-bye before the pain lessened?

At least her father's trips had been shorter ones to England or France. Jed's were to distant ports in the Orient. Almost a whole year out of their lives each time he sailed away.

To think she had prayed for this moment when Jed had entered their lives, had even planned a marriage on the advantages of such a relationship. Now she wondered how she would bear it without him.

How was it possible for one person to make such an impact in such a short time? Why hadn't she made the most of every moment they had together? Were there enough good memories now for her to draw on in the lonely months ahead?

Or what if this was the journey where he would finally meet that one woman who would rival his love for the sea? Would he even come back to them again?

She squeezed Garrett's hand. "Time to go, sweetheart."

"Can't we wait 'til the boat sails?"

His leaving was agony enough without watching the ship he was on sail away.

"No, honey, we have a train to catch."

Caroline took a final long, lingering look at the sleek black ship. The crew had begun to unfurl its bright-red sails as they prepared to hoist anchor and catch the tide.

"Good-bye, my love," she murmured. "God be

with you, and may you have a safe journey. Come back to us. We'll be waiting."

Garrett was quiet on the return trip from San Francisco. He had stopped crying, but his face was puckered in a pout. He finally found his voice to ask, "Granddad, how come men want to sail the ocean 'stead of staying home with the people who love them?"

"Often, son, they don't have anybody who really loves them."

"But Grandma and Mama really loved you, and you sailed away."

"That's how I made my living, Garrett. The money to build a house for them, feed them. Like Jed, I wasn't married when I went to sea. By the time I met your grandma, I had been a seaman for over ten years.

"She was the prettiest gal on either side of the Mason-Dixon line. But the sea was in my blood by that time, and your grandmother understood that. Some people just aren't cut out to be farmers or ranchers. Going to sea is a good life if you like the water."

"I sure didn't like that river water. Does sea water taste better?"

Despite her melancholy, his question brought a slight smile to Caroline. "I'm afraid not, Garrett. Sea water is salty. You can't drink it."

"You can't drink river water, either, 'less you want to puke." Garrett sighed deeply and gazed out the window.

By the time they returned to Napa, the sun had set. Nathan knew the route so well that moonlight was enough to light the road ahead.

There was no sign of Buffer when they reached the barn, which was unusual. Neither Nathan nor Caroline were that concerned, though, because he never strayed too far from home.

But his absence troubled Garrett, especially when Buffer hadn't returned the following morning.

Dejected, Garrett went outside and sat down with his elbows propped on his knees and his chin in his hands. "Sure don't seem fair to have to have your dad and your dog leave you on the same day," he grumbled.

The morning passed slowly for the two depressed individuals. After lunch Nathan persuaded Garrett to accompany him to the mill, but Caroline chose to stay home. She wanted to go upstairs and have a good cry alone.

Upon entering her room, she paused at the sight of the open door connecting it to the room Jed had been using. She walked to it and stood in the doorway, her gaze sweeping the room. His presence had made it seem so alive, but now the room had never looked so empty.

She moved to the bed and ran her hand along the curved metal footboard, then opened the closet door and saw that he had left some of his clothing behind. Impulsively, she buried her face against the shirt he had worn when they were wed. The faint aroma of cigar carried to her nostrils, and her tears began to fall.

Sobbing, she ran back into her room and threw herself down on her bed. She slid her hand to her stomach and rubbed it gently. It was too soon to know for certain, but if her suspicions were correct, their baby would be born before Jed returned.

CHAPTER
27

Later, she listlessly went back downstairs. She sat down at the piano, but no matter what she played, the music failed to soothe her. She slumped down and laid her head on her arms.

Soon, through her gloom, she sensed she wasn't alone. Startled, she bolted up and turned her head. Jed stood in the doorway.

Was she imagining him. "Jed! What are you doing here? Didn't your ship sail last night?"

"It did, but without me. And I missed the train you came back on, so I had to wait for the next one. I have something to say to you that I should have said sooner. So I resigned and left the ship."

"You resigned your commission on the *Redheaded Belle*! But you love that ship, Jed." Her heart began pounding in her breast. "Does this mean you don't intend to go back to sea?"

"There are other ships."

Another false hope. But she'd been given a second chance to confess her love to him, and she wasn't going to let him leave again without doing so.

"What's so important to cause you to come back?"

"Caroline, Lord knows I've given you enough cause to dislike me. But I don't want . . . I mean . . . I can't go on with our current arrangement."

Her heart stopped. "So . . . you want out of the marriage?"

"Let me finish," he grumbled. "I've rehearsed this damn speech all the way from San Francisco!

"When I agreed to your marriage demands, I intended to honor them. But I find it impossible."

"You find *what* impossible?"

"To make this damn speech, if you keep interrupting! Dammit it, Caroline, I want us to have a *real* marriage—not a polite arrangement for Garrett's sake. I want to be a real husband to you, and I want you to be a real wife to me—not just a cook and housekeeper."

Her whole body was quivering. She wanted to fling herself into his arms. This was a Jed she had never seen before. His sweet talk and smooth control had shattered to the point where he was having trouble putting words together in a sentence. But he still hadn't said the words she yearned to hear from him.

"No woman has ever touched the deep part of me that you did, Caroline. It scared the hell out of me, because I knew I would have to choose between you and my love for the sea.

"And yesterday, when I stood on the deck of that ship and watched you walk away, the choice suddenly became clear to me. *I'm in love with you, Caroline.*

"For the past month, I've told myself it was simply

physical attraction. I let my body take command, when I should have been listening to my heart.

"I love you, Caroline. I'm madly, insatiably in love with you. I can no longer even imagine a life without you. I want a *real* marriage. I want us to be a *real* husband and wife."

She wanted to shout for joy, to cry from happiness. And talk about sex urges! She had never desired him as much as she did this moment. She wanted to strip off her clothes and his, and make love to him on the spot.

Savoring the moment, she feigned being shocked. "You mean in the *real* biblical sense of the word?"

"Of course, I mean that!" he literally shouted. "That has to be part of a marriage if—" He stopped and stared at her with an enlightened gleam in his eyes. "Why, you little vixen! You're teasing me, aren't you?"

She walked over to him. Their gazes locked as she opened the buttons of his shirt. "Tell me, sailor, have you ever made love on a piano?"

Devilment gleamed in his eyes. "Can't say that I have. Do you have something in mind, Miss Caroline?"

She slipped the shirt off his shoulders. "You bet I do."

He swept her up in his arms, and she slipped her arms around his neck as he carried her to the stairway.

"And for the record, sailor, the name's *Mrs.* Caroline Fraser. And I *definitely* have something on my mind. You're about to find out just how much of a wife you married, because I've decided to give my rival, the sea, a real battle. So batten down the hatches—for I've not yet begun to fight."

Jed turned on his side, leaned on his elbow, and cradled his head in his hand. He gazed down at Caroline's face. The sight of her lovely lips, still slightly swollen from kissing his, reminded him of their sweetness, and he gently traced them with his fingertip.

Having confessed their love with every shared kiss, they now were content to just lie in the afterglow of their lovemaking, their legs entwined.

"When did you realize you were in love with me?" she asked.

He lay back and drew her closer to his side, their heads side by side on the pillow.

"I don't really know. But you were always on my mind. You know how you sometimes hear a haunting song? You don't know the name of it, but its strains keep running through your head. You were that melody, Caroline. I had to come back to tell you I love you, no matter what you thought of me. I couldn't imagine being away from you for eleven months."

He shifted to his side and brushed an errant strand of hair off her cheek. "Now it's your turn. What about you?"

Her delightful giggle brought a grin to his face. "I think it was when I looked up in that restaurant in San Francisco and saw you. Like Rory told me when she first saw Garth: 'From the moment that big, beautiful man walked in the door, I was in love.'

"My mind was so clouded with fears of losing Garrett that I didn't listen to my heart. Even quarreled with my nasty alter ego."

"Your nasty alter ego?" He chuckled.

"Oh, yes. I carry on conversations with my image in the mirror."

"And you admit to it!"

"Don't you sometimes talk to your image in the mirror?"

"Well, I suppose so . . . But, honey, I don't expect an answer."

"It's a way of playing devil's advocate with myself. I never get a positive response, but you were our main topic of conversation."

"No wonder my ears have been burning," he teased. "Honey, in the future, discuss me with *me*. You might get better answers. I know me better than she does."

"Was Captain Beningham upset when you told him you weren't sailing with him?" Caroline asked.

"I wouldn't say he was happy to hear it, but he said he understood since we're newlyweds."

"Does he have someone to replace you?"

"He had someone in mind, because he suspected that I wouldn't be coming back."

"What gave him that idea?"

"When he saw us in Sacramento, he knew I had finally met the woman who rivaled my love of the sea."

Caroline was skeptical. "Now, how would he know that?"

"Apparently everyone guessed it but us. Clay told

me that we were fooling ourselves if we didn't believe we were in love."

"So did you mean it earlier about intending to take
a different ship and return to sailing?"

"The sea could never draw me away from you, my
love." He cupped her cheek in his hand. "I never want
to spend another day away from your side. Though I
am unemployed at this time, I have three definite
options. Nathan said he'd like to expand the sawmill
and would need a strapping young fellow like me to
run the whole operation for him."

"And what did you tell him?" she asked.

"That I would think about it."

"And the second option?"

"Clay told me their neighbors, the Palmers, are
moving back to Illinois. He wants to purchase their
land and expand Fraser Keep, bring in some different
grape cuttings from Italy and Germany. He's pretty
excited about the idea, and so are the rest of my
brothers."

"And what did you tell him?"

"That I would think about it if I didn't go back to
sea."

"And the third option?" she asked.

"When we were in Sacramento, Leland Stanford
offered me a position with the railroad. He said he
was impressed with me and was looking for a man
he can trust." He chuckled. "Ironic isn't it? Stanford
looking for an honest man."

"So which offer are you considering?" Caroline
asked.

"Which one would you be the happiest with?"

"Jed, you've already given up the thing you love the most. I want *your* happiness. I'm just thankful you aren't gone for the next eleven months."

"Well, I'm not even considering Stanford's offer. If I took it we'd probably end up being millionaires, but I doubt I'd enjoy the role of an entrepreneur and the bustle of a city like Sacramento or San Francisco."

"What about Fraser Keep? I know what your family means to you, Jed. I love them, too. If that's what you want, we'll go there," she said, fearful of what his answer would be.

"Well, that's my first choice. The thing is, I made a promise to someone I love very much that I would never take him away from his granddad. So being a man of honor, I have no choice. I'll be learning the lumber business if Nathan wants to expand."

Caroline sat up. "You're a fraud, Jed Fraser! A sneaking, lowdown fraud! You had me worried sick, when you never had any intention of leaving here."

"My, what a suspicious woman you are, my dear. Here I was attempting a quiet and intelligent discussion of our future with my wife."

"Quiet discussion, indeed! You aren't fooling me one bit Oh, I'd like to . . . to . . ."

"To what?" he asked.

"To kiss you." She rolled over on him. "Jedemiah Fraser, I love you so much." She kissed him.

Then she kissed him again . . . and again . . . and again . . .

Caroline was in the kitchen preparing dinner when Nathan returned. "Whose horse is in the stable?" he asked. "It looks like that chestnut from the livery in Napa."

"It is, Father." Her eyes misted with tears of joy. "Jed's come back. He's not going to sea. He wants us to have a real marriage."

"And you agreed to it?"

"Oh, yes, Father. I love him so much. And he loves me."

He hugged her for a long moment, then kissed her on the cheek. "I'm very happy for you, my dear. My faith in that young man has been completely restored. Where is he? I want to welcome him home."

"He's upstairs bathing. Where's Garrett? I can't wait to tell him the good news."

"He's still moping. We didn't see a sign of Buffer today. When we got back, Garrett headed for their favorite spot in the hope of finding him."

"Could something serious have happened to him?"

"I hope not. This is the longest he's stayed away."

"I can't bear to think of it," she said.

"Think of what?" Jed asked, joining them.

"Welcome back, son!" Nathan said.

"Thanks, sir." The two men shook hands.

"Caroline, what's wrong?" Jed asked.

"We're concerned about Buffer, Jed," Nathan said. "He wasn't here when we returned last night, and he's been missing all day."

"Has he stayed out overnight before?"

Nathan shook his head. "Not when we're home. He's always been waiting for us when we return home."

"It's my fault," Caroline said. "I thought of taking him with us, because I knew how depressed Garrett would be when he said good-bye to you. Then I changed my mind because of the long train ride. I thought he'd be better off here."

"You were right, honey, so don't blame yourself," Nathan said.

"Where's Garrett now?" Jed asked.

"He went to their favorite spot in the hopes of finding him."

Jed nodded. "I know where that is. I'll go and bring him home."

"I'll go with you," Caroline said. "I know seeing you will cheer him up."

"I'll stay here in case one or both of them return," Nathan said.

After a short walk they found Garrett sitting in a shady cove, hugging his knees to his chest.

As soon as Garrett saw Jed, he jumped to his feet. Jed knelt down and Garrett ran into his arms, hugging and babbling excitedly.

"I thought you were gone for a long time! I thought you might not come back, just like Buffer. How come you didn't sail away on that big ship, Dad?"

"Because I could never be happy anywhere again until I was with you and your mother."

"You mean that, Dad? You really mean you're gonna stay and never go away again?"

"That's right, Garrett. We're a family, and families stick together, no matter what."

Garrett sighed with joy. "Boy, if only Buffer was

here I'd be 'bout the happiest kid alive." Then his eyes saddened. "Do you suppose he's hurt, or sick? He didn't seem sick when we left him."

"I think it's too soon to give up hope. If he's not back by tomorrow night, we'll ride into Napa the next day and post a reward to find out if anyone has seen him."

"Really?"

"You bet, pal."

"Right now, I think we should go back to the house, honey," Caroline said. "Your grandfather is waiting for us."

Garret suddenly lifted his head. "Listen. Do you hear that? That sounds like Buffer's bark." He jumped up.

"I think you're right." Jed rose to his feet and saw Buffer racing toward them.

And under the watchful eye of their mother herding them, four puppies wobbled behind, trying to keep up with him.

"It's Buffer!" Garret shouted. "He's come home!" He took off at a run.

"And look what he's brought with him." Jed reached down a hand and pulled Caroline to her feet, then slipped his arms around her waist and drew her back against his chest.

Nestling his cheek against the perfumed sweetness of her hair, he grinned as they watched the reunion between their son and his dog, with the four puppies hopping and nuzzling in the fray.

"I wonder who they belong to? None of the men at the mill have a dog," Caroline said.

"Could be she's part wolf. If so, that means she's here to stay."

"What makes you say that?" she asked.

He pressed a kiss to the side of her neck. "Because, my beloved wife," he said lightly, "just like the Fraser species, a wolf mates for life."

"There's just no end to your gems of wisdom, my love." She cuddled deeper into his arms.

"Like it or not, Mrs. Fraser, it appears our family's growing daily."

Caroline slipped a hand to her stomach and with a secretive smile murmured, "Oh, you have no idea, Mr. Fraser."

Catch up with love...
Catch up with passion...
Catch up with danger....

Catch a bestseller from Pocket Books!

Delve into the past with *New York Times* bestselling author

Julia London
The Dangers of Deceiving a Viscount
Beware! A lady's secrets will always be revealed...

Barbara Delinksy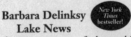
Lake News
New York Times bestseller!
Sometimes you have to get away to find everything.

Fern Michaels
The Marriage Game
New York Times bestseller!
It's all fun and games—until someone falls in love.

Hester Browne
The Little Lady Agency
New York Times bestseller!
Why trade up if you can fix him up?

Laura Griffin
One Last Breath
Don't move. Don't breathe. Don't say a word...